MORGAN'S MERCENARIES
II
LOVE & DANGER

"I'm scared this time, Culver."

He glanced over at Pilar's face, drawn with worry. "Maybe," he said huskily, "you have more to lose this time around."

She saw the expression on Culver's face. His eyes had softened, as had the set of his mouth. When he realized she was watching him, his features hardened. Pilar wanted so badly to tell him how sorry she was, but it would do no good. Just being this close to Culver made her ache with desire. Despite the harshness of the intervening years and circumstances, she wanted him now as she had the first time their eyes had met. Pilar didn't fool herself this time, however.

She would never allow Culver to know she still wanted him. They lived in two very different worlds. The two could never truly meet and bond. Her world wouldn't allow it.

Dear Reader,

The holiday season is upon us—and we're in the midst of celebrating the arrival of our 1000th Special Edition! It is truly a season of cheer for all of us at Silhouette Special Edition.

We hope that you enjoy *The Pride of Jared MacKade* by *New York Times* bestselling author Nora Roberts. This is the second title of her bestselling THE MACKADE BROTHERS series, and the book is warm, wonderful—and not only Book 1000, but Nora's eightieth Silhouette novel! Thank you, Nora!

The celebration continues with the uplifting story of *Morgan's Rescue*, by Lindsay McKenna. This action-packed tale is the third installment of Lindsay's newest series, MORGAN'S MERCENARIES: LOVE AND DANGER. I know you won't want to miss a minute!

This month's HOLIDAY ELOPEMENTS title is a poignant, stirring story of the enduring power of love from Phyllis Halldorson—*The Bride and the Baby*.

Holidays are for children, and this month features many little ones with shining eyes and delighted laughter. In fact, we have a fun little element running through some of the books of unexpecting "dads" delivering babies! We hope you enjoy this unexpected bonus! Don't miss *Baby's First Christmas*, by Marie Ferrarella—the launch title of her marvelous cross-line series, THE BABY OF THE MONTH CLUB. Or Sherryl Woods's newest offering—*A Christmas Blessing*— the start of her Special Edition series, AND BABY MAKES THREE. Last, but not least, is the winsome *Mr. Angel* by Beth Henderson—a book full of warmth and cheer to warm wintry nights with love.

We hope that you enjoy this month of celebration. It's all due to you, our loyal readers. Happy holidays, and many thanks for your continued support from all of us at Silhouette Books!

Sincerely,

Tara Gavin
Senior Editor

Please address questions and book requests to:
Silhouette Reader Service
U.S.: 3010 Walden Ave., P.O. Box 1325, Buffalo, NY 14269
Canadian: P.O. Box 609, Fort Erie, Ont. L2A 5X3

LINDSAY McKENNA

MORGAN'S RESCUE

Silhouette®

SPECIAL EDITION®

Published by Silhouette Books
America's Publisher of Contemporary Romance

To the women of the Blue Heron Group: Rhonda Pallas Downey,
Andrea McShane, Dr. Gail Derin and Veronica Vida, who have been
such wonderful and inspiring role models to and for me: I honor your
quiet, unobtrusive walk through my life and am grateful.
And to Karen David, world-famous numerologist, spiritualist
medium and shamanka. It's great to have such an old, dear friend of
eighteen years! I love you and so enjoy our friendship. It gets better
and better with every year—good thing you have a fax machine now!
Thanks for "being" there!

SILHOUETTE BOOKS

ISBN 0-373-23998-X

MORGAN'S RESCUE

Copyright © 1995 by Lindsay McKenna

LINDSAY McKENNA

spent three years serving her country as a meteorologist in the U.S. navy, so much of her knowledge comes from direct experience. In addition, she spends a great deal of time researching each book, whether it be at the Pentagon or at military bases, extensively interviewing key personnel.

Lindsay is also a pilot. She and her husband of twenty-two years, both avid "rock hounds" and hikers, live in Arizona.

Dear Reader,

In 1983, when I first published *Captive of Fate* with Silhouette Special Edition, I had no idea I'd continue to write over thirty novels for Silhouette Books. Now, Special Edition has hit 1000 great romance novels, and I'm thrilled to be a part of a wonderful, continuing tradition.

I have always loved the freedom to write what inspires me. At Silhouette, my interest in the military has been nurtured and supported enthusiastically. With Silhouette's support, I helped to create the subgenre of military romances. It has met with resounding success—thanks to you!

That is why MORGAN'S MERCENARIES: LOVE AND DANGER is an achievement not only for Silhouette Special Edition but for readers who have loved the Trayhern family since LOVE AND GLORY. And everyone, judging from the thousands of letters I've received over the years, fell in love with Morgan Trayhern and Laura Bennett.

Well, after all those years of pleading to see what happened to Morgan, Laura and their family, I have created a four-book series that answers all your questions! This series came about because of *you,* and I hope it gives you as much pleasure reading it as it gave me to write it. So don't think that your heartfelt thoughts and feelings about an author's characters don't count with her and her editors—this is living proof that it does!

I hope you enjoy MORGAN'S MERCENARIES: LOVE AND DANGER.

Warmly,

Lindsay McKenna

Chapter One

Pilar Martinez stood quietly before her old boss, who frowned at her from behind his massive desk.

"Pilar," Hector Ruiz said, opening his short, pudgy hands toward her, "I know you will not want this assignment." He sighed, then sat a little straighter in his well-padded executive chair. "As your old friend, I asked you to come into Lima today to see me. To talk of this problem—together."

Pilar moved to the leather wing chair that Hector was gesturing for her to make herself comfortable in, her low-heeled shoes making no sound on the thick maroon carpeting. How long had it been? She mused as she sat, crossing her legs beneath the skirt of her pale pink business suit. Ten years ago, she had stood in this same office, a young woman whom everyone said belonged back in her native village with her family, not in the governmental halls of power.

Pilar studied her old friend and mentor. Hector had been like a father shadowing her life then, protective of her youth and naïveté as the daughter of the Spanish ambassador—a Castilian nobleman—and a Quechua Indian housemaid. Unlike most of Peruvian Society, Hector had held no prejudice against her as a mestiza. Instead, he had treated her with unfailing kindness despite her mixed-blood ancestry, and for that she would be forever grateful.

Now, she noted, perspiration shone on Hector's wrinkled brow. Though he was short and fat, Hector possessed a certain vanity about his appearance. He liked jewelry, and several heavy gold and diamond rings studded his stubby fingers. His suits were of the finest fabrics and craftmanship yet they managed to hang on him poorly despite every effort by his tailors to correct their fit. His shoulders were simply too round and slumped, no matter how much padding the tailors added. He looked a little as if he were wearing football pads, Pilar thought with a secret smile.

"It has been a long time," she agreed softly, smoothing her skirt's silk fabric across her thighs. She took the white leather purse from her shoulder and placed it in her lap, draping her fingers across it, as she smiled at Hector over the expanse of his desk. The huge mahogany piece dwarfed him, but Pilar knew that the rule in Peruvian business—and even more so here in the halls of the country's government—was that the importance of the person was related directly to the size of the office and the desk within it. As if for extra insurance, a gold pen set shone conspicuously from its place on the gleaming desk top. Behind Hector framed color photos of his family, ten in all, lined a shelf. Many diplomas and certificates of accomplishments adorned the rich mahogany walls, and the windows overlooking Lima provided an appropriately impressive backdrop, framed by wine damask drapes. Everything about Hector's office testified to his power.

"Too long," Hector agreed, then nodded at the approach of his secretary. "Ah, here is Manuela Gomez. She brings us good, rich coffee and some cookies."

Pilar turned slightly to see Hector's secretary, now in her fifties, enter the sumptuous office, a silver tray in her hands. Manuela was tall and thin, her black-and-gray hair drawn back severely into the chignon at the base of her neck that Pilar recalled from years ago. Ever conservative, she wore a dull gray business suit with tasteful pearl earrings and a simple choker of pearls. The secretary studiously avoided Pilar's steady gaze as she carefully placed the silver tray on Hector's desk.

"Thank you, Manuela," Hector said with a smile as he lifted his steaming cup. "Come, Pilar, have a taste. The finest coffee in Peru."

Hector seemed unaware of Manuela's cold, fleeting look as Pilar reached for the bone-china cup, but Pilar didn't miss the implied judgment in the other woman's eyes. Evidently the passing years hadn't softened Manuela's feelings about a mere mestiza being treated royally in her boss's office. The secretary made an about-face, much like a well-schooled military officer, and left as quietly as she had come. Forcing herself to shift focus, Pilar settled the saucer in her left palm and picked up the delicate cup, savoring the black coffee's fragrance. She took a small sip.

"There is nothing like a good cup of coffee," Hector said happily, reaching for a chocolate-covered cookie. "Here, Pilar, help yourself to some of these. You're as thin as a rail. I think you take after your mother."

She smiled a little at Hector's flattering reference to her beautiful mother, thankful again for his lack of disdain toward her heritage. Instead, Hector treated Pilar with the warmth and respect due any old friend. "Thank you, but I have just had lunch."

"So," Hector said with a sigh, leaning back against the tan leather behind him, "after your husband Fernando died, you are the manager of the finest Paso Fino breeding farm in Peru? I hear your horses take the blue ribbons no matter where you show them. That is quite a compliment to you as a trainer."

She bowed her head slightly. "Working with horses suits me well, Hector."

"It's your Incan blood," he said, waving the cookie expansively in the air. "You were always quiet and gentle—like a deer, I thought when we first met. I have heard at some of the embassy parties about your taming of that rogue stallion, El Diablo—and that you are the only one who can ride or handle him. He's earned quite a reputation in the horse circles. I was with the Sepulvedas the other night at a dinner for our president, and they were complaining loudly how you swept the championships, gathering all the major awards with that black devil."

"Perhaps the Sepulveda family, with their wonderful Paso Fino breeding stock, has gotten too used to winning everything?"

Chuckling indulgently, Hector lifted the cookie toward her in a salute, then popped it into his mouth. "Mmm, this chocolate is the best. These are my favorite cookies. Are you sure you won't have any?"

Laughing lightly, Pilar said, "Hector, if I ate those, I would not fit into my riding clothes!"

He grinned affably and leaned forward for another cookie. "Very well, I will eat one for you, then."

Despite his cheerful banter, Pilar felt the tension building in her. It wasn't anything obvious, just the familiar tightening sensation that had so often served as a red flag to warn her of danger. But Hector was not dangerous. No, if anything, he'd saved her life a number of times in the past and acted as something of a paternal figure. She'd not seen him in several years, since her most-recent service to her country, but because of the horse circle she was in, she'd heard news of him at the parties she was forced to attend from time to time. Of course, Hector never forgot her birthday, in late May, and she never forgot his mid-December one. They always exchanged cards and gifts. And Pilar would always love him fiercely for his unflinching loyalty to her—despite her blood.

"Well . . ." Hector sighed, eyeing the last cookie on the silver tray. "I must say no to the last one. I'm trying to lose some weight. My doctor says my cholesterol level is too high, and I must cut out fat. Did you know that chocolate, the rich gift of the cocoa bean, is very high in cholesterol?"

"That's why I don't eat much of it," Pilar said, quirking her eyebrows at him.

With another sigh, Hector sipped his coffee and set it aside. "Even my wife, Carmellita, is making the chef produce low-fat meals for me." He wrinkled his nose. "Of course, we are invited to so many embassy parties that there is still good food to eat."

Her mouth stretched into a full smile. "Hector, you always find a way to get what you want."

Looking pleased, he laced his fingers across his protruding belly. "Yes, I do, Pilar."

"One of your skills."

He nodded. "I'll take that as a compliment." He paused, his face turning suddenly serious. "But now we must talk of business."

Pilar's stomach tightened another notch. "Yes," she murmured.

"You were a part-time undercover agent for us off and on for many years, Pilar, and your work was always above reproach. I considered you my best female agent."

Heat rose from Pilar's neck to her face at the glow in Hector's dark brown eyes. She knew he would never make such a statement lightly. "Thank you," she said.

"You gave us three years of superior service. When your father died, it was hard on you—as it was for all of us who wept at his loss. And of course I know there were, ah...let us say, extenuating circumstances for your leaving government employ." He frowned and looked up at the ceiling. "I was pleased when you agreed to help us three years ago, when Enrique Ramirez captured two of Morgan Trayhern's men." He rolled his head to the left and pinned her with a dark gaze. "Without you to help lead Jake Randolph and our special team into Ramirez's fortress, their rescue could have been a disaster, Pilar.

"Maybe," he continued, waving his hand in the air, "there are people here who would dispute that, but I don't. You were the reason for the success of that mission. You know the jungle, and you know Ramirez, because your village exists in his shadow. You knew Ramirez's trails and activities and were able to identify his thugs. Some may hold up their noses at your Incan blood, Pilar, but I never have. You have the sixth sense that good agents must possess. I think your mother's blood running through you has contributed as much as your father's to your becoming one of our finest agents. I do not take lightly what you bring to our table, Pilar."

"Thank you, Hector." It was unlike him to be so lavish with compliments. Instead, like her mother's people, he tended to believe actions spoke louder than any words could. Pilar realized he must have a great favor, indeed, to ask of her.

"You came out of retirement, and your job as manager of the Paso Fino farm to help us then, and I was greatly relieved when you said you would."

"Only because of you, Hector, and you know that."

"Yes, yes," he murmured, offering her a fatherly smile. "And I appreciated your loyalty to me. Our government has worked with Morgan Trayhern quite often over the problems of cocaine from the coca fields in the mountains sent north to the United States."

"Yes, I know." Her mother's village, which made its living by agriculture, had nearly been coerced by Ramirez's thugs to turn away from their usual crops and grow coca for the express purpose of producing cocaine. Had it not been for the elders, including her influential grandmother, Aurelia, the village might have fallen for Ramirez's cajoling and trinkets. Instead, it was one of the few communities in the mountainous region that had not been gobbled up by the man.

Hector took out a linen handkerchief and mopped his perspiring brow. "Pilar, you are like my own daughter, you know that?"

Her stomach tightened even more. "Hector, you said the same thing to me three years ago when Morgan Trayhern's men were captured by Ramirez." She placed the cup and saucer back on the silver tray.

"Yes, yes, I did." He carefully refolded the handkerchief and placed it in his back pocket. "What I tell you now is to be held in total confidence. Do you understand that?"

"Of course," Pilar murmured. She clasped her hands on top of her purse. Hector's expression had become pained. "What is going on, Hector? I don't think you looked this worried when Trayhern's men were captured. It must be very bad."

"It is, it is, Pilar." He stood up and lumbered around the desk, his gaze never leaving hers. "You are like a daughter to me, Pilar," he repeated, "and God in Heaven knows—" he raised his hand in testimony "—I don't want to ask this of you. You have always been so loyal and honest. You are young and beautiful, with a lifetime stretching before you.

I hate to even talk of this incident, but I must. I fear you are the only one who can help us.''

He leaned against the edge of his desk, very near her chair, his voice lowering with feeling. ''You know that our government interfaces on all levels with the United States. We have worked with their FBI, their CIA, DEA and so on, over the years. Now we have military specialists from the army and Marine Corps down here helping our troops wipe out the cocaine connections. And you know that Morgan Trayhern's people were asked to participate in the defending of certain villages near Ramirez's mountain fortresses.'' He looked at her intently. ''You remember meeting Morgan?''

Pilar nodded somberly. ''Of course, Hector.''

''He is a man of immense integrity. Like you and me, Pilar.''

''Yes, he was. I liked him immediately.''

''His word is his bond,'' Hector agreed. ''I could always count on Morgan to be honest. He never played word games or hid a secret agenda as so many of the other government people we deal with do. Do you recall that after you helped free his men from Ramirez's prison, he sent a huge donation to your village as thanks?''

''I won't ever forget it,'' Pilar said, closing her eyes in thought. She had met Morgan Trayhern at a party at the American embassy a month after his men had been freed. He'd asked specifically to meet her, to thank her personally for her help in leading the troops successfully through the hazardous jungles and mountains to Ramirez's hideout. Morgan's intensity had impressed her. Never had she met a man so profoundly loyal to the people he employed. The depth of his concern for them, unmatched even by Hector's warmth and caring, had shaken her.

Morgan had toasted Pilar in front of all the officials, generals and ambassadors, openly acknowledging her help.

And she had stood, champagne in hand, blushing and longing to run away. She had never liked the limelight, but Morgan had gently wrapped his hand around her arm—as if he knew she might bolt—and raised his glass, his voice ringing with emotion as he gave her the lion's share of credit for the mission's success.

Later, he had pulled her aside and asked if she would consider working for Perseus. Pilar had been honored, but her days as an undercover agent were over. After the pain of the events that had first caused her to leave her country's service at twenty-one, she'd sworn never to resume that role, so she had turned Morgan down. Never would she forget his probing gaze as he'd silently studied her—as if he could look inside her head, inside her heart, and know what she was thinking and feeling. Only one other man had ever affected her that way. But with Morgan she had felt none of the panic or anxiety that the other man had aroused, only the burning focus of his care and perception.

Morgan hadn't been daunted by her lineage, either. In fact, he'd applauded her Indian blood. One of the reasons she had taken the mission in the first place was because of the Eastern Cherokee heritage of Wolf Harding, one of the two men captured by Ramirez. And she'd told Morgan the truth about that decision. It didn't matter whether Wolf was North American or South American, they shared the same blood. Morgan seemed to intuitively understand her reasoning.

When he'd asked what he could do to thank her, Pilar had been dumbfounded. No one had ever asked that of her before, so she'd had no words for him. Morgan had placed his hand on her shoulder and said he would think of an appropriate way to repay her courage in laying her life on the line for his people. Two weeks later, Pilar had been back at work at the horse farm when she'd received a check from Perseus for twenty-five thousand dollars. An accompanying letter from Morgan explained she was to use the money for her village in whatever way she felt was needed.

And every year since then, a check for the same amount had arrived. Pilar took the money to the council of elders of the village, which included her grandmother, and in three years, the local children had a schoolhouse and a teacher. Books had been bought, classes organized, and now a vocational school was being built to serve the entire region, where Indian children could learn not only to read and write, but other marketable skills as well. All thanks to Morgan Trayhern's unending generosity.

Pilar opened her eyes. "What do you want of me, Hector?" she asked steadily.

"It concerns Morgan."

"Oh?"

"Yes." He sighed. Again, he took out his handkerchief and mopped his brow. "Something very bad has happened," he muttered. "I'm afraid Ramirez and Garcia have conspired to kidnap Morgan from his home in the United States and to take his wife, Laura, and their son, Jason, as well."

Pilar was instantly on her feet. "Oh, no!" Her purse slid off her lap. Shaken, she leaned down and retrieved it. "When did this happen, Hector?"

"Not long ago." He shrugged lamely. "We were contacted immediately, and my office has been working feverishly to help Perseus with its efforts to locate them. The good news is that Laura was found at Garcia's estate on Nevis Island, in the Caribbean, and Jason, their small *niño,* was found in Maui, Hawaii."

Pilar's stomach tightened into a knot, and she pressed her palm against it. "*Dios,* Hector. Are they all right? What about Morgan? Have they found him? Is he dead or alive?"

He held up his hand. "One question at a time, Pilar." He wiped his brow. "Laura was rescued first, and now I've received word that Jason is safe, too. The Pentagon just intercepted a satellite message, and they've been able to confirm that Morgan is being held at Ramirez's stronghold near your village."

Pilar's stomach screamed with pain, and she swallowed against a dry throat. "Oh, no...." She inhaled sharply. "He's alive?"

"We don't know."

"Knowing the snake that Ramirez is, Morgan is alive but very badly tortured," Pilar said bitterly, pressing a hand to her forehead. "Not Morgan Trayhern. Of all people, Hector. He is a good man. A man with a generous heart." She sank back into her chair, glad for its support.

Hector moved to her side and patted her shoulder gently. "I know, Pilar. I know. I'm aware of his generosity to you and your village. I don't know too many men in this world with such strength of loyalty to others. It grieves me badly in my heart of hearts to know that Ramirez has him hostage."

Shutting her eyes, Pilar tried to stop the anguish threatening to rise from her stomach into her throat. "He's such a fine person," she said in a choked voice. "You saw what Ramirez did to the two men we rescued?"

"Yes," Hector murmured heavily, moving back to his former position against the desk. "The Indian almost died. Ramirez is a monster when it comes to drugs and torture methods."

"Ramirez hates Morgan," Pilar whispered, looking up at her former boss. "He even threatened to come into our village with his men and kill all of us. He did that to another village near us."

"That is why you are here, Pilar," Hector said in a low voice. "I must ask for your help once again. I need you to lead one of Morgan's finest operatives to the fortress. We are afraid if we go in with special troops, a second time,

Ramirez will kill Morgan. Ramirez will be expecting us to use the same tactics. He knows we will try to rescue Morgan if we locate him. Luckily, right now, we believe Ramirez has no idea that we have done so.

"That is where you come in, Pilar," continued Hector, settling more heavily against the solid mahogany. "We want you to go back to your village. Don the clothes of your people and go undercover, saying you're the daughter of a farmer from one of the villages Ramirez controls. They don't know everyone from those communities, so you should be safe enough in that regard. Lead this agent to Ramirez's fortress. A special team in several helicopters will wait well outside Ramirez's sight and hearing."

"What do you want me to do then, Hector?"

"We want you to penetrate the fortress, Pilar. Find out where Morgan is being kept. If he is alive or dead."

"And then this special team will fly in and take him out?"

"Yes." He frowned. "This mission will be much more dangerous for you, Pilar. Last time, you led a contingent of troops to the fortress and stood back while they made the assault. This time it is different." He gave her a keen look. "Your life will be in direct jeopardy. There will be no immediate and assured rescue if you get into trouble. But you'll be going in with one of Morgan's most trusted mercenaries. Two against Ramirez. The odds are not fair, I grant you, but if we are to have a prayer of rescuing Morgan, we must do things differently and surprise Ramirez completely. I'm sure he will be expecting troops as last time and will have prepared accordingly.

"Many people from these villages serve as his eyes and ears, as you know. You must have as little contact with anyone as possible. If you must talk to people, tell them this white *Norte Americano* has hired you to take him into the jungles to carry on his botany work. Morgan's mercenary will pose as a biologist from Stanford University in California, and you as his guide. The local people will accept that explanation. Scientists are always coming to our country for such reasons.

"You are to make your way through the jungle and into the mountains to his fortress, *El Nido del Águila,* the 'Eagle's Nest.' Enter the fortress and find Morgan."

Pilar wrinkled her nose. "Any woman entering *El Nido del Águila* is a target, Hector. You know that."

"Yes, yes, I do know it. But someone must get in and verify that Morgan is there."

"This plan is very dangerous, Hector," Pilar said with great deliberation. "I have a daughter to raise. I cannot just throw responsibility aside without serious promise from you—from the government of Peru—that you will care for her monetarily if I am killed."

He stared at her. "Then you will take this assignment?"

"Only because Morgan is involved. Hector, I do not want to put my life on the line. My daughter, Rane, is eight years old, and she is my world—" Her voice broke. "I know my grandparents will care for Rane while I take this mission. But if Ramirez catches me, I have no doubts about what will happen to me, Hector. I have seen his cruelty. If he even suspects that I'm a government agent, he will drug me and wring the truth out of me. He will rape and kill me, then send his men to my village to kill everyone. He will kill Rane and my grandparents. I have seen the devastation he can wreak."

"The government of Peru has already signed papers on your behalf, Pilar. I told them that if you took this mission, generous monetary provisions had to be made for your daughter and village."

"Yes," she said, studying Hector. "I won't do it otherwise. I can't. . . ."

Hector moved around his desk, pulled open a drawer and produced a legal-size document. "Here, read this. If you agree with the provisions, Pilar, then sign it."

Her hand trembled slightly as she took the heavy, official-looking document. In it, the Peruvian government promised to protect her family. A stipend of one thousand dollars a month would be provided for Rane until she was eighteen years old. Rane would be sent to the university in Lima to get a degree, with all expenses paid. Permanent troop protection would be offered to the village, should Ramirez find out where she had come from. Her grandparents would be placed in a protection program and kept safe.

Pilar studied every clause carefully. Finally she looked up. "I want Rane to have a full scholarship to Harvard University, Hector. If Ramirez discovers my real name and connection, the government is to take Rane to the United States. She is to be provided three thousand dollars a month until she graduates, with payments to stop once she gets a job. She will be given a new name and identity. I know Ramirez well enough to know he would try to track my daughter down and kill her out of revenge."

"It will be done," Hector promised, taking the document and quickly writing the new clauses into the contract and initialing them. "Anything else?"

"I want my grandparents to receive a monthly check from the government of Peru for five hundred dollars until the day they die. Just because they're placed in a protection program doesn't mean they will be cared for. Government people could dump my grandparents into some small town and leave them without a way to survive."

"Very well," Hector murmured, again writing hastily. He looked up and handed her the document. "Sign, please."

Pilar took the pen. She stood and placed the document on the polished surface of Hector's desk, her stomach quivering with fear. If it weren't Morgan Trayhern's own life at stake, she would never take this mission, risking her beautiful daughter, the child created out of pure love. But she owed Morgan. Scribbling her signature, she realized the enormity of her decision.

"There...." she murmured, handing the document back to Hector. "It is official."

"And legal." Hector placed the document aside. "I will make sure that all these things are done should you be killed, Pilar." He opened his hands. "But of course we will do everything to prevent that from happening in the first place. We will do our best to ensure contact with you via radio. The special troops assigned to this mission are the best we have. And one of Morgan's best mercenaries will be at your side."

Pilar sat down. "You must be speaking of Jake Randolph, then. Remember? He was with me when I led the troops to the fortress before."

"Er...no, it isn't Jake. He's at Perseus, running the company in Morgan's absence. It is another man...." Hector pulled a file toward him and quickly opened it. "Ah, yes. And this is so fortunate, Pilar—you have worked with this man before."

Frowning, Pilar said, "I've worked only with Jake Randolph from Morgan's company."

"No, no, you misunderstand." Hector beamed happily and held up a color photo. "You must remember Culver Lachlan? He used to be with the CIA. You two worked together for three months and—"

Pilar gave a cry, standing up so swiftly that the heavy chair she was sitting in was nearly knocked over. Her fists knotted and she stared, frozen, at the face looking back at her from the photo.

Hector frowned. "Pilar? What is it? You look as if you're going to faint. *Dios,* are you all right?" He quickly dropped the photo and rushed around the desk. Slipping his hand under her elbow, he helped her back into the chair. "Come,

come," he coaxed, "sit down. There...that's it." He straightened and gave her a confused look. "Pilar, you look as though you've seen a ghost. What is it? Surely, you remember Mr. Lachlan? He was the last agent you worked with before you had to quit." He patted her shoulder. "Pilar?"

Tears rushed to her eyes as she sat rigidly, only vaguely aware of Hector's attempts to comfort her. Oh, no, no... how could this be? Could fate be this cruel? Her mouth had gone dry and her throat constricted. Tears blurred the world around her as she struggled to control her rampant feelings. *Culver.* How she had tried to put him out of her heart and mind. *Culver Lachlan.* The name sent a bittersweet river of feelings coursing through her, including a terror, and anxiety in her stomach that nauseated her.

"*Dios,* Pilar, let me get you a glass of water. You look so pale. Stay still. Stay still and I will be right back...."

She barely heard Hector leave her side. All her focus, all her rage, sadness and guilt were aimed at the photo lying on his desk. It had been years. Eight long years... Pressing her cool, trembling fingertips to her brow, Pilar tried to rise above the rush of emotions released by the unexpected sight of that photo.

Alone in the office, she stood on wobbly knees. Leaning across the desk, she forced herself to take the photo and turn it around, though her fingers seemed to burn where she touched it. *Culver Lachlan.* His name went like a knife to her suddenly aching heart. Eight painful years of trying to forget. How could he suddenly be thrown back into her life?

Suddenly panicked, Pilar acknowledged with a horrible realization that by signing those papers, she had been stuck not only with the mission, but with Lachlan. She forced herself to look at the photo. He was a giant of a man at six foot five, brawny and strong as his Scottish ancestors before him. He was square jawed, with a thick, bull-like neck, broad, powerful shoulders and a barrel chest. He was built as stoutly as the finest Paso Fino. Solid. Hard. Dangerous. Oh, how dangerous he had been to her young, vulnerable emotions! Though he'd been only twenty-five at the time himself, but he'd been far from innocent to the ways of the world as she had been.

Much as she wanted to, Pilar couldn't forget the imposing shadow Culver had cast on her life. But the man in the photo looked different from the Culver she remembered. Here was a hardened warrior with a face like armor itself, the pale blue eyes devoid of emotion.

Jerking back her hand, Pilar stood hypnotized by the photo, wanting to wrench her gaze from it, but helpless to do so. Her heart was pounding like that of a frightened animal relentlessly pursued by a jaguar. She saw a coldness she'd not seen before in Culver. His mouth... She quivered internally, recalling his mouth upon her own, hotly, swiftly taking hers, stealing her breath, stealing her very soul with those scalding, spiraling kisses. Now that mouth had become a thin, harsh line, no longer revealing any softness.

"Pilar?" Hector came rushing back into the room with a glass of water, the liquid slopping onto his hand in his hurry. "Here. Drink this...."

She sat down and accepted the glass as Hector hovered anxiously, wringing his hands. He was breathing hard, and she felt bad to have caused him such distress. After sipping the water dutifully, she handed it back to him.

"Th-thank you, Hector. I will be all right now."

"Are you sure? I thought you were going to faint, Pilar."

"This agent, Lachlan..."

"Yes?" Hector set the glass down on his desk, near enough for her to reach it if she wanted to. He circled the desk and sat. "What about him?"

"Do—" In spite of herself, her voice broke. "Do I have to work with him?"

"There is no one else. Is there a problem here, Pilar? I thought you would be overjoyed to know that an agent you had worked with undercover before would be helping you again. You already know each other, and he seemed to like you. I recall he did try to contact you after that mission. You're a team already, Pilar, and I believe it will serve you well."

Pilar felt torn as never before to divulge the shaming truth to Hector. But the look of fatherly anxiety on his face stopped her. She could tell no one. Not even him. Only her grandparents and Fernando, her now deceased husband, knew the truth. Not even Rane knew—nor would she ever know. Pilar's throat ached with tension from holding back unshed tears. She wanted to weep violently, like the sudden thunderstorms that popped up and rolled across the hills above the jungle, sweeping everything clean. But if she cried, Hector would only worry more.

"Pilar?"

"It's all right," she managed to whisper. Picking up the glass of cool water again, she sipped it.

" You do not trust this man?"

"I . . . trust him. . . ."

"What then?"

"Are you sure he's with Morgan's company?"

"Very sure. Jake Randolph called me personally to tell me he was available. Jake, too, felt it was a good thing you two had worked together before."

Touching her throat, Pilar whispered, "And he wanted to come on this mission knowing I would be his partner?"

Hector shrugged dramatically. "Jake and I did not talk about that. He just said that Lachlan was available and would take the mission."

"But he's been told I'll be on it?" she persisted.

Hector began to relax a little, some of the tension draining from his features. "Of course, Pilar. He was briefed as much as you have been."

Faintness rimmed Pilar's vision, but she fought it off. The desire, heartbreak, rage and anguish refused to be stilled within her, and she felt like a volcano erupting inwardly. Only the cool solidity of the glass clenched between her hands gave her some semblance of sanity in that moment. Pilar couldn't believe Culver would go on a mission with her. Not now. Not ever again, after what had happened.

"Wh-when will he arrive?"

"Tomorrow afternoon at three. We'll pick him up at the Lima airport."

"And where do you want us to meet?"

Hector sighed and brought out a large manila envelope stamped Top Secret. "Only one other person and I know the contents of this envelope, Pilar. I helped formulate the plans contained within it, including specific and detailed instructions of anything you need to know. This mission has the strictest degree of secrecy because we know there are moles on Ramirez's payroll.

"Please be very careful with the contents of this envelope. Read it where no one will disturb you. Provisions have been suggested for Rane while you are gone, and we will make sure your employer has no inkling of why you're leaving for two weeks. We've arranged to have one of our agents call the farm and ask them to fly you to Argentina to pick up a mare that will be bred to El Diablo. The owner will think you are in Argentina, preparing the flight for the mare. Of course, we'll have a mare show up at the farm when you return to maintain your cover."

"Good," Pilar whispered as she nervously touched the thick, heavy envelope.

"Here," Hector said with a frown, handing Lachlan's photo to her. "Put it in there with the rest."

Woodenly, she did as she was instructed. "Are you sure he knows he's going to be working with me?" she couldn't resist asking again.

Hector gave her a strange look. "I'm positive. Jake Randolph said he would brief Lachlan immediately after our phone call. I told him I would try to talk you into taking this mission." He touched the phone at his right hand. "As soon as you leave, I'll call Jake to tell him you've signed the contract."

"I see." Pilar took a deep, unsteady breath and got to her feet. She gripped the edge of the desk for a moment, reorienting herself.

"Pilar," he said worriedly, "is there something I should know? You are acting strangely, and it isn't like you. Is there a problem with this agent? I personally went over his file from the CIA and Perseus. He has an impeccable record and was given the highest marks when he left The Company. You will see that for yourself, though." He pointed to the envelope beneath her left arm. "His complete dossier is in there for you to peruse."

Alarm spread through her. "And what about me? The information on me?"

Hector shrugged. "He will be given the same."

Alarm became panic. "What of my family?" *What of Rane?*

"All the usual information."

Her heart plummeted. Would Culver know? Would he suspect? He couldn't. He just couldn't. Pilar tried to focus on her legs, willing strength into her wobbly knees. "Very well, Hector, I'm going to go home."

"Good," he said, getting up. He came around the desk and threw his arm around her shoulders briefly. "Be careful, Pilar. I know you are an excellent agent. And you have much to live for. You've got that beautiful daughter...."

Tears flooded her eyes as she hugged the older man affectionately. "I'll be very careful," she whispered. "Just knowing you're behind me, Hector, gives me hope."

He released her and looked at her worriedly. "This is one mission we cannot fail. I know the walls have ears. I pray to God I have taken every possible precaution to ensure the safety of you and your family."

Pilar nodded, sniffed and turned away. If she didn't leave, she was going to cry in earnest. For herself. For the fear she felt about the mission. As she walked to the door to let herself out, she knew she had to tell her grandparents what was happening. Even though the mission was classified, she had to get Rane to the safety only they could provide.

As she walked down the long, polished hallway, Pilar hoped Hector had already provided those outlets on her behalf. He knew how much family meant to her. She'd already lost her mother and the two men in her life she'd loved with a fierceness that defied description. Her father had passed away. And Culver? He'd probably thought she was dead. Or wished she was. She knew he would never forgive her. Not even after eight years.

Her hands felt damp and cold as she stood waiting for the elevator that would take her to the first-floor lobby. It was January, the beginning of summer in South America. Although Lima was the country's largest city, and its capital, it wasn't nearly as large as New York or Buenos Aires. Still, people in impeccably tailored business suits traversed the halls as she stepped from the elevator and headed toward the revolving glass-and-brass doors. Pilar hated the city. It was her Indian blood, she knew. To her, cities meant congestion, chaos, pollution and stress—people hurrying and scurrying everywhere.

Catching a taxi outside the complex, she directed the driver to take her to the train station, from where she would head south, out of the city. Rancho Verde was a mere hour away from all this craziness, but right now, Pilar longed as never before for its peace and open spaces. She felt suffocated in the cab, even though the windows were down, allowing the warm salt air of the Pacific to waft through, lifting strands of her shoulder-length hair.

What was she going to do? How would Culver react to her? She tipped her head back against the seat and closed her eyes. She could almost feel his hatred. His anger. Could she blame him? No. But then, he never would have understood, either. He could be stubborn, immovable and highly opinionated. He had walked into her life like a tank blasting away, and she had been soft and malleable in response. And then things had gotten out of hand. Completely.

Sighing, Pilar pressed her hand against her brow. What was she going to do? She had signed a contract she had to fulfill. And she *wanted* to fulfill it, because Morgan deserved her help. But how was she going to do it with Culver at her side? She would be terribly distracted, she knew. And distraction could get her killed. Rane would be in danger, too. What if Ramirez found out the truth of her identity? Her precious daughter's life would be on the line as much as her own—as would her grandparents'. *What was she going to do?* And how, with Culver's glowering, menacing presence, was she going to hold herself together long enough to rescue Morgan?

Chapter Two

Culver is coming. Culver is coming. The words echoed through Pilar's thoughts with each beat of her thorough-bred mare's galloping hooves. Desperate to do some-thing—anything—to quell her growing anxiety, she had placed a jump saddle on Honey, a lovely, seventeen-hand-high chestnut, her favorite mount at Rancho Verde. But as she and Honey circled the largest of the horse farm's pipe-enclosed training arenas, Pilar's mind refused to stray from the coming meeting.

The day was warm and slightly damp, with the tang of salt in the air. The Pacific Ocean was less than a mile away, and humidity tended to settle in the lower elevations. Rancho Verde was a dream come true—the largest horse farm in Peru, immaculately kept by the Antonio and Cecelia Navarro family—and Pilar longed to find her usual peace of mind through work. But it was three o'clock, and she couldn't escape the knowledge that Culver would even now be landing at the Jorge Chavez Airport in Lima. Hector would be meeting and briefing him, then, according to her orders, she was to meet him at seven tonight at Hotel of the Andes, one of Lima's finest four-star palaces.

Honey snorted as she cantered slowly, guided by Pilar's sensitive, gloved hands. Riding brought Pilar a sense of freedom she otherwise never seemed able to achieve—except in visits to her grandparents' village. A black, velvet-covered hard hat protected her head in case of falls as she put Honey through her paces over the two-to-three-foot jumps. But Honey was so steady that Pilar never worried about that possibility. The arena was quiet, for the afternoon and early evening here were considered siesta time, and no one worked. Only Pilar couldn't rest. She hadn't slept well last night, either, her dreams entwining with haunting nightmares from her shameful past.

The sky was cerulean blue, with a few white wisps that reminded Pilar of Honey's flowing flaxen mane as they cantered about the enclosure. Tall trees, grown scraggly from the frequent winds off the ocean, hugged the arena, and a cooling breeze chased away the worst of the early summer heat. The hacienda itself, constructed of pale yellow stucco with a red, Spanish-tile roof, was situated below the training grounds in a small vale. From their higher position, the various arenas for the jumpers overlooked the surrounding, tree-covered hills and Pilar could see the sparkling deep blue of the Pacific in the distance.

She guided Honey with her legs and a slight change of weight on the saddle as she took three jumps in a row. Each time the mare gathered and collected the energy in her hind legs, Pilar felt as if she were on a powerful, living spring. The big, easygoing mare trusted Pilar implicitly, sailing effortlessly over another two-and-a-half-foot jump.

A combination jump, consisting of a pool of water and a four-foot barrier, was next, requiring Honey to stretch to her maximum length as well as jump "big." Just as Pilar steadied the mare for the exercise, the back of her neck prickled. A red flag. Why was she sensing danger? She had little time to assess the warning as she lifted upward, knees jammed tightly into the rolls of the saddle, riding easily on the horse's withers as they approached the combined jump. Honey's front legs rose and she soared like the Andean condors that floated over her grandparents' village. For a moment the mare seemed to have wings like Pegasus. As Honey landed solidly on the other side of the jump, Pilar gently pulled on the reins.

Squinting against the western sun, she looked toward the buildings that housed the tack and stables. Her hands were wet, the gloves slightly slippery on the double reins as the mare came to a halt. The animal's ears went instantly forward—toward the same area Pilar was studying. The prickling sensation at the back of her neck was a sure sign of trouble, Pilar knew. That internal warning system—which her mother had attributed to her spirit guardian, a jaguar—had saved her life a number of times when she'd worked undercover. So now she strained to see past the blinding sunlight to the stable area.

Nothing moved. As expected, the farm help were enjoying siesta. A few horses hung their heads out of their roomy box stalls and looked around, but none were snorting or appearing alarmed. One of the older dogs, a black-and-white mongrel Pilar had rescued from Lima long ago, moved with a limp down the breezeway between the stalls. Frowning, Pilar lifted her hand and touched the back of her neck. Rubbing it, she again swept her gaze along the long, rectangular barn area. She saw no one. But she felt someone watching. Watching *her.*

Compressing her lips, she gathered up the reins. Perhaps if she ignored the sensation, it would go away. Maybe it was merely anticipation over having to meet Culver tonight. Her stomach had been on edge ever since Hector had dropped his bombshell. And her heart . . . well, her heart felt as if Culver's own massive, powerful hand was relentlessly squeezing it. After all, what was she going to say to him? That she was sorry? It seemed such a lame, weak word at this point. Blowing out a breath of air in exasperation, Pilar tried to return her focus to Honey and the remaining jumps, but the sensation of being watched refused to go away. Danger was present—and it was very near.

Culver Lachlan stood just inside the breezeway of the stables, watching Pilar Martinez ride a magnificent chestnut jumper. He scowled as he eyed her, struggling to control those wild feelings that had first erupted in him when Jake had ordered him to take this mission. Pillar was like hot butter in a skillet, so effortlessly did she move in rhythm with her horse. It was obvious she loved to ride. And Culver remembered all too well seeing that same pure joy on her face a long time ago. A joy that he'd— *Stop it,* he ordered himself harshly. *Stop remembering. It won't do any good. She left you when you were down for the count.*

But no matter how much he wanted to hate Pilar for what she'd done to him, Culver couldn't bring himself to feel it. The voice inside his head coldly announced that she had used him for her own means, gotten what she wanted and abandoned him.

Well, what the hell had he expected, anyway? She was a woman, and the women in his life had always been as unstable as C-4 explosives. He'd never had good luck with them. Still, Pilar had seemed different. His gaze never left her as she rode at a canter around the arena, taking the jumps with ease. Even at this distance, Culver could see that the twenty-two-year-old ingenue he'd fallen hopelessly in love with eight years ago had become a woman, blooming with the full-blown beauty of a mature rose compared to the sweeter, less-complex bud—and still able to take his breath away.

Was Pilar's ebony hair still long? He couldn't help but wonder. Were her eyes still those of the jaguar that roamed the Peruvian jungles? She had the most arresting eyes Culver had ever seen. Her Incan heritage made them almost black, but Culver had found out quickly that he could determine Pilar's emotions by watching for sparkles of real gold in their depths.

Over the three months they'd worked together, he'd learned to love watching those huge, luminous eyes, slightly tilted, again by her Incan heritage, shift from near black to a rich, golden brown. His heart twisted in his chest. How deeply his feelings ran—even now. It was stupid, he knew. He was thirty-three years old—old enough to know better. *Face it,* he reminded himself cruelly, *she was a young college girl out for a fling.* She hadn't wanted commitment. She'd wanted the high adventure and pulse-pounding sensuality of combining passion with life-and-death work.

Shifting his weight to his other booted foot, Culver rested his shoulder against a large, wooden support post and absorbed the sight of Pilar as she rode. Memories came flooding back—so many of them painful. Why had she run out on him in his darkest hour? All he'd wanted was Pilar at his side. He'd been scared, seeing his whole twenty-five years of life flash before his closed eyes. Yet as soon as they'd made it to the hospital, she'd disappeared. The last memory of Pilar he had was of her running alongside the gurney as the ambulance attendants raced with it toward an operating room. He'd been bleeding to death. Pilar had been crying, gripping his limp, nerveless hand. Her long, luxurious hair had been damp and twisted into strands, the expression on her face one of sheer terror, and those lips... Culver groaned. No one had a mouth quite like Pilar's. Full and almost heart-shaped, it had drawn him like a hummingbird to a rosy bloom filled with sweet nectar.

With a sigh, Culver crossed his arms over his chest. It was agony to be here. God knew, he'd fought Jake about this assignment. He wanted no part of teaming up with Pilar—not after what had happened. How could he trust her? His heart certainly couldn't. After he'd nearly died in that hospital, he'd tried many times to contact her. And to what end? Hector would merely say Pilar was undercover and couldn't be contacted, and eventually Culver had gotten the message. After all, even undercover agents came off the job to rest once in a while.

Pilar's canary yellow breeches showed off hips and long legs as slender as he remembered. At this distance, he couldn't see her face clearly, but the outline of her form was unmistakable, and unwillingly he acknowledged the tightening in his lower body at the memory of her. Culver drew in a deep, ragged breath and closed his eyes. How he'd tried to forget the feel of her warm, sleek body against his. Forget her small, delicate hands restlessly roaming his chest, his shoulders, eliciting fire storms as she caressed him, her eyes big in wonderment. . . .

"Stop it!" he snarled aloud. He turned, hoping no one had heard him, but the breezeway was empty. An old, limping dog approached him, wagging its tail. Angry at himself for allowing the vault of memories to spill out from beneath his steel control, Culver leaned over and patted the dog's head absently.

He had no time to waste. He had to let her know he was here. It was the last thing Culver wanted to do—face the sight of rejection in her eyes. He'd never really cared what anyone thought of him until Pilar came along. She was different, exotic—like the heady fragrance of the orchids that laced the jungle trees. And when she'd opened to him, he'd believed he'd met the woman who could fulfill him on every conceivable level. Like an orchid stretched fully into bloom, she had given herself to him, allowing him to inhale her dizzying fragrance.

To this day, Pilar haunted his dreams. He still had torrid, sensual dreams about her touch, the way she looked at him, that caressing smile that shot through him like hot sunlight, letting him know he was the center of her world. Well, it wasn't so. He'd stupidly made the assumption that Pilar felt about him the way he did about her. Culver had never fallen in love with anyone before Pilar—or since. Maybe that's why she was always in his heated, humid, jungle-like dreams like some ethereal fog that would reach out, tease him, and yet as he tried to grab it and embrace it, would dissolve upon his contact. Or, maybe the silent, dangerous jaguar who owned the jungle.

Anxiety riffled through him. Humiliation. Desire. He felt all those things as he decided to step from his hiding place and walk to the pipe fence where Pilar could see him. How would she look at him? Hector had said she knew he'd been assigned as her partner for this highly dangerous mission.

As he pushed away from the beam and straightened, Culver felt the weight of worry press down on his broad shoulders. A terrible anxiety was building in his chest. No matter how angry or hurt he was about how Pilar had treated him, he didn't want her placed in a situation where she could be killed. As he stepped out of the breezeway into the sunlight, Culver knew in the depths of his aching heart that he would still step between her and an oncoming bullet—as he had once before. He walked slowly toward the arena.

He felt a certain satisfaction in knowing she didn't realize he was here. Pilar was at the other end of the arena, having just finished a series of jumps. She had brought the thoroughbred from a canter to a walk. As Culver placed one booted foot on the fence's lowest railing, he saw her dismount. Frowning, he watched her intently. At five foot three, she was short next to the giant horse she rode. He laughed to himself, remembering their height difference. The first time Pilar had seen him, her dark eyes had widened enormously and she'd said in Spanish, "You must be a giant from a special place on earth."

Her low, breathless voice had sent tingles through him. Pilar had never met someone from Scotland, and the awe combined with curiosity in her gaze had made him feel special and powerful. At the time, Culver had been expecting to work with a hardened veteran woman agent. Instead, he'd found this wild, exotic orchid bud preparing to burst open to the world at large, and he'd wanted to be the one to watch each of her beautiful petals unfold, to reveal the honeyed depths of her womanhood.

Culver shook his head. In the eight years since, he'd waited for the memory of Pilar to disappear. But as he stood at the fence, watching her pat the thoroughbred, he realized with a terrible, sinking feeling that every emotion he'd had eight years ago was just as brilliantly alive within him today, burning fiercely and without apology. Running his fingers through his short dark hair, he wondered what he would say to her. Blazing anger paralleled an aching need.

Something happened. Culver felt it before he actually saw Pilar react. She had been petting the horse, praising it, when suddenly she turned on her booted heel and looked down the length of the arena—toward him. His heart thudded once in his chest to underscore, even at this distance, the intensity of her gaze. How he wished he could see her expression. Culver shook his head. To hell with it; the time had come. Bending down, he climbed between the rails. Sand and sawdust covered the arena, and his rough-out boots sank into the mixture as he straightened to his full height and squared his shoulders.

Pilar gasped, her hand contracting on the reins. She had to be seeing things! But she wasn't. Her eyes widened as she realized Culver Lachlan was walking down the arena—toward her. Her heart skipped a beat as panic set in. Her breathing became ragged. *Culver!* The word shot through her like an arrow—striking straight to her soul. An ache began to pool in her lower body with memories of Culver's strength and incredible tenderness as he moved deeply within her, branding her his for all time.

Tears raced into her eyes, but just as quickly, Pilar forced them away. Culver must not see her cry. He must not know how she really felt. Her hands grew sweaty as she stood by the horse, rigid with an unsettling mix of anticipation, fear and need. As he walked slowly toward her, so much came careening back to her. The sound of his laugh, low and deep, like the reverberation of a medicine drum. His pale, sky blue gaze, which sent heat jagging through her like bolts of lightning teasing the jungle canopy above her village during a storm.

The color photo of Culver she'd studied was no match for the real thing. He was still a giant to her, built sturdily, of good strong bone, as he used to say. How many times had she lain against him? Felt the weight of him upon her like a warm, secure blanket? No feeling in the world matched that of Culver on top of her, his body a shield. He always felt more stable, more solid than she. Pilar gulped as each step brought him closer. What was she going to say to him? What *could* she say? He'd never understand nor forgive her for what she'd done. Worse, if he knew the whole truth, he might try to take from her the one thing that mattered most in the world.

Culver was not conventionally handsome. He'd once said that his face was carved from the rugged granite cliffs of his Scottish home. But Pilar adored those craggy features. Now crow's-feet marked the corners of his eyes, and slashes on either side of his mouth gave new depth to his face. His cheekbones were high, like her own, but his face was square, with a hawklike nose that reminded her of the harpy eagle, a huge aggressive white eagle that plummeted like a dive-bomber through the Peruvian jungle to snatch a monkey for its dinner.

Pilar tried to steady herself, but it was impossible. Already she could feel strength ebbing from her with each wild heartbeat. Culver's eyes looked merciless. Pilar knew from experience that a deep, dark blue meant he was angry, while they became lighter with happiness. Right now they were a stormy cobalt, and the set of his mouth frightened her. How warm, exploring yet powerful that his mouth had once been against hers. As big as he was, when Culver kissed her, he'd taken her gently, inviting her to surrender herself to him. Then his kiss would deepen, becoming hotter and more frantic, until their mouths clung together with passion.

Shakily, Pilar removed her hard hat, and the black hair she'd coiled on top of her head spilled in a cascade about her shoulders. It was nowhere near the length it had been when she'd been Culver's lover. But right now, it seemed as if the eight long years between then and now had not occurred at all. Pilar felt pinned by his gaze as he moved ever closer. She trembled inwardly with a violence that frightened her. Oh, to be touched by him in that special way once more! How many nights over the years had she tossed and turned, aching to feel his strong hands caressing her damp skin as if she were a high-strung thoroughbred in need of a gentle touch to soothe her fractiousness?

Pilar's mouth grew very dry as Culver closed the distance. Only belatedly did she realize he was wearing Levi's, rough-out boots and a short-sleeved, white cotton shirt that outlined his magnificent chest and shoulders. There was nothing weak about Culver. He was macho in a way few men would ever be, in Pilar's opinion. As always, his skin was darkly bronzed, a tough shield, seemingly capable of challenging any harshness the world had to offer. A lock of dark hair tumbled across his lined brow, which was covered by a light sheen of perspiration in the summer heat.

One of the many things Pilar had come to love about Culver was his loose, elastic gait. His athletic build was his heritage, he'd told her. He came from a line of warriors who'd repeatedly challenged the kings of England. So many nuances from past conversations jammed Pilar's spinning senses as Culver came to a halt no more than six feet away. She felt the hot, angry rake of his gaze, like a wildfire burning from her black leather boots up across her thighs and abdomen, over the gentle curves of her breasts. Then his eyes locked with hers, and Pilar felt her lips part as she stared back at him, seeing the good and the bad, his weaknesses and strengths. Culver wasn't perfect by any means, and he had a nasty temper when things didn't go his way. She strove to shield herself from that anger now, fairly boiling in his dangerously darkened eyes.

"You're early," Pilar heard herself say faintly. Honey moved restively, as if sensing her confusion and anxiety, and she turned and placed her gloved hand on the mare's sweaty neck to soothe her.

Culver stared at Pilar, struggling to hold on to his anger. When she'd removed her hard hat, her delicious hair had showered around her, blue black as a raven's wing. The straight, shining strands framed her small, oval face to perfection, while Pilar's dark eyebrows reminded him of the thin crescent of the waning moon, accenting her luminous eyes framed by thick lashes. Her nose was fine and thin, and he knew it came from her father's side of the family—the Castilian aristocracy. But her slightly parted mouth was his undoing. Without a speck of lipstick, it was like a ripe, exquisite fruit begging to be picked.

Culver gathered his raging feelings. "I wanted our meeting to be private," he growled. How he ached to step forward, reach out and caress her highly flushed cheek. Pilar's skin had a golden, dusky tone, heightened by the blush in her cheeks, which gave her an endearingly helpless look. But she was far from helpless, as he knew all too well. She was a government agent and a damn good one. If not for her quick thinking, tough mind and ability to focus, he wouldn't be standing here today. Pilar's face appeared soft and vulnerable on the surface, every expression there for the reading, but he knew she was hard beneath that exterior. Hard and cruel. Selfish. Self-serving.

The short-sleeved white blouse she wore outlined her curves to perfection. Culver wondered just how many lovers Pilar had had since he'd taken her virginity. Plenty, he told himself angrily. She was petite, slender and even more graceful in her movements than he remembered. Instead of being an equestrian, she should have been a ballet dancer, though her height might have been a detriment to that career.

Nervously, Pilar pulled off her leather gloves. "I was to meet you at seven," she protested weakly. Inwardly, she cringed. If she didn't do something, she feared she would burst into tears—or throw herself into his arms. And the expression on his face spoke not of forgiveness, but of bitterness and anger.

Culver deliberately placed his hands on his hips and slowly looked around. "Yeah, I know." Dammit, why did she have to look at him like that? He could see hurt reflected in her eyes—hurt and...desire? Yes, desire of all things. After what she'd done to him. "You might as well know up front, Pilar, I didn't want to work with you."

Hiding the pain his words caused, she tucked the gloves beneath the brown belt that circled her waist. "I expected that. I asked Hector if he was sure you knew I was going to be the other agent." Pilar forced herself to look up at him. "I knew you wouldn't like it."

"No."

She gave a slight, pained shrug. "Well, what's important is Morgan."

"Is that why you volunteered for this? Did you have an affair with him, too?"

Stunned, Pilar stared at him. "What?"

"You heard me."

Pain gripped her heart. "I—uh, no, I had no affair with Morgan."

"Given the circumstances," Culver continued, "the thought crossed my mind. I know why I'm here. The man saved my life, and I owe him. But I wonder just what the hell you owe him to get you to agree to take a mission with me."

Anger erased Pilar's hurt. She glared at him. "You haven't changed at all, Culver. Not at all! You are the same pigheaded person I knew eight years ago!" She tugged gently on the reins, turning Honey to head her toward the barn.

"Hold on," Culver rasped, reaching out and grabbing Pilar's upper arm. Though careful not to hurt her, he put enough pressure in his grip to bring her to a halt. Her head snapped up, her eyes going black with fury.

"Don't touch me!" Pilar cried, jerking out of his grasp. *Dios,* why did he have to touch her? She backed away, breathing raggedly, and raised her fingers to the place his massive hand had covered. "Don't *ever* touch me again, do you hear me?" she rattled, her voice off-key. Tears stung her eyes, and Pilar forced them back. She saw contriteness come into Culver's eyes, but it never reached his rugged features or the set slash of his mouth. "Don't do that again," she whispered brokenly. "Not ever..."

Culver stood, breathing hard, his hands curled into fists at his sides. "Stop acting like I hurt you, Pilar. I didn't, and you know it."

Pilar tried to focus her spinning senses. Culver's contact had been completely unexpected—the only thing that could make her drop the shield she hid behind. He didn't realize how evocative his touch was, or that it made her want to surrender to him—all over again. Instead, he was taking her response just the opposite—as an indication that she couldn't stand his touch out of hatred or disgust.

Her heart swelled with anguish at that knowledge, and Pilar drew herself up to her full height. She allowed her hand to drop from the arm Culver had touched, but she was unable to keep her voice from trembling as she said, "We have to work together. I accept that. What I don't accept is you thinking you own me. You don't. And don't you dare touch me again. My reasons for helping Morgan are my own. Truth never needs a defense, Culver, and I don't have to spill my heart to you any longer." Pilar saw her words hit him like bullets ripping into his flesh. The pain showed in his eyes, no matter how impassive his face remained.

What they had shared long ago, she was discovering, was still just as vibrant as ever. A miraculous thing had occurred after they'd made love that first time on a luxurious carpet of grass near that pond. From that moment on, Culver had not been able to veil his true feelings from her.

Now Pilar read the pain in his eyes and regretted her words. The last person she wanted to hurt was Culver. She'd already hurt him more than anyone in her life, and she could barely live with that knowledge even to this day. Pain was something she'd known a great deal about, and she'd promised herself to avoid causing it to others, yet the very person she loved most in the world was the one she'd hurt the most. Pilar ached for Culver, wanting to take back her words but knowing she didn't dare. If she didn't erect some kind of barrier now, she would be lost.

"Fine," Culver growled. "Let's get out of this sun and into the barn. We have a lot to discuss before I go to the hotel tonight."

Nodding jerkily, Pilar brought her mare along with her. So much remained unsaid, yet she could say nothing. It was obvious Culver hated her for what she'd done. If he could not forgive her for that, he would never forgive her for the far worse transgression she'd made. She'd been so young then—and a product of the culture that raised her, despite her Harvard education. But how could Culver be expected to understand that—to know the full extent of the pressures brought to bear on her then?

Looking back now from her more-mature perspective, Pilar could see that the decision she'd made eight years ago might have been wrong—and in making that decision, she might innocently have committed a transgression far worse than the one that had originally caused her to flee from Culver's bedside on that awful night.

Chapter Three

Culver tried like hell to ignore the gentle sway of Pilar's hips as they made their way back to the barn's breezeway. He stood back and watched as she put the sweaty mare into cross ties and unsaddled her. Such anxiety showed in Pilar's dark, beautiful eyes. Still, he couldn't keep his gaze from dropping to her mouth—and couldn't prevent the heated memories of taking that soft, luscious mouth from rushing back to taunt him.

"Why didn't you wait and meet me at the hotel?" Pilar demanded breathlessly as they made their way to her office, a small house near the barn, after the horse had been put away. The sun was lower in the west now, the trees beginning to cast long shadows across the property. She pushed several errant strands of hair from her eyes.

Culver kept his gaze on her as she opened the door to the tiny white stucco house with its red tile roof. "I don't trust the Peruvian government. I flew in early, just in case."

Glancing up at him, unable to stop her inner trembling, Pilar moved quickly into the coolness of her sumptuous, yet homey office. Culver looked out of place in it—clumsily large compared to the delicate furniture the owners had installed for her. "Hector is someone you can trust," she said, hesitating at the kitchen entrance.

"I had my luggage sent on to the hotel," he said. "And I contacted Hector."

Her stomach wouldn't settle down. "I have things I must do."

Lowering himself to a Queen Anne couch, Culver shrugged. "Go ahead, then. I'll wait."

Pilar hesitated. His rugged features were unreadable as he surveyed his surroundings. She needed to *think*, but his presence made it nearly impossible. She got herself a glass of water from the apartment-size kitchen and took it into the bathroom with her. First, a cooling shower to wash away the grime of the day's riding. Then she'd be ready to head to her apartment in Lima.

Culver ordered his body to relax, with little success. He'd never dreamed he'd see Pilar again, and he knew he was still emotionally in shock. She hadn't changed at all—except to become more beautiful, more confident and more desirable, dammit. The college girl had grown into a stunning woman. Frowning, he thought of the anguish in Pilar's voice when he'd pulled her to a stop. And it had been anguish—real pain. My God, how much did she hate him, to flinch from his touch like that?

Wiping his mouth, Culver looked around Pilar's serenely elegant office. It was atypical for Peru, he supposed. The furniture wasn't the dark, ponderous Spanish style, and small plants lined the window, where sheer, pale green drapes had been drawn back to allow the north light to enter. The furniture was as graceful and diminutive as Pilar, the couch and two chairs leaving plenty of the floral, Victorian-design carpet visible. The walls also had been painted a pale green and were hung with prints of Amazonian orchids. He scowled.

On a bookshelf across the room, he saw several framed photos. Pushing himself up, Culver moved toward them. A large gold frame held the photo of a black-haired girl with light brown eyes, smiling for the camera. She wore a pale pink dress with lace at the collar, and a dark pink ribbon held her hair back. Culver sensed something oddly familiar about the child, who he guessed must be around seven or eight. *That smile.* Culver's fingers burned as he replaced the photograph on the shelf. It was Pilar's smile. A bitter taste filled his mouth. Pilar's child. She had married, obviously. Or had she?

A sickening feeling invaded Culver as he took in the next photo, where a tall, gray-haired man held the same child, Pilar next to them, smiling. Happy. Looking around, Culver wondered where this man was. If, indeed, Pilar was married to him. Divorces didn't go down well in South America. Women who tried to divorce their husbands could end up dead in the perverse macho traditions of the culture. Violence against South American women was a common, everyday occurrence. How had Pilar gotten away unscathed?

Then Culver laughed bitterly at himself. Pilar had gotten away from him, hadn't she? He'd been the one mortally wounded by their relationship, after all, not her. Setting the second photo back in place, Culver noted sounds coming from the hall then heard the shower running. A crazy urge to shed his clothes and join Pilar in that shower was nearly his undoing. Somehow, he had to get a tighter grip on his emotions. He would never have believed he still had this much feeling left for Pilar.

It had hurt so damn much when she'd cried out like that as he gripped her arm. She was the last person on the face of this earth he wanted to hurt—even now. Quirking his mouth as he wandered into the kitchen and got himself a drink of water, Culver decided he was crazy. Pilar had hurt him, not the reverse. He'd loved her, and she had wounded him—forever.

Returning to the living-room sofa with the glass of water in hand, Culver tried to be patient. Jet lag was pulling at him, and he was exhausted by the events of the past forty-eight hours. Suddenly the couch seemed so inviting that he put the glass aside and stretched out. Closing his eyes, he told himself that he was going to rest for only a moment.

Pilar dressed hurriedly in a dark blue cotton shirtdress—one of a few simple outfits she kept in the closet at her office. She belted it with white leather, then slipped into comfortable white sandals. Her briefcase was packed. Where they were going, she wouldn't be doing much paperwork. An hour had passed since Culver had blasted back into her lonely world, and her heart was still beating out of control, underscoring her surging emotions. Oh, why had he touched her? Memory of his roughened, caressing fingers moving across her body made her stop what she was doing and take a deep, unsteady breath.

Culver appeared older, more mature, naturally, but also harder. The look he'd given her, so cold and unfeeling, was one she'd never seen from him. Pilar knew she deserved it, and accepted it with a confirmation of her guilt. It would serve neither of them for him to know the full truth. *Ever.* Turning, she picked up her briefcase, shut off the light and walked down the hall toward the living room.

A sudden sound stopped her—and stirred a familiar chord deep within her. Snoring. It was Culver snoring! Her mouth curved tenderly for a moment. Whenever Culver slept on his back, he snored. How many times had he awakened her with his snoring? But with a nudge from her hand, he'd turn onto his side without waking and the snoring would stop. The memory was warm, filled with love. Pain flared on the heels of it. How many years had she slept alone? How many times had she awakened during the night and reached out for Culver's comforting presence, only to find him a figment of some dream?

Releasing a little sigh, Pilar told herself to get moving. She had much to do before they left Lima. As she stepped quietly into the living room, she saw Culver's long frame draped across the couch. He was asleep, his thick arms crossing his chest, one leg dangling over the end of the couch, the other sprawled out next to it. In sleep, he looked less harsh. Less threatening, Pilar realized. She knew she should wake him, but something begged her not to do it just yet.

As if an invisible cord tied her to him, Pilar moved even closer, to within a few feet of the couch. Culver slept deeply, his snoring ragged. No longer were his lips pressed into a dark slash of accusation. This mouth was the one she remembered, the one she'd kissed hundreds of times in their short, torrid months together in the jungle. For the first time Pilar remembered Culver's smile, and the feeling it inspired in her, as if the sun itself were smiling down at her.

As he slept, an errant lock of dark hair had curled slightly on Culver's now-smooth brow. No longer was he scowling. How wonderful he looked while sleeping! Pilar stood, feeling her heart tear open as she absorbed his less-threatening pose. The ache to reach out and nudge that strand of hair back into place was powerful. Swallowing hard, she moved to the end of the couch. She couldn't touch him. She mustn't. She could never kiss that wonderful mouth again.

"Culver?" His name came out so softly that Pilar thought it couldn't possibly awaken him.

Instantly, Culver sat up, his reflexes slow with grogginess. As soon as he saw Pilar, he froze. She stood hands clasped in front of her, in a tastefully conservative blue dress. Her hair was sleek, falling to a slight wave just below her shoulders—a magnificent cape to frame her oval, dusky features. Culver frowned and rubbed his face savagely.

"I must have dozed off," he growled thickly.

"The flight to Peru is long," Pilar whispered, a catch in her voice. Automatically, her fingers had risen to rest against the base of her throat as she stared down at him. The white cotton shirt was stretched to its limits across his broad back and shoulders as Culver sat, his hands draped across his knees. She tried to smile, but didn't succeed. "We need to get going."

"Yeah," he rumbled, pushing himself to a standing position. How lovely Pilar looked in the simple, yet businesslike dress. Well, wasn't she a businesswoman? Somehow, her wilder side and love of horses didn't jibe with what she wore now. Then he saw the edge of a dark leather thong, mostly hidden by the collar of her dress.

"You still wear that jaguar amulet?" The words were out before he could stop them. He saw the shock on Pilar's face.

"Why...yes, I do." Nervously, she fingered the leather thong. Had Culver forgotten nothing about her? Maria, her mother, had been a jaguar priestess to her people—a woman of great healing power and authority. The jaguar ruled the jungles, respected as much as it was feared by the Quechua people. When Pilar was born, she had been given the amulet, a small leather pouch that contained the hair of a jaguar her mother had faced in the jungle and mesmerized with her song of power. The jaguar had allowed her to take hair from its coat, proof that Maria had met a jaguar and, more importantly, lived to tell about it. The Indians respected anyone who assumed his or her power from an animal protector. Pilar had grown up knowing the jaguar was her spirit guardian, watching over her as long as she wore the medicine bag.

Culver managed a grimace. "I haven't forgotten much at all," he admitted thickly, as if in response to her unspoken question.

Pilar forced herself to move, to reorient back to the present. "Come on. My car is in the garage."

"Let's take my rental car."

Pilar agreed with a nod, deciding it wasn't worth arguing over.

Culver moved to her side and picked up her briefcase.

"You don't have to do that," she protested.

"I want to." He gave her a look that warned her he wasn't in the mood for arguments.

Opening the door, Pilar hurried through and locked it behind Culver. "I'll drive," he said firmly, walking toward the barn area, where he'd parked the large, dark green Buick in the shade. He and small cars didn't get along, Culver acknowledged as he put Pilar's bag in the trunk and managed to fold his bulk into the luxury car. It was still siesta time—five o'clock. The sun was hanging very low in the west, and the verdant slopes of the mountains were spectacular as they drove down the long dirt road that would eventually take them to the highway.

"Once we get to the hotel, we'll talk about our plans to rescue Morgan," he said, glancing at Pilar. She sat stiffly in the seat, her hands clasped tightly in her lap.

"Why not now? The hotel could be bugged."

He shrugged. "I thought you said you trusted Hector."

"I trust *him,* but the government has moles. He said that himself."

"It's a thought," Culver murmured, slowing down for a Stop sign. The four-lane highway into Lima wasn't busy at this time of day. Most people stopped work and rested for siesta, and Culver had always thought it a good idea. After all, who was worth anything brainwise after two or three o'clock on any given day, anyway? The South Americans had it right on this one. He pulled onto the highway and accelerated. Turning on the air-conditioning, he said, "This mission is dangerous. You know that."

"No one knows it better than I do. Ramirez has killed people at our village because we wouldn't bend to his demands."

"He's a sadist," Culver growled. He gave her a worried look. "I told Hector I didn't like his plan of sending you into Ramirez's fortress alone to locate Morgan."

"I don't like it, either, but it's not an option, is it? Who else can do it? They certainly won't let you in." She opened her hands to convey her helpless feeling.

His own hands tightened on the steering wheel. Culver was nearly oblivious to the natural beauty surrounding them. The blue Pacific shimmered off to their left, since Lima occupied prime beachfront property. But Culver's heart was centered on Pilar and her wonderful low, breathy voice. As she leaned forward slightly, the cascade of her hair hid her expression, and he longed to reach over push those thick, silky strands behind her delicate ear.

"How someone as murdering and black as Ramirez has survived this long is beyond me," he said grimly. "The last time I locked horns with that bastard was when I was with you, eight years ago."

Pilar felt faint. Was Culver going to bring up their past? She prayed he would not. She wasn't sure she could stand it. "He continues to be the most powerful drug lord in Peru," she said in a halting voice. "His methods haven't changed. He still prefers rape and tortures."

Culver felt anger. "I don't know if I can let you go into that compound...."

harsh tone, Pilar twisted to look in his direction. Culver's face was set, his mouth a hard line. "What do you mean?"

He shrugged, his voice taut. "No woman deserves that sort of treatment. Not even you."

The coldness of his voice shattered her. Pilar turned away, pretending to look out at the landscape flashing by. The implication in his tone was clear: she deserved something—something bad—for leaving his side when he'd been near death. Knotting her hands in her lap, she held back any response. Even if Culver knew the whole truth, he wouldn't understand.

"I saw a couple of pictures in your office," Culver muttered. He glanced at her profile, clean and somehow innocent. "Who are they?"

A lump formed in her throat, and Pilar felt herself go cold with fear. Moisture sprung to her palms. "They..." She struggled to breathe. "They are my daughter and my husband."

"I thought so."

The syllables were like shards of glass being ground into her flesh, hurting her as nothing else could. It hurt to breathe. It hurt to even be alive in that moment.

"When did you get married?" Culver hated himself for asking. It was none of his business, but he had to know.

"Uh...eight years ago." Pilar squeezed her eyes shut, the anguish too much to bear.

"What's his name?" he demanded harshly.

"Fernando."

"But you still use your last name, Martinez. Why?" He felt the pressure of anger and betrayal in his chest. Eight years ago, he had loved Pilar, while she'd had this man on the side, hidden from him. She had lied to him with her body, with the kisses and looks he could have sworn were for him alone.

Touching her brow, Pilar whispered, "Fernando died of a heart attack two years ago. I—I took my name back at that time."

"And the girl? She's yours?"

A knifelike pain stabbed her heart. "Yes, Rane is my daughter."

Compressing his lips, Culver stared straight ahead. He heard the tears choking Pilar's voice and wondered about them. Could she possibly feel any remorse over what she'd done to him? The picture congealed before him, and Culver realized he'd been some kind of lovesick fool to have fallen in love with Pilar. She had been two-timing him. He was sure Fernando hadn't known about him, either.

It was on his lips to ask her why she'd done it. How she could have. Culver would have bet his life then that Pilar was not only an innocent, but completely honest with him. *Face it,* he told himself, *you took one look and it was all over.* He'd fallen as surely as if someone had struck him with a sledgehammer. In truth, Culver knew little about Pilar. They'd had the CIA mission to complete, and their days had been spent on guard, with only occasional nights of torrid embraces whenever they could feel safe enough. They hadn't made love all that many times due to the danger that had always surrounded them. And Culver vividly remembered each of those melting experiences. Any other woman's kisses paled in comparison to the rich depth of those he'd shared with Pilar. He'd shared his soul with her. She'd sold his soul to the devil.

Tears flooded into Pilar's tightly shut eyes as she kept her face carefully positioned so that Culver wouldn't suspect the depth of her heartbreak. Even now, despite what she'd done to Culver, he seemed protective of her. He'd stepped in front of her and taken a bullet meant for her eight years ago—and had nearly died in the process. She'd left him in the hospital. Alone. Her lips parted, the lower one trembling as tears wet her lashes before she forced them back once more. How long she could hold their destroyed dreams and shattered hopes at bay, Pilar did not know.

Finally, their approach to Lima claimed Culver's attention. Driving in the frantic traffic of Peru's capital always felt like dodging stampeding bulls. The Hotel of the Andes was one of the finest in Lima, and as they drove up to the elegant entranceway, a porter in a light gray uniform met them, opening Pilar's door with a flourish. The young man smiled and welcomed her. Nodding, Pilar climbed quickly up the white marble steps, with many tourists, mostly North Americans, bustling around her.

Gripping her shoulder bag, she reminded herself to stay on guard. They were government agents and therefore potential targets. She gazed out at the thick traffic clogging one of Lima's main arteries, the avenue in front of the hotel. It was seven o'clock; siesta was over. Those who had rested through the afternoon's heat were back at work. Sometime between ten and midnight, everyone would eat dinner. Pilar wasn't hungry in the physical sense, but as she looked at Culver, she felt like a sponge, dried out by lack of emotional sustenance. Somehow, simply gazing at Culver's imposing, implacable figure fed her renewed life.

How long had she felt depressed? Pilar was stunned to realize she'd been living beneath a dark cloud ever since she'd left Culver. She'd thought she'd recouped, moved on. Certainly Rane had provided a bright patch in what she now could see as an otherwise dreary world. As Culver walked toward her, she could see him looking around, all his senses on alert, as hers were. He had the look of a condor, with his regal power and watchfulness.

Culver fluidly moved up the steps toward Pilar. Without thinking, he started to reach for her arm, to lead her into the hotel. At the instant panic in her eyes, he dropped his hand.

"Come on," he muttered, stepping through the door.

The lobby was spacious and sumptuous, with sparkling crystal chandeliers highlighting the thick gold carpeting and white marble surrounding the registration area, where three clerks, dressed impeccably in the gray uniforms, waited. Pilar stood quietly at Culver's side as he checked himself in under the assumed name printed on his passport: John Kensington. Pilar smiled to herself at the inappropriate plainness of the name for someone with such an imposing presence.

Once registered, Culver shook his head at the porter and lifted his suitcase in his left hand. He looked at Pilar. "Come on," he said.

Pilar walked at his shoulder to the elevator, feeling a different type of tension around Culver as the doors slid open and they stepped aboard. He pushed the button for the fifth floor and they began to ascend.

"I don't like this place," he growled, watching the numbers light up in sequence as the elevator rose.

"Hector thought it would be safe."

He sent her a derisive look. "You keep saying that."

She glared at him. "He's been like a father to me. He's always been there for me."

With a nod, Culver watched the doors open, then looked both ways down the hall before easing out of the elevator. "Stay behind me," he ordered.

Pilar was mystified by his sudden caution. She was about to protest when she heard the slight click of a door opening behind her. Turning, she saw a man with a submachine gun step into the hallway from one of the rooms.

"Look out!" she shrieked, shoving Culver to one side.

Culver jerked around, his eyes narrowing. Two men in business suits charged out of a room not more than a hundred feet from them. Pilar was in front of him, her body a shield for his. Damn her! Dropping his suitcase, he grabbed her shoulder and hauled her toward the exit door fifty feet away. His fingers tightened on the soft fabric of her dress as he literally threw her ahead of him. What was wrong with her, putting herself in the line of fire?

Bullets pinged and snapped around them as Culver ducked and ran, pushing Pilar ahead of him. The machine guns had muzzle suppressors, muting the sound. Bullets stitched an angry path beside his feet, and Culver dug his toes into the thick carpet, hurtling forward, sending Pilar crashing against the wall. She cried out as she hit it, but Culver was already shoving the exit door open. Twisting, he jerked Pilar past him and into the stairwell.

"Run!" he roared between ragged breaths.

Still stunned from the impact, Pilar staggered backward, then caught herself. She saw the terror in Culver's eyes. Sagging against the cold, concrete wall, she dug in her purse and produced a small handgun.

"Give it to me!" Culver yelled, holding out his hand, his shoulder against the door. At any moment, the henchmen would be upon them. "Get out of here. Run down to the first-floor exit!"

Pilar tossed the gun to him, turned and started down the stairs on wobbling legs. Her breath was coming in sobs as she reached one landing then another. Though her hand was clenched on the cool metal railing, she nearly fell when she heard the rattle of gunfire above her. Where was Culver? Her mind spinning, Pilar realized she had to get to the rental car. It was still in front of the hotel, she was sure; but were the keys in it or had Culver pocketed them?

She heard sudden heavy footsteps descending behind her. Culver? Or was it? Panic pushed her rapidly down the final staircase to the exit door and freedom. Gasping, she spotted the Buick and ran toward it.

A car's brakes screeched as Pilar ran in front of the vehicle. The driver honked and cursed, but Pilar ignored him as she reached the rental car and jerked open the driver's-side door. Yes! The keys were still in the ignition! Getting in, she started the engine. Where was Culver? Was he hurt? Dying? *Oh, Dios, please, get us out of this alive....*

Pilar backed the car out just as Culver burst from the exit door. She honked, and he halted, turned and ran toward her, gun in hand. As he leapt into the passenger side, she jammed her foot on the accelerator, nearly ripping the door from his hand as he slammed it shut.

"Get down!" he roared, his hand suddenly on the back of her head, pushing her below seat level. Bullets popped through the window, showering them with glass.

Peering out, Pilar yanked the car into the traffic, weaving and accelerating at the same time. She was aware that Culver's hand had left her hair. He had twisted around, looking out the shattered rear window.

"Keep going. Keep going. I don't see them."

As much as she hated Lima because it was such a big city, Pilar had grown up here, and she knew every back alley and side street. She drove relentlessly, making sudden turns to avoid red lights. For nearly an hour, they wove their way through the city, until finally they were out in the country once more, the lights of Lima behind them.

Pilar had been trembling for half an hour. Wind whipped through the damaged rear window, chilling her taut nerves. She could feel Culver's tension as if it were her own. Her mouth dry, she managed to say shakily, "I think we've lost them, don't you?"

Culver glanced at Pilar in the dusk. "I think so," he said, noting how pale she looked with the wind whipping her hair wildly around her face. He could see small rivulets of blood near her temple where flying glass must have struck her. Her lips were parted, her eyes huge with terror. Without thinking, he reached over and stroked her cheek, wiping at the blood. "You're hurt...."

Pilar gasped as Culver's rough fingers touched her, sending electric tingles racing across her skin.

Jerking back his hand, Culver cursed richly. He hadn't meant to touch Pilar. She'd made it all too clear that she wouldn't welcome it, and now that same look was on her face, making him feel like hell.

"I—I'm okay. It's just a scratch. Are you okay?" Pilar whispered tremulously.

"I'm fine," he snarled. Relaxing for the first time, he said, "It looks like your friend Hector screwed us royally."

Gasping, Pilar darted a look at him before returning her eyes to the road. As darkness fell, the traffic around them became very light. "What are you saying?"

"That Hector gave us up to Ramirez's men."

"No!" Pilar cried. "No, that is impossible!"

"Do you have a better explanation of what went on?" He glared at her.

"Not right now. But we need to stop. I need to call Hector."

"Call him?" Culver couldn't keep the derision out of his voice. "You want to call him so he can run a trace on where we are and finish us off?"

"Listen to me, Culver, Hector is *not* our enemy!"

"Yeah, and at one time I thought you loved me, too."

Pain sheared through Pilar, so unexpected and shattering that she braked and pulled the car abruptly off the road onto the berm. Turning toward him, she rasped, "I can't help the past, Culver. I live in a hell because of it. But that was then, and this is now. We must call Hector. He's our only contact in the government. Without him, we're alone, and we're going to need coordinated help if we have a prayer of rescuing Morgan. You know that!"

Culver was breathing hard, the air seeming to sear his lungs as he held Pilar's raw gaze, taking in the anguish that burned in the depths of her eyes. Her voice was raspy, and as a flash of headlights momentarily illuminated her, he thought he saw tears glistening in her eyes. No, it was impossible. The seemingly innocent college girl who had played him for a fool would hardly be crying now.

"Look, the Peruvian government is riddled like buckshot with moles," he said in a low, guttural tone. "You know that and so do I. Hell, that's what damn near got me killed eight years ago, Pilar. Or have you conveniently forgotten that, too?"

Pilar felt as if he'd slapped her. "Stop it! Stop it! I have forgotten nothing, Culver. Do you hear me? *Nothing!*" She was sobbing for breath. Fists clenched, she rattled, "I know our government isn't trustworthy. But Hector is!"

"We should head out to your village in the jungle," he snapped. "Leave Lima, Hector and everything else behind."

"I can't do that."

"Why the hell not?"

"Because," Pilar rasped, "my daughter is at my apartment in Lima. I *must* go back, Culver. I can't leave her there."

Culver raised his eyes heavenward. "For God's sake, why didn't you tell me that?"

"I was going to leave you at the hotel and go pick Rane up." Pilar swallowed hard, her voice sounding worried. "Culver, what if they know where Rane is? They could take her hostage...."

"Then where the hell were you headed just now?"

Pilar felt as if she were being physically assaulted, his words raining on her like blows. "I was going to take you to my village, to my grandparents' hut. You'll be safe there."

His mouth compressed. "And then what? You were going to drive back to Lima alone for your daughter?"

She smarted beneath his glare. "Yes."

Culver swore and sat back.

"I know you don't want to be here. I know you don't want to do this mission with me." Her voice cracked. "I was just trying to make it easier on you—"

"Easier?" He turned, gripped her shoulders and shook her. "What the hell's easy about this? Nothing. Not a damn thing. But you aren't going back into that snake pit without me. You hear me? Next time, talk to me—let me know what's going on in that head of yours. I'm not a mind reader, Pilar, as you well know. I thought I knew you at one time, but I don't. I never did." He released her and his mouth flattened. "I thought I knew you...but I've learned. So from now on, you tell me what you're thinking, damn it."

Swiping at the small trickle of blood on her cheek, Pilar drew in a deep, unsteady breath. "All right, I'll tell you what I think. I have to go back to Lima and pick up Rane. I think we should try to call Hector from a pay phone somewhere after we know she's safe. Then we'll take her to my grandparents in the village, where she'll be protected." Her skin seemed burned where Culver had gripped her, but she felt herself drawing an odd sort of strength from his action—and the need to protect her that still seemed to run deep in him.

"Don't tell Hector where we are or where we're going. Most of all, we have to keep your daughter out of this. Taking her to the village is a good idea."

Shaking in earnest, Pilar raised her hands and struggled to steady her emotions. "Rane is so young. What if they've taken her? I've tried so hard to protect her, to—"

"Okay," Culver said harshly, unbuckling his seat belt, "move over. I'm going to drive. Don't worry, we'll get your daughter. She'll be fine."

Pilar eased her hands from her face and looked at him. She had expected Culver's expression to be harsh and emotionless, but it was anything but. His narrowed eyes gleamed with an unexpected tenderness that she had thought she'd never see again. "Y-yes," she whispered, opening the door. "You drive."

Chapter Four

Pilar tried to gather her strewn emotions as Culver drove steadily back toward the lights of Lima. It was ten o'clock—dinnertime for most of Lima's residents—and traffic had once again become light. Taking a handkerchief from her purse, Pilar wet it with her saliva and tried to wipe away the remnants of blood on her temple and cheek.

Nearly all of her attention was centered on Rane—getting her out of Lima and to some semblance of safety. Just having Culver in the car with her steadied her frayed nerves somewhat. She stole occasional glances at his rugged profile, which reminded her of the Andes—relentlessly harsh yet beautiful, suggesting a stoic loneliness. The tight line of his mouth revealed that he, too, was worried. They hadn't spoken since night had fallen, the darkness like a cocoon in which to hide their thoughts and feelings.

Culver broke the silence as they once again approached Lima. "Tell me the best way to get to your apartment."

"We should probably take an indirect route, using small side streets," Pilar suggested.

"I'm in agreement. We don't want to risk being seen by one of Ramirez's men again."

"You think it was his men who tried to kill us?"

"No question in my mind." Culver shot her a glance. Beneath the streetlights, Pilar's face appeared taut and colorless. She had wiped away the telltale blood at her temple, but her eyes were wide, and he could see terror and anxiety in them. Even now she was beautiful. They'd almost been killed. He could have lost her. His heart squeezed in pain at the idea. No, he didn't want to lose her. Despite all she'd done to him, she still managed to look innocent—and vulnerable—as if life hadn't hardened her as it had him.

Culver digested those discoveries about Pilar. Her hair was windblown, in mild disarray around her soft, oval face, and she seemed untouched by the unfolding events except for her concern for her daughter. On that point, Culver agreed with her. No child deserved to be caught in the cross fire between adults. Pilar's daughter was too young to protect herself, and her safety had to come first, before their own.

Pilar began giving him directions as they entered Lima. "It's an apartment east of the city. My housekeeper, Alexandra Somoza, lives there with us," she explained as they wound their way through quiet back streets tightly lined with houses.

"Good, then Rane has someone to take care of her."

"Yes," Pilar whispered unsteadily, "she does."

"So you think your grandparents' village is the best place for her?"

"It's safer there."

"Why not leave her with Hector?"

Pilar heard the derision in Culver's voice and met his eyes momentarily. "Hector would put her in a safe house if I wanted, but Rane is sensitive, and I know she would be frightened. No, I want her with people who love her. She's used to going out to the village on weekends with me. My grandparents love her dearly. They will see to her safety."

"There's a possibility Ramirez or the mole inside the government knows exactly where your grandparents live."

"I know that." Pilar touched her aching temple. "It's a risk I have to take. I don't see a better option."

"We can't take her with us."

"No!" Pilar didn't mean to sound so alarmed, but she couldn't help herself. "Rane has been protected all her life. She knows nothing of what I once did for a living. I want my daughter to be able to sleep at night without nightmares."

"Did you have nightmares after you quit your job as an agent?"

Pilar avoided his sharp look. A lone car passed them as they moved down a curving side street. "I have them to this day, sometimes," she whispered.

"Part of the trade."

"Isn't it, though." Pilar gave Culver more directions, then murmured, "I don't know how you continue to be an agent."

His smile was cutting. "I was about to turn in my resignation to Jake when this thing began to unfold," he admitted. "I've had it. All I want is to get back to the land, where I belong."

"You talked of wanting to live with my people at one time," Pilar reminded him quietly. Culver had confided in her during their three months together that he'd fallen in love with her village and the jungle. She glanced at him shyly. "What would you rather be doing?"

Culver shrugged, never losing his awareness of passing automobiles. "I'm not sure. Some of my ancestors were Scottish seafarers who sailed the world, so I think it's in my genes to travel. But we always had an anchor, a homebase to come back to after wandering.'' His mouth flattened. ''I guess that's what I'm missing most now—a home.''

Pilar absorbed his words. This was the first time Culver hadn't treated her coldly. He was more like his old self, the person she remembered from so long ago. ''I...never knew much about your background—before.''

His laugh was sharp. ''Yeah, we didn't spend too much time doing background checks on each other, did we?''

Heat rushed into Pilar's face at his words. They had been thrown together on a makeshift CIA mission, and the moment their eyes met, they'd both felt the undeniable electricity. The ache to touch Culver, to find out what it would be like to kiss him, had become almost an obsession to Pilar that first month. Once some of the danger eased, they had come together like the sudden thunderstorms that gathered so quickly and unexpectedly over the Peruvian jungle. Pilar had never forgotten that first time—nor any of the times they shared. Those memories were the stuff her dreams were made of. Even now.

Culver saw how his comment had hurt Pilar. She had turned her face away, pretending to look out the window, but the shame in her expression was clear, arousing an anger directed mostly at himself, but also at her for her ability to affect him at the deepest levels. What they'd had, while it lasted, was the best thing he'd ever experienced. He no longer knew what Pilar would call their coming together, but for him, it had been love. Pilar had brought her virginity, her innocence to him, had walked trustingly into his arms, her eyes guileless. And he'd taken her that humid jungle night, surrounded by the aphrodisiac fragrance of orchids clinging to the surrounding trees. To this day, Culver could not separate memories of her from the heady, exotic scent of those rare flowers. Nor did he want to.

''Turn here,'' Pilar said in a choked voice. ''We can park a block down on the right.''

"I don't want to stop in front of the apartment," he warned. "They could be waiting for us."

"We're two blocks away."

Culver nodded, respecting Pilar's intelligence as an agent. Despite her overriding fear for her daughter, she was keeping a cool head. "I thought your skills might be a little rusty, but they don't seem to be," he murmured, braking and pulling into a parking space in the block she'd indicated.

"I am rusty, as you put it," Pilar admitted as he shut off the engine. Gathering up her purse, she unsnapped her seat belt. "I can use all the help you can give me."

Culver nodded and looked around the quiet, darkened neighborhood. "This is one of the wealthy sections of town, if my memory serves me," he said in a low tone.

"Yes, it is."

"I'm glad you did well for yourself, Pilar."

His words cut her to her soul. Compressing her lips, she opened the car door as she said, "Fernando was one of the finest, most gentlest men I have ever known. He cared for us. He protected us." She choked back the rest as she glared over at Culver, recognizing the jealousy in his darkened eyes.

"I cared for you, too. I protected you. But I guess that wasn't enough, was it?"

Pilar wanted to cry at the pain in his voice, but now was not the time. "It's the past," she cried softly. "Let it go!" Leaving the car, she hurried down the sidewalk, her hand in her purse, touching her pistol. If only she could shield herself from Culver's angry sniping as easily. She knew she had it coming, and she felt helpless to protect herself.

As she climbed wrought-iron steps that she knew led to an alley that would take them to her apartment building, she felt Culver's presence. Glancing over her shoulder, she saw him approach soundlessly, his strides much longer than her own. His face was set and unreadable, but she could sense the anger throbbing around him. Well, he had every right to be angry.

"Take it easy," he growled, coming up to her side. "Slow down." His gaze moved ceaselessly, casing the street as they walked. Many areas weren't lit by the sparse streetlamps and he and Pilar stuck to the shadows. Large apartment buildings rose on either side of them, and small trees lined the boulevard, with a few concrete benches at bus stops. Culver longed to reach out and touch Pilar's arm—just in case. Matching his stride to her much-shorter one, he remained on her streetside.

Pilar tried to check her panicked pace. Culver was right. She would look out of place and could draw attention to them if Ramirez's men were watching. Her shoulder brushed Culver's arm, and she jerked away, inhaling sharply. Touching him was like tapping into a secret compartment hidden in her heart, revealing a glowing coal from the past that refused to die, reminding Pilar of all she had forfeited.

"Is there a rear entrance to this place?" Culver asked in a low tone.

"Yes, this way." She turned onto a narrower sidewalk lined with tall bushes that offered perfect cover. She led him to a door the janitor used.

Culver stepped ahead of her. "Give me your gun."

She pulled it out of her purse and handed it to him. The small pistol looked like a toy in Culver's hand. He motioned for her to stand back, away from the door. So many of the ingrained habits of being an agent were flooding back to her. Never directly approach any door—approach from the side so you won't be hit if someone begins firing through it from the other side. Her heart took up a staccato beat as Culver pressed himself against the wall next to the door. With his left hand, he pushed it open, then stepped inside. She was amazed by his agility, despite his size.

"Come on," he said harshly, signaling for her to hurry inside.

Few lights illuminated the building's basement, but Pilar could see enough to lead Culver to the freight elevator. "This will take us up to the tenth floor, where my apartment is." She stepped in, Culver following closely.

He shoved the pistol into the waistband of his jeans and pressed the button. "Ten. Is that the top floor?"

"Yes." Pilar wrung her hands in worry. Was Rane safe? What would they find? She pressed her hand against her eyes.

"She's going to be okay."

Culver's thick, low voice was as comforting as a touch. Pilar dropped her hand and looked up at him. "How did you know?"

His smile was one-sided. "It may have been eight years, Pilar, but I haven't forgotten much about you."

In that moment, as the elevator slowly rose, Pilar realized how badly she'd needed to hear something kind from him. She let out a breath of air. "I'm so worried about Rane...."

"My gut tells me she's okay. Just relax." Suddenly Culver ached to reach out, slide his arm around Pilar's small, tense shoulders and pull her against him. He knew he could give her solace. Just as quickly, he wondered if he was crazy or if jet lag was affecting his senses. Much as he wanted to be angry as hell at Pilar, his heart had other notions.

As the elevator slid to a halt and the doors opened, Culver again went on guard. The hall, with walls of highly polished mahogany, was empty at this time of night. Everyone must be inside, eating. As he and Pilar moved soundlessly down the corridor, Culver could smell various meals being cooked, and his stomach growled. Despite the danger, he was hungry. But food would have to wait.

"The next door on the left," Pilar whispered, coming alongside Culver. Unable to help herself, she hurried ahead, her key in hand.

"Wait," he ordered, holding out his arm to stop her. He empathized with Pilar's anxiety but wasn't about to allow a lapse of security because of it. Ramirez's henchmen could be waiting just inside that door, submachine guns ready. He saw no sign of forced entry or anything else to indicate a struggle. Slipping the key into the door, Culver turned the brass doorknob quickly and stepped into the apartment.

Pilar was on his heels. Everything looked fine. She could hear her housekeeper, Alexandra, moving about in the kitchen. Her heart dropped with relief, and she looked over at Culver, who was tense and alert, the pistol raised.

"It's all right. I hear Alexandra. It's fine...." She shut the door, locked it and tried to pull herself together.

Her fifty-year-old housekeeper poked her head around the corner as Culver slipped the pistol back into Pilar's purse. "Ah, there you are! Rane and I were wondering what had kept you so long at the rancho." She halted and observed Culver. "And who is this?"

Pilar almost smiled at her housekeeper's sudden imperious attitude—like a guard dog spotting a stranger on her territory. "This is Señor Culver Lachlan. He's—"

"I've got a mare to breed to El Diablo," Culver said, interrupting Pilar. Above all, he didn't want their cover blown—not even to the housekeeper. The woman had steel gray hair piled atop her head, and her thin face was pinched, but her dark brown eyes looked kind.

"Er...yes," Pilar said, hurrying across the simply furnished living room. "Where is Rane?" She had to see for herself that her daughter was really alive and well.

Pointing toward the kitchen, Alexandra said, "In there refusing to eat her vegetables, but eating the noodles as if she's famished."

Culver began to relax a little. He watched Pilar hurry across the room and disappear through the swinging kitchen door.

Alexandra smiled primly. "*Señor,* would you like a meal? You are *Norte Americano,* no?"

"I am," he said, easing away from the door. "And yes, I'd like to eat, but—Señora Martinez and I are in a hurry."

"Oh?" Alexandra raised her thin, almost-nonexistent eyebrows.

"Business," Culver said. "But I will take you up on a cup of good Peruvian coffee, if you have some."

"Black?"

Culver grinned a little. No one drank good coffee with cream or sugar down here, he knew. "Yes, black."

"*Bueno.*" Alexandra swept a rangy arm toward the couch. "Please be seated, Señor Lachlan. I will serve you in here."

Culver nodded. As the housekeeper disappeared into the kitchen, he took a better look around the condo. Either Pilar was making very good money or, more likely, she had married into money via Fernando. A photo of the man graced the mantel of the alabaster fireplace, along with a photo of Rane. Culver forced himself to look at this important part of Pilar's life, then quickly turned away.

Fresh flowers of all varieties filled an antique pitcher on a Queen Anne table in the center of the living room. The furniture was all Victorian and very feminine, without a trace of a man's presence anywhere. Sheer ivory-colored drapes covered the windows, flanked by thicker curtains in a print featuring pink rosebuds and greenery. Culver noticed some toys strewn about near the couch and a red rubber ball against the wall. A doll, very old and obviously very loved, sat on the couch itself.

Everything about Pilar's apartment spoke to him of serenity. He wasn't surprised. Wasn't that one of the many gifts she'd given him? Pilar had always been a calming influence on him simply by her presence, he acknowledged as he slowly sank onto the couch. Absently, he picked up the doll. It had a brown Indian face and long, black yarn hair twisted into two braids. Its clothes were straight out of an Indian village—colorful, simple and utilitarian. Culver handled the doll with reverence, noting it had weathered many years of active loving. The little girl had probably had it for her entire seven years of life.

Culver heard the sound of a child's delighted laughter. Then, for the first time since his return to Peru, he heard Pilar laugh. His chest constricted and his hands tightened around the doll momentarily. How he missed that breathy, earthy laughter. He could close his eyes and see her laughing, joy glistening in her eyes, her luscious mouth curved upward to show even white teeth. When Pilar laughed, it was without reserve—the laugh of a woman in touch with Mother Earth.

As the recurring ache squeezed at his heart, Alexandra marched back in, a silver tray in hand, arranged with coffee and several small sandwiches and cookies. "*Señor,* you must eat something before you go. Señora Martinez insisted. She has taken Rane to her bedroom to pack some clothes. She said she would be out very shortly." The housekeeper set the tray down and poured him the coffee with a flourish. "Now, you must eat."

Culver smiled. "*Gracias, señora.*" Alexandra flushed a little at the genuine enthusiasm in his voice, then turned and headed back to the kitchen. Culver wasted no time eating all four of the sandwiches, surprised at his appetite. The coffee was hot, rich and fragrant, and it warmed his inner chill. The pleasant refreshment reminded him of another thing he'd loved about Pilar—her thoughtfulness toward others. She was such a dichotomy. How could she be so kind, yet leave him near death in a hospital and disappear from his life without so much as a word? With a shake of his head, Culver picked up one of the cookies.

He had just finished his second cup of coffee and the last of the cookies when he heard a child's giggling. Twisting around on the couch, he saw Pilar, now dressed in a white cotton blouse, jeans and flat, brown leather shoes, appear with her arm around her daughter. Worry marred Pilar's expression, although she was smiling—no doubt for the child's sake. Rane was a tall, slim little girl. Culver was surprised at how tall she was for her age. She had her mother's huge eyes, but in a much lighter shade of brown. Her hair was rich and black, pulled smoothly into braids that hung down her narrow chest. Rane's eyes danced with laughter, and Culver thought for an instant how much the daughter resembled her beautiful mother.

"Rane," Pilar said, resting her hand gently on her shoulder, "I want you to meet Señor Lachlan. Culver, this is my daughter, Rane." Nervously, Pilar searched Culver's face, watching a gentle smile break the hard line of his mouth as Rane, with her typically bold and friendly ways, walked up to him.

"You have my dolly," she said, pointing to it.

"So I do," Culver answered, smiling. He leaned over and handed Rane her doll. "I think you take her everywhere with you."

Rane tilted her head. "How could you know that?"

"She looks much loved."

Rane giggled, turned and ran back to her mother, throwing an arm around her and hiding her face.

Pilar smiled and placed her hands on her daughter's head and shoulder. "It's all right, sweetheart. Culver won't hurt you. He's a *Norte Americano*. Remember, I showed you on the map where he lives?"

Rane peeked at Culver. "He's a giant, Mama! He's so big!"

Culver smiled a little more broadly. "I guess I am."

Pilar colored fiercely and knelt down, smoothing her daughter's fine hair away from her brow. "Now, listen to me, Rane. We are going on a trip, the three of us. Señor Lachlan is going to take us home to see Grandmother Aurelia and Grandfather Alvaro. Won't that be fun? You'll get to see Grandma's chickens and pigs again."

Rane eased back and became suddenly serious. She wrinkled her nose. "Mama, can I ride the donkey? Last time you said I was too little." She stood back and pointed to her legs. "See how I've grown? My legs are longer now. Can't I ride the donkey?"

Culver watched the joy in Pilar's eyes as she conversed with her daughter, vivid proof of her love. The child was friendly, open and enthusiastic, but looked as if she was going to be much taller than her mother when she grew up.

"Perhaps," Pilar cautioned as she straightened. "I will leave it up to Grandma to decide whether or not you can ride that old, bossy donkey. You wouldn't want to fall off, would you?"

Rane pouted and walked over to the couch, not far from Culver. "You always say I'm too small, Mama."

"Wait," Pilar said with a sigh, "and someday soon you will grow up big and tall."

Rane turned her head toward Culver. "Like Señor Lachlan?"

Wincing inwardly, Pilar whispered, "Exactly like Señor Lachlan."

"I'm ready if you are," Culver said, rising.

"I've got our bags packed."

"Thanks for the food. I was hungry."

Pilar felt herself melting in response to the genuine warmth glowing in his eyes. "I grabbed a sandwich myself as we packed." She held out her hand. "Come, Rane."

Rane galloped like a frisky filly around the coffee table and grasped her fingers. "Let's go, Mama! Hurry! I want to see Grandma and Grandpa!"

Culver asked in a lowered voice, "Have you told the housekeeper anything?"

"Only that we'll be visiting another an Argentinian horse farm to look at a mare, and we'll be gone for two weeks."

"She knows Rane will be at the village?"

Pilar grimaced. "No, I told her she would be with us. When we use one."

Culver nodded his approval. If Ramirez realized Pilar was part of this mission, his goons could come in here and scare information out of the old housekeeper, putting the girl in jeopardy. He saw the pleading look in Pilar's eyes to say nothing more in front of her daughter. "Okay, let's get going. I'll bring the luggage."

Pilar sighed softly. Rane was sound asleep in her arms. They had taken Pilar's second car, an older Volvo, and had made it two hours out of Lima, on their way to Tarapoto, without further mishap. Overhead, the night sky sparkled with stars. This stretch of road was devoid of other cars, and she relaxed almost to the point of dropping off to sleep herself. Culver had taken advantage of the thermos of coffee she'd brought, drinking it steadily to stay awake.

"It won't be long," she promised him softly as she rested her hand across Rane. Her daughter was so lanky that her small, sock feet rested against Culver's massive thigh, but he didn't seem to mind. In fact, Rane had gravitated to him. Pilar wasn't surprised. She had gravitated to Culver, too.

"Good," he rumbled, rolling his shoulders to release the tension accumulating in them. "I'm dead on my feet."

"I know you are," she said, giving him a worried look. The sudden intensity of his gaze at her words caught her by surprise. Just as abruptly, he turned his attention back to the road ahead. They were now climbing into the hills, far from the Pacific. "I don't know how you do it. I never did...."

"What?" Culver saw such peace in Pilar's face now that her daughter was safely in her arms.

She sighed softly. "I was always amazed at your untiring spirit. You never seemed to give out or give up." Pilar laughed a little and looked at him with tenderness. "Remember? I was always the one who had to rest. You were always ready to push on."

"Yes, I remember." Culver felt his heart beat hard in his chest at her intimate look. Pilar had a way of making him feel he was the center of her universe when she talked with him. He felt that way now. Bitterly, he reminded himself it was a facade—just part of the pretty packaging of Pilar Martinez.

"I'm scared this time, Culver."

He wrenched himself out of his self-pity. "What?" He glanced at her once more, and saw that her face was drawn with worry.

"I'm scared as never before." Pilar gazed lovingly down at her sleeping daughter and gently caressed her hair. "I have an awful feeling about this mission. I have from the start. Ramirez is evil. He has no heart in his chest. He kills as naturally as we breathe."

Culver checked the urge to reach out and touch her sagging shoulder. "Maybe," he said huskily, "you have more to lose this time around."

"Rane is my life," Pilar admitted in a broken whisper, as she studied her daughter's sleeping face. "She's taught me so much about giving and taking love. She has helped me heal in so many ways. I'm sure she'll never realize all she's done for me, and it doesn't matter." Her hand stilled on Rane's small shoulder. She saw the expression on Culver's face. His eyes had softened, as had the set of his mouth. When she realized she was watching him, his features hardened again. Pilar wanted so badly to tell him how sorry she was, but it would do no good.

Instead, she said, "Tell me about your home in Scotland, Culver."

"You didn't know much about me eight years ago. Why is it important now?"

She felt the cutting edge in his low tone. He refused to look at her, and she was glad for the cloak of darkness that hid her reaction to his biting words. "You talked of wanting a home," she persisted. "Are you going to return to Scotland?"

"My grandparents live there—I have relatives in Scotland and England. But my folks live in Colorado." His mouth twisted. "I guess the Rockies were as close as they could get in the U.S. to the Scottish moors and mountains. I like isolated places with lots of trees, and I like people who work with the earth and respect it."

Tentatively, she asked, "Do you have brothers or sisters?"

His hands tightened on the steering wheel. A part of him was wary of Pilar's attempt to weave more intimacy into their relationship. She was so personable, but where did the right to know and the right to privacy begin and end? With Pilar, the boundary was all too blurred. "I have four brothers and one sister, Mary."

"And does she live in Scotland?"

"No. In Durango, a small town in southern Colorado, near my folks."

"Is she married?"

"Yes. She's got two kids."

Pilar smiled a little. "Then you're an uncle."

He nodded. "They're good kids. Mary's divorced, but she has custody of them, and Bob, her ex-husband, sees them on weekends." He wanted to ask about Pilar's marriage to Fernando, but decided he'd rather not know. Why stab his heart with another ice pick? Was he a masochist or something?

Pilar stroked Rane's arm gently and watched her sleep. It was on the tip of her tongue to ask if Culver was married. Had he found someone, as he so richly deserved to do? Someone who could care for him the way he was capable of caring? Pushing a strand of hair out of her eyes, she released an unsteady breath. Just being this close to Culver made her ache with desire. Despite the harshness of the intervening years and circumstances, she wanted him now as she had the first time their eyes had met. Pilar didn't fool herself this time, however. She would never allow Culver to know she still wanted him. They lived in very different worlds. The two could never truly meet and bond. Her world wouldn't allow it.

"We'll be in Tarapoto in about forty minutes," she said into the silence. Looking at her watch, she saw it was three in the morning. Darkened jungle hugged the two-lane highway now, silhouetted against a starry sky.

"Good, because I'm ready to keel over from lack of sleep."

"How long has it been?"

"A good thirty-six hours."

"Do you want me to drive?"

"No, you have Rane on your lap. Don't wake her."

"If I talk, does it help you stay awake?"

His mouth quirked. "Yes, talking helps." And God help him, he had so many questions he wanted to ask Pilar. "I remember one time you saying your father had royal blood?" He glanced at her.

Pilar stirred. Talking might help keep him awake, but she wasn't completely comfortable being the target of his attention. "My father was an aristocrat from Spain—an ambassador to Peru."

"And he married your mother, Maria?"

"Yes . . . Mama was a Quechua medicine woman." She opened her hand and studied it. "I was an only child and very much loved."

"I imagine," Culver said, "you lived a life of luxury." A life-style he couldn't have given her at twenty-five.

"Yes," she agreed. "I grew up at the consulate in Lima, surrounded by servants. Later, my papa sent me to America for college."

"And you went to Harvard," he confirmed, remembering.

Pilar nodded.

"Was it hard moving back and forth between North American society and this one?"

She sighed and nodded again. "You know how it is down here in South America. At Harvard, I didn't have to endure the kind of prejudice I experience here. People can be cruel. Manuela, Hector's assistant, for example, hates me."

"Why?"

She heard the dismay in his voice, and it gave her the courage to tell him the story. "Because I'm mestiza—what you might call a 'half-breed' in the U.S. You see, Manuela comes from a rich family of pure Castilian lineage. When she saw me leaving Hector's office one day shortly after I became an agent, she turned to a friend and said, 'Imagine mating a fine Paso Fino stallion to a donkey from the barrios of Lima. What you get is her.'"

"The bitch."

Pilar felt the grating anger in Culver's voice. "The words cut me deeply," she admitted, surprised by his response in her defense. "I guess I should have been used to such remarks by then, but I could never seem to harden myself in that way. I tried to hold my head up and keep my shoulders squared, as my mother counseled me. She was a housekeeper at the consulate when she met Papa. They fell in love, even though everyone said it was wrong."

Culver nodded. He was familiar with South American prejudice. A woman was considered the property of her husband. A daughter's entire fortune and life was tied to the man her father chose for her to marry. "Are your parents still around?"

Pilar felt sadness overwhelm her. "My wonderful Papa died when I was twenty-one. It was one of the worst days of my life. He died suddenly, of a heart attack. He was only sixty."

"And your mother? What did she do without the shield of your father between her and Lima's rich?"

Pilar smiled grimly. "She fled Lima and moved back to the village where she was born. Without Papa's powerful presence, Mama didn't want to stay where she wasn't welcome. Five years later, she died suddenly, without warning. Now," Pilar whispered, "all I have left are Grandmother Aurelia and Grandfather Alvaro."

"And you got out of your career as an agent when?"

Squeezing her eyes shut, Pilar managed to say in a strained tone, "I joined at twenty-two, as soon as I graduated from Harvard. I was part-time in only three years. I— I quit after our mission."

Culver heard what was not said. She had married Fernando, a man twice her age—probably chosen by her father for her when she was ten or twelve years old. Fernando was a man of obvious wealth and station. Well, Culver couldn't fault Pilar for that, could he? She was mestiza, considered an outcast by the well-to-do of Lima with their aristocratic Spanish blood. Her father had been rich, and she wouldn't marry below her station, even with her half-breed blood. No, old Fernando had been a far more appropriate suitor than Culver had been. Hell, he'd been a twenty-five year old CIA agent with five thousand dollars in savings, no aristocratic breeding and without the sort of future prospects Pilar had wanted.

Bitterly, he acknowledged a certain understanding of her decisions. Looking at Rane, her beautiful daughter, he figured Pilar must have had at least had six years of happiness before her husband died.

"If something does happen to you," he said, "will Fernando's family take care of Rane?"

Shaken out of her state, Pilar stared at him. "Fernando?"

"Yes."

She frowned and gave him a questioning look.

Culver motioned to the girl. "If you die, will your husband's family take care of Rane?"

"Oh . . . yes, they will."

His eyes narrowed. "You aren't sure?"

"Well," Pilar stammered, flustered by the question, "of—of course they will."

Culver was puzzled. Why should such a simple question make her so rattled? Pilar wasn't the kind of woman who was easily shaken. But she had a characteristic habit of pushing the hair from her eyes when she was nervous, and she was doing that now. Why? It didn't make sense, but Culver was too damned tired to try to figure it out at the moment. All he wanted was a mat on the floor of a hut and a good night's sleep.

Chapter Five

Culver barely stirred. Somewhere in the distance, voices were speaking Quechua. Children were laughing and playing. A rooster very near let loose with a raucous crowing to where he lay. The smell of woodsmoke permeated his exhausted senses and he became aware of the hard earth beneath him, the blanket woven of llama wool folded under his head as a pillow.

Something warm and soft met his hand as he stretched his arms and yawned. Culver pried open his eyes, his groggy brain slowly recalling his mission. On the heels of that realization came the memory of arriving at Pilar's grandparents' village about four this morning. They had been shuffled off to a small thatched hut with little preamble, though Culver remembered meeting Aurelia, Pilar's grandmother, who had led them to the hut.

He recalled Pilar's surprise and panic at having to share the floor of the hut with him. What had she thought he was going to do? Make love to her? This time at least he'd been too bone tired to be wounded by her rejection of him. Instead, he merely stumbled into the hut, lay down in the far corner on a mat and drew up a blanket for a pillow. Almost instantly, he'd spiraled into badly needed sleep.

What was he touching? The gloom in the hut was nearly complete. A blanket hung across the entrance, with only a fine line of sunshine peeking around its edges. As his eyes adjusted, he realized with a start that it was Pilar who lay so close to him. She was still asleep, he saw as he eased up onto one elbow. The soft light stealing around the blanket washed lovingly across her form.

Pilar lay on her back, her hands clasped near her breasts, a blanket drawn up over her. How beautiful, how achingly desirable she looked. Culver couldn't help himself as he leaned over and threaded his fingers through the tangled black hair near her face. The hut's dim lighting accentuated her Incan ancestry, from her high cheekbones to her broad, unmarred brow. She was thirty-two years old, yet, he marveled, she had changed very little from the time he'd first known her. Maybe it was her ageless Incan blood.

Her hair spilled like a dark flow of moonlit water across a small pillow beneath her head. The strands felt like warm silk, just as he recalled. His fingertips tingled as he eased the strands back to get a better look at her face. Her skin was dusky and velvety soft. Did he dare touch her? How badly he wanted to. Culver wanted to do more than that. Her lush lips were parted, begging to be kissed.

It would be so easy to lean over and graze those lips. His lower body tightened with hungry need. With undeniable memory. Culver allowed his hand to rest lightly against the crown of Pilar's head. Belatedly he realized that Rane, who had slept in Pilar's arms last night, was gone. Having no idea of the time, he guessed that the girl had long since

awakened and was probably out happily running around
with the village children.

His gaze moved back to Pilar. How small and innocent
she looked in sleep. Last night, they'd nearly died, yet as her
breasts rose and fell slowly, she looked supremely untouched by life. Culver's fingers moved as if they had a life
of their own, lightly stroking her silky hair. All he had to do
was lean over and place his mouth against hers. The driving desire almost shattered his massive control.

Pilar murmured in her sleep and rolled onto her left side.
The blanket slipped, revealing her shoulder. Her white
blouse was wrinkled, but Culver didn't care. Pilar could
wear the most expensive of gowns or nothing at all and she
still looked just as beautiful in his eyes. Her hair tumbled
gently downward, caressing the curves of her face and slender neck. Her hand stretched outward, connecting softly
with Culver's chest, his skin tightening instantly where her
fingers rested. He marveled at her reaching out for him,
even in sleep. Then he scowled. Probably for Fernando, not
him. It hurt to be realistic about it, but Culver strove to be
ruthlessly honest with himself. It didn't pay to be an ideal-
ist, as he knew from hard experience. Pilar had taught him
well.

Her breath was shallow and moist against his skin. He'd
shed his shirt last night in the heat of the hut. Now her
breath tickled strands of hair on his chest. Her fingers lay
slightly curled against him. *So innocent.* The words, the
feeling, flowed through Culver. In sleep, Pilar trusted him.
Taking in a deep, ragged breath, he recalled as if it were
yesterday how Pilar used to sleep in his arms—peaceful as
a newborn baby. She'd felt completely safe, protected by
him. Even with the danger that had swirled around them,
she had slept quietly in his arms.

They had had each other, he realized, sadness blanketing
him as he studied her small, delicate hand. An automatic

trust had sprung up between them, and it had translated into the abandon with which they had made love. He released a long, painful breath as he stared down at Pilar. What could he have done differently to keep her? How many times had he asked himself that question? What had he done wrong to chase her away?

It was true that he wasn't rich or aristocratic. As he studied Pilar, he tried to be sensitive to the plight of a South American woman. The husband was the autocratic ruler here. Marriages knew no equality. Women became so much chattels, allowed no life of their own, no hopes or dreams outside their kitchens and the raising of large broods of children. A husband was considered macho if his wife had many children, for that showed his sexual prowess. And the concept of machismo included making the wife bow to the husband's needs and demands.

Culver sighed. He'd lived in South America off and on for a decade now, and he'd often been disgusted by the way men treated women. Among the Quechua, women were respected as equals, so they didn't suffer as the rest of South American women did. It was a Spanish problem, not an Indian one. Intellectually he could understand that Pilar had been no less trapped by the male-dominated environment than any other South American woman. Her only hope was to marry someone rich and affluent and thereby escape some of the worst of the daily drudgery. Money would provide the services of a maid and housekeeper, and among the rich, families tended to be smaller.

Culver knew how intelligent Pilar was. He'd always respected her savvy—a combination of her American Liberal-arts education and her deeply rooted Incan heritage. Still, how could she be expected to come back to this village with her royal blood and marry a dirt-poor farmer? She lived precariously between two opposing worlds.

Leaning over, unable to help himself, Culver lightly touched Pilar's arm, the skin firm, warm and velvety beneath his fingers. So she had married some old man for his money. Fernando had probably been promised Pilar, anyway, falling for her blazing beauty and youth. How could Culver blame her for finding her own way to avoid the cultural quagmire that threatened all women down here? His mouth tightened. Maybe that was why he had such a hard time staying angry with her.

"Mi querida," he whispered near her brow, as he had once called her so often. *My darling.* She had always been his darling—a beautiful, rebellious survivor of a woman.

Pilar stirred. She heard Culver's deep voice rustling like leaves nudged by a breeze. Her dreams were lush. Fulfilling. He was touching her, moving his roughened fingers slowly up and down her arm. His breath feathered across her brow and cheek as she heard the endearment, and her heart opened like a flower starved for sunlight as his mouth pressed lightly against her hairline. She loved her dreams, for in them, she could be with Culver again, laughing, playing and loving without the burden of the terrible price they had paid.·

A slight moan came from within her as she felt herself being eased onto her back. Culver was with her, and that was all she needed. His hand was warm and supportive on her shoulder, and she felt him trace her collarbone. Something was wrong with the dream, though. She was wearing clothes. Usually in her dreams, she was naked and standing beside a deep, dark blue pool with rich green grass beneath her feet. Culver was naked, too, drawing her into his massive arms, smiling down at her with that predatory smile that made her blood sing with anticipation.

"Mi querida...."

Where did dreams end and reality begin? Pilar could feel his lips bestowing a series of small, moist kisses on her forehead. Each touch of his mouth sent a delicious tingling sensation from her head right through her to her very core.

The dream felt so real. More so than ever before. Somewhere in the background, she heard a rooster crowing. Something wasn't right. Pilar dragged herself out of her deep, languid sleep. As she began to surface to awareness, she realized she could still feel Culver's hand on her shoulder, caressing her, and his lips continued to trail along her temple.

She slowly lifted her lashes. Though still caught up in the remnants of sleep, her vision blurry, she could smell Culver's naturally musky scent. No dream had ever been this real. A small, startled gasp escaped her, and she groggily looked upward—into the burning intensity of Culver's light blue eyes. He studied her in the intervening silence. Her breath caught. He was so close, so close.... Wildly aware of the gentle pressure on her shoulder, she felt as if she were drowning in the desire she read in his eyes. His expression was no longer hard or distant. No, this was the man she had once known so intimately. His lips were parted, his vulnerability clear.

Pilar's body throbbed as if in a fever state. The ache within her grew with each wispy, ragged breath she took as she stared wonderingly up at Culver. He wanted her, with a raw, naked need. She wanted him no less. Dizzied by his nearness, by the power of him as a man, Pilar lay helplessly snared within this embrace, her skin still tingling where he'd kissed her brow. Only inches separated them. Would he kiss her lips? Pilar saw the intent in his eyes as his gaze shifted to her mouth. She felt his grip on her arm tighten further. How badly she wanted his kiss. If kissing Culver would make her world right, Pilar would have surged forward those few inches and kissed him first.

Then, through the flimsy hut walls, Pilar heard Rane laughing with the wonderfully joyous freedom of a child. *No.* Her own tough reality came rushing back like a shower of ice water. She couldn't kiss Culver, though every cell in her body screamed out for his mouth's caress. If she did, she would be lost. Her carefully constructed world, which she'd worked so hard to keep in place, would shatter like a crystal glass beneath the blow of a hammer.

"Please . . ." she whispered unsteadily, "please don't kiss me, Culver. . . ." Instantly, she saw his eyes narrow dangerously, anger replacing the desire. His hand drew back from her shoulder, and inwardly, she wept for the loss of that cherished sense of effortless intimacy. His mouth tightened once more into a hard, uncompromising line. Regret tunneled through Pilar as Culver shifted away and sat up, his legs crossed.

How masculine he looked with his magnificent chest and shoulders exposed. He had the beauty of the deadly jaguar—lethal power mingled with an oddly heady promise of letting her feel that strength, become part of it. Pilar knew Culver's magical sway over her could kill her, too; as surely as jaguar. What little was left of her wounded heart couldn't stand the pain of sharing with him and losing him. She'd barely survived the first time; she didn't have the strength to survive him again.

Bitterly, she sat up, the colorful wool blanket spilling into her lap. She hurt for Culver, knowing her words had injured him. She reached her hand toward him.

"I—I'm sorry, Culver. I wish . . . I wish so many things were different. . . ."

Culver sat, stunned by her rejection. They had been so close to kissing each other. So close to touching once more. He saw the regret on Pilar's still-drowsy features. Her hair was tousled wildly around her face, and he ached to pick up a brush and stroke those silky strands, taming them back into place. How many times had he dreamed of brushing Pilar's hair? Feeling those strands slide between his fingers, so full of life and shining like a raven's wing? Too many, he angrily reminded himself. Why the hell had he tried to kiss her when she'd made it all too clear that she no longer wanted him?

"It won't happen again," he said harshly, forcing himself to his feet. The hut was gloomy and he looked around for his shirt, finding it crumpled up in the corner on one of the woven mats that covered most of the hut's dirt floor. He saw that blankets covered the windows as well as the door, accounting for the murky lighting. He leaned down, jerked up his shirt and threw it across his shoulder.

Pilar got to her knees, trying to fight off the sleepy confusion that still held her. "Culver, it's not what you . . ."

He glared at her as he stalked to the entrance and jerked open the blanket. "I said it won't happen again. Let it go, Pilar."

Even after he'd stridden angrily away, Pilar remained kneeling, devastated. Rubbing her hands against her arms, she bowed her head and fought back the sobs that threatened to well up from deep within her. It hadn't been a dream. But how had she ended up on his side of the hut? The dwelling was very small, the type an elderly person lived in alone, but last night, they'd been dizzy with exhaustion. Her grandmother had brought them to the nearest empty hut. Pilar was grateful for her grandparents' care. She remembered Aurelia placing a blanket over the still-sleeping Rane after Culver had gently placed the girl on one of the mats.

Pilar had lain on her side, facing her daughter's back. She vaguely remembered Culver lying down on the opposite side of the hut, but that was all. She looked slowly around the place now. How had she managed to get over here, to his sleeping mat? Stymied and a little frightened of the evident strength of her own subconscious, she realized Culver had remained where he'd slept. At some point, she knew, Rane had awakened and left the hut, but Rane had had the benefit of a much better night's sleep than they, since she'd slept in the car all the way from Lima. Looking down at her watch, Pilar saw it was nearly ten in the morning already. Her heart ached with longing for Culver. She had to apologize to him. At least if he had been the one to come to her side of the hut . . . But no. It wasn't his fault. It was hers— again.

She heard the sound of Rane's laughter, once more, this time mingled with the deep rumbles of Grandfather Alvaro's somewhere nearby. Rousing herself, Pilar knew she had much to do today. First, she would go for a swim in the small, beautiful pond ringed by rushes where the villagers sometimes bathed. Being in her mother's village always made her feel safe. Pilar knew she wasn't—not with Ramirez's fortress a mere twenty-five miles away—but the serenity of her people still created that sense of security, deserved or not.

Easing to her bare feet, she stretched fitfully. She picked up all blankets they'd used, folded them carefully and stacked them in a corner. She savored the familiar scent of woodsmoke as she left the hut. Blinking in the strong sunlight cascading down through the trees, she looked around and spotted Grandmother Aurelia leaning over a tripod cooking pot, stirring the contents. Dogs and children were playing here and there throughout the tiny village of barely a hundred people. The elderly remained close to their huts, the women working on llama-wool weavings and the old men sitting and talking nearby.

The air was fresh and clean here, the humidity high. Touching her usually straight hair, Pilar smiled, knowing it would soon become wavier in the damp air from the nearby jungle. The village was situated just above the jungle, on the slope of a mountain. Below them a thick, dark green canopy stretched to the horizon. Down there, Pilar thought with a shiver, lay Ramirez's fortress. Down there, too, somewhere beneath the shining foliage, Morgan Trayhern waited for his rescuers.

Abruptly, Pilar blocked the automatic images of Morgan being tortured. Thinking about it wouldn't help Morgan, it would only weaken her with fear. She saw Aurelia straighten and look over at her. Her grandmother's dark brown face was lined with age, but the kindness of her smile and the love shining from her eyes soothed Pilar's battered heart. She lifted her hand in greeting, then hurried toward the edge of the village to prepare herself for the day.

Culver sliced through the pond's icy water, each stroke like an explosion, releasing a little more of his anger and hurt. He swam naked, rinsing away the grime of the past forty-eight hours. His feet touched the pebbled bottom and he stood. Closer to shore, sand lined the floor of this oval-shaped pond, fed by icy streams from the craggy Andean mountains that towered over the village. Culver's skin roughened with goose bumps as he walked to the edge of the pond. Though it was midmorning and summer, the air was still cool at this elevation. Scooping up a handful of sand, he scrubbed his body with it. Nothing cleaned like sand, and as he washed, unbidden thoughts sprang to mind of that other pool—one he and Pilar had discovered somewhere deep in the jungle northeast of Lima. They had scrubbed each other's backs with sand much like this.

Muttering a curse, Culver wondered why he couldn't staunch the relentless cascade of memories about Pilar and himself. Leaning down, he sluiced off the sand, his skin feeling vibrant, warm and tight from the scrubbing. To get at his feet and legs with the refreshing sand, Culver took a seat on the grassy bank, noting the herd of llamas, in all colors and sizes, feeding below on one of the verdant hillsides. The village was perfectly situated between the mighty Andes, their snow-covered, granite peaks thrusting to the heavens above, and the humid jungle, close enough for the villagers to gather its rich array of fruit and nuts.

Yes, this village was a virtual Shangri-La, in Culver's opinion. The only fly in the ointment, he thought as he sat on the bank, scrubbing his feet, was Ramirez's fortress in the lush jungle below. He looked up into the deep blue sky, accented with long strands of thin, white gossamer clouds. More than once he'd entertained the thought of living here—but that had been eight years ago, with Pilar the woman he would have shared this tranquil farm life with. He knew some of his friends might think him crazy, but others, like Jake Randolph and Wolf Harding, understood his need to sink his roots deep into the earth and revel in a simpler, more natural existence. The sun warmed his damp back, and he smiled. It was a perfect day. Well, almost.

Sighing, he rinsed off his legs and got out of the water. Shaking his arms and hands, he allowed the slight, playful breeze and the sunlight to dry him. He knew he'd miss this coolness once they entered the jungle. Frowning, he retrieved his jeans, sat on a fallen log and pulled them on. His hair dripped with water and he pushed the damp strands back off his brow.

A sound caught his attention, and he snapped his head toward the well-worn path the villagers took to the pond. His heart thudded. Pilar stood uncertainly, a towel in her hand. The expression on her face told him she was as surprised as he was. Scowling, he said, "Come on, I won't bite."

He reached for his shirt and shrugged it over his shoulders as he watched her walk hesitantly toward him. The path ended at the pond, near the log where he had left his socks and boots. Pilar looked so soft and innocent as she picked her way delicately along the trail. Culver wanted to look away, to ignore her. Impossible. She was barefoot! He allowed the corners of his mouth to lift momentarily. Here, she was free to be her natural self. The villagers never wore shoes unless they had to, and he knew Pilar disliked them. It was her Incan blood longing to be free of such civilized confinement.

As she drew near, he saw the wariness in her eyes. Could he blame her? No. Feeling foolish, Culver hurriedly tugged on his boots and tied the leather laces into double knots.

"The water's cold but fine," he said gruffly, looking up as she halted in front of him.

Pilar nodded. "Culver, I owe you an apology—"

"You owe me nothing," he snarled, getting to his feet. He shoved the tails of his cotton shirt into his Levi's, with angry movements.

"I do. Please," she begged softly, holding out her hand, "hear me out."

He glared at her. "Why should I?"

Pilar held his glare. "Have we moved so far apart that we can no longer talk? I remember—"

"That's the past," he snapped. Putting his hands on his hips, he said in a low, vibrating voice, "It's the past, and that's where you want to keep it, isn't it, Pilar? God help me, but I don't have the control I wish to hell I did when it comes to you. This morning was a mistake." *A terrible mistake.* His mouth flattened as he saw his words landing like fists, their impact clear on her vulnerable features. Angry at his lack of control, he snarled, "Let's just make the best of this, okay? I don't like it any more than you do, Pilar. I'm human, too, dammit, in case you don't remember."

Pilar stepped forward, touching his arm. As her fingers curved around Culver's powerful bicep, she felt a vibration go through him and saw the shock register in his eyes at her unexpected gesture. For a moment, the hardness and anger in them dissolved. "Please," she begged in a raw voice, "I know I'm hurting you by being around you. I don't mean to, Culver. *Dios,* if there was anything I could do to stop the pain I give you, I would...."

Helplessly, she held his narrowed gaze. He stood like a magnificent bronze statue of a hero, proud, wounded, yet holding his head high, tolerating her hand on him. It took everything Pilar had to keep tears from streaming down her face, but she couldn't keep the sound of them out of her voice as she spoke.

"It was my fault back at the hut. I—somehow, I rolled over after Rane got up. I should have stayed on my own side, Culver. Please, forgive me. I don't blame you for what happened this morning. It was my fault. Do you hear me?" Trying to steel herself against the suffering that had come into his eyes, Pilar forced herself to release his arm. When she did, it was almost as if Culver suddenly sagged before her. The rigidity went out of him, like a punctured balloon deflating.

"I don't blame you," he said hoarsely after a moment of tense silence. "I shouldn't have touched you, even if you touched me."

Pilar's eyes widened. "I touched you? In my sleep?"

Culver grimaced and looked above Pilar's head, studying the Andes's snowy peaks. "I made the mistake of touching your hair, that was all. You turned toward me and your hand fell against my chest."

Pilar dragged in a breath. "I see...."

He gave her a sad smile, the anger bleeding out of him. "I'm sure you do. You always did, Pilar. Maybe it's that jaguar blood of yours trying to entrap me—mesmerize me like before. I don't know."

Pilar's hand went to the small medicine bag that hung around her neck. "Do you think I did it on purpose?"

"No, of course not. You were asleep." Culver raked his fingers through his drying hair. "I don't blame you, Pilar. You're looking at me like some lost lamb. Stop it! I can't roll back the past, and neither can you.'' Frustration tinged his voice as he gazed at her. ''The past is the past. It's over and done. Destroyed.''

''Yes,'' she whispered faintly, closing her eyes, unable to stand the terrible grief shining in Culver's eyes.

''Hell,'' he muttered, ''take your bath and meet me back in the village. We've got a lot of planning to do before we head into that jungle.'' Turning on his booted heel, he strode down the path.

Breathing raggedly, Pilar opened her eyes and watched Culver stalk off. Even wounded as he was by her decision, he treated her with respect. A South American man would not have tolerated her behavior as he had, though a Quechua man would. Culver was a good man. An honest one. A man with a large and forgiving heart. Much like Fernando. Pushing her hair back from her face, she sat down on the log to undress.

The day was exquisite, but Pilar felt raw. Her heart was weeping. She could feel it pounding in her chest as she removed her blouse with trembling hands. As she closed her eyes to her feelings, she saw Culver's face—proud, fierce and defiant, yet with a tenderness burning in his eyes that made her want to weep for what they had lost. And it had all been her fault. Hers alone.

Chapter Six

Culver was busy setting their army-issue, two-way radios onto a special frequency when Pilar came back to the village. It had been brought in by a CIA helicopter from Lima—one that Hector did not know about. Rane, curious seven-year-old that she was, sat companionably near him in the dirt, watching him solemnly. She was a living, breathing miniature of Pilar, as far as Culver was concerned.

In front of him, on a clean blanket, was spread the array of state-of-the-art equipment they would take into the jungle with them. Don Alvaro, Pilar's grandfather and village shaman, well into his nineties, sat opposite them on a wooden chair, rocking slowly back and forth, his dark brown eyes flicking from Culver to the equipment and back to his great-granddaughter.

"You need these machines?" Don Alvaro finally asked in broken English.

Culver looked up. "Yes." The tall, thin old man was weather-beaten, his tobacco-brown skin, stretched tight across high cheekbones, and deep lines at the corners of his eyes attesting to his time working the corn and potato crops on the terraced hillsides. Yet he emanated the aura of power befitting his role as leader of the village.

"You challenge Don Ramirez, eh?"

Culver's hands stilled over the radio he was holding. How much had Pilar told her grandparents? Very little, he hoped. He wondered if she'd told him they were going to try to rescue Morgan. She must have. He chose his words carefully as he continued to assemble the radio.

"We're here on a secret mission, so I can't say much."

"Ahh," Don Alvaro murmured. His face stretched into a shining smile as he caught sight of Pilar walking toward him. "She walks like the jaguar she was born to become, does she not?"

Culver scowled, barely glancing in Pilar's direction. She was drying her hair with a thin white towel, the long black strands shining in sunlight dappled by the trees among which the village had been erected, to provide a modicum of summer shade, as well as protection against the winter's rainy weather.

"Yes, she's a jaguar all right," he muttered.

"You know," Don Alvaro continued pleasantly, gesturing toward Pilar, "that my wife, Aurelia, performed a special ceremony for Pilar's parents in order to bring her spirit into being." He beamed. "Once in every generation, if you are from a jaguar medicine clan, a special spirit child is brought forth to carry into the future all our knowledge, experience and ceremonies." His smile grew tender. "Pilar is our great hope."

"She doesn't live with you. How can she help your people?" Culver thought of her job at the horse farm and wondered how often she came back to the village, and if she was aware of her responsibility.

Chuckling, Don Alvaro slapped his knee. "You have lived among us many years, my friend. Surely you know that we are shamans?"

Culver placed the radio headset before him on the blanket, and Rane handed him the plastic bag containing the second unit. She smiled brightly up at him, and he couldn't help but smile a little in return. The child was innocent, and she came from Pilar's body—a body he had once loved.

"I know among the Indians you have medicine people," he answered slowly, again glancing to check Pilar's continued approach. She had draped the towel around her shoulders, the white creating a dramatic contrast with her dusky, golden skin and black hair. Culver knew she wasn't even aware of her ethereal beauty, which must have any number of men falling at her feet in adoring admiration. And her lack of vanity only added to the depth of his unwanted feelings for her.

"We are not ordinary people," Don Alvaro corrected, rocking in the chair. "Shamans are different. We travel to the other worlds. We fly to the past, work with the present and can see into the future. Medicine people heal with herbs, ceremony and songs. We do a great deal more." He lifted his hand. "Pilar possesses such skills. She can fly because she is a priestess to the jaguar."

"Really?" Culver looked up at the old man, not certain how to take his confidently spoken statement.

"Mmm, but my granddaughter is afraid to embrace her power. Aurelia tells me to be patient with her—that in time she will become one with her gifts."

"And when she does, what will happen?" Culver attached the mike to the headset.

"She will be able to move at will into the other worlds and help others. She will become a healer, which is her true calling in this lifetime."

"Not a horse manager?"

Chuckling indulgently, Don Alvaro said, "My son, her destiny was decided long ago." He gestured to the sky. "The moon and stars were right. The energy came, and life was breathed into my daughter's womb. Pilar was sent to us with a purpose. She rides horses and works at a rancho, but it is temporary." He frowned. "I am afraid there is great danger ahead of her, though. She is coming to a fork in her life path. If she chooses wrongly, she will leave us forever."

The calmly spoken words got Culver's instant attention. He stopped assembling the second radio, and narrowed his eyes speculatively on the old man. Don Alvaro had sunk back into the creaking old rocker, a sad look on his face as he studied Pilar. Culver believed that shamans possessed magical, inexplicable qualities. As a CIA agent stationed in Lima, he'd met such a shaman once, who had taken him to a jungle clearing and given him a drink called *ayahuasca*— the vision vine. He remembered heaving his guts out, time after time, while the shaman whistled and sang for hours on end. Finally, Culver had lain on the damp jungle floor, caught up in a series of vivid images. . . .

Culver sat apprehensively with a group of six other CIA agents in an oddly open area in the middle of the jungle. Don Gonzalez, the shaman who had promised to induce a vision of the future, had given him a blanket to sit or lie on. The moon was full, and it was near midnight, the jungle producing a virtual symphony of sounds around them. Because he'd experienced many things and had traveled the world in his twenty-four years, Culver treated this ceremony with deference, willing to approach it with an open mind. Don Gonzalez squatted in the middle of the circle of men mixing the "vision vine" herb in a bowl, whistling and singing.

The other agents, all Peruvians, sat solemnly, their legs crossed, their attention on the old shaman. Don Gonzalez's white hair shone like a startling halo around his head, the luminescence of the moon powerful in this meadow in the midst of the moist, fragrant jungle.

To Culver's surprise, the old shaman brought the ayahuasca first to him. His bony hands thrust the nondescript wooden cup toward Culver.

"Drink, my son," he urged.

Taking the cup, Culver stared down into the dark brown liquid.

"All of it," the shaman commanded with a flourish of his hand.

Without hesitation, but with some misgivings, Culver pressed the rim of the cup to his lips and drank. Surprisingly, the liquid was sweetish tasting and thick. As he finished gulping it, he saw the shaman's black eyes sparkle.

"Tonight you will meet your destiny," was all Don Gonzalez said as he moved away to refill the cup for the next recipient.

At first Culver became violently ill, his spasming stomach muscles contorting his body. As again and again he was sick with great shuddering heaves, he worried that he'd been poisoned. But gradually his body calmed, and he began to have the urge to lie down. He'd heard many things about ayahuasca, and the Peruvian agents swore by it. Culver noted the reverence with which the other agents, his friends, treated the experience. He knew shamans' powers were held sacred here.

The shaman began to whistle and sing again shortly after everyone had drunk from the cup, three of the other men getting sick as Culver had. The singing seemed hypnotic, and Culver finally gave in to the urge and lay down on his *back, staring up at the sky. A warmth began to permeate him, starting in his toes and working slowly upward. In his mind, he knew it was impossible—at midnight, the jungle would be growing cooler, the inevitable, shroudlike fog appearing between the layers of tree canopy that covered its vast reaches. Still, the sensation of warmth was pleasant and lulling. The Shaman's singing was rhythmic, and soon Culver felt himself drifting into a state of deep relaxation.*

Whatever it was, this altered state felt good. Warmth crested like small ocean waves toward the top of his head. As soon as it entered his skull, he felt a terrific whirling sensation, as if he were being sucked into a powerful whirlpool. The shaman's singing changed, growing higher pitched, and Culver felt his body changing with it, lengthening here, shortening there. Beneath his closed eyelids, lights began to flicker like blinking dots of sparkling color. At first they had no form, but soon they began to coalesce.

The lights throbbed, gathering intensity and purpose, and Culver felt a power radiating from the golden glow as it slowly took shape. He watched, mesmerized, as a female jaguar formed from the light and walked out of the radiance down a jungle path. Culver felt her incredible power and purposefulness as she trod silently on the huge pads of her feet. Her coat glowed like the sun, the thick, black crescent markings speaking of her silent, deadly power.

He found himself standing on the same jungle trail, directly in the path of the jaguar. Culver knew he should feel fear, for he'd seen a jaguar kill a man once. This cat was thickly muscled, low to the ground and unquestionably deadly. But as he awaited her approach, an incredible calm filled him. When she saw him, she halted about six feet away. Lifting her magnificent head, she studied him in the building silence.

Culver felt hypnotized by the jaguar's intense gaze. Suddenly, her nearly black eyes turned gold, the black becom-

*ing a mere pinhole in the center. As soon as that happened,
he felt himself being pulled forward, hurtling toward her at
a terrific rate of speed. He started to scream, but it was too
late. Everything went black. At first he felt cramped, almost suffocated, but as he adjusted to the darkness, he felt
the powerful beat of a heart against him, then the thick bone
of curving ribs. In that moment, he realized he was inside
the jaguar. Somehow, he'd become her! He was the jaguar.
The power he felt was unlike any other he'd ever experienced. This feeling was wild, primeval—untrammeled animal power of the highest degree—and he felt the jaguar's
confidence as she began walking again with her languidly
graceful gait.*

*Somewhere in his distant mind, Culver remembered what
the natives had often told him about the jaguar: how she
would hypnotize her chosen prey simply by looking at it with
her mesmerizing eyes, pulling its spirit out of its body, ren-
dering it incapable of movement. And that was how he'd felt
when she'd looked at him with those stunning eyes—para-
lysed.*

*Darkness fell over him again, and Culver felt himself be-
ing propelled out of the jaguar. In the next moment, he was
back in his own body, staring at her on the jungle path. The
jaguar switched her tail, blinked slowly at him and turned
away, dissolving into the glistening clouds she'd originally
come out of. He stood watching the golden clouds as they
began roiling, shifting in new and different ways.*

*The face of a young, beautiful woman appeared. She was
laughing and dancing naked by a dark green pool surrounded by grasses, and wild, colorful orchids hung from
nearby trees. She was the jaguar, Culver somehow knew, but
in human form. Her hair was long, almost to her waist, and
shone like sparkling moonlight on water. Her graceful arm
movements reminded him of the hula dancers of Hawaii.
Her body was slim, untouched and virginal, and each sway*

of her hips stoked a fiery heat building in his loins. He no longer cared if she really was the jaguar. He moved toward her, wanting to mate with her, wanting to expend this deep, animal feeling that possessed him, that he had become.

When she turned and saw him, she laughed, the low, throaty purr of a jaguar greeting her returning mate. Her eyes were ebony, shining as brightly as a thousand full moons. Her lips curved in welcome, and she opened her arms to him as he approached. Walking into them, wrapping his around her, feeling the moist, sensuous heat of her body collapsing joyfully against his made him growl—like a jaguar. He guided her down onto the thick, luxuriant grass and found himself naked beside her. Wherever she touched him, purring, her fingertips roaming searchingly across him, tiny, volcanolike fires seemed to erupt. He'd never ached for a woman this way before. He was tied in knots of fire, wanting to bend double with the pain of his need.

Her eyes danced with joy and she began to kiss him from his chest downward. He lay on the carpet of grass, its cool dampness a stark contrast to the branding heat of her lips as they reverently caressed his skin. He wanted her on a primal level, and yet, as she stroked him, rubbing sinuously against his body, he felt that something sacred was taking place between them. Culver had never experienced the hunger of desire combined with the sort of spiritual fire that seemed to surround them. Sex was sex. Or was it?

As the jaguar woman moved on top of him, allowing him to enter her, he felt a terrific shift within him on so many levels that he had no words for it. He could merely feel, with a purity that was much more than sex. Whatever power this mystical woman possessed was something so sacred that he'd never, in all his life and travels, encountered it before. He felt tears leaking from beneath his closed eyes as he reveled in the juxtaposition of animalistic need and punity in their consummation—two separate souls being brought into a sacred oneness that left him in awe of their magical coupling.

The golden clouds enveloped him, and suddenly the woman was no longer beside him. The clouds roiled again, turning dark and threatening above him as he lay naked and sweaty on the grass. Lightning bolts ripped from the churning sky, striking him in the chest, in the region of his heart. Blackness engulfed him, and he felt himself tumbling wildly through the storm's grasp like a leaf ripped from a tree during one of the jungle's powerful afternoon thunderstorms.

Though he was being buffeted by the clouds and lightning, Culver felt a horrifying sense of loss. Never had he felt such grief and such a soul-deep deprivation. The sense of abandonment, of being torn from the woman who had made him feel whole, became a well of grief tunneling through him, making him gasp for air.

Culver was gasping, his heart pounding, sweat running off his brow in rivulets, when he felt a hand on his chest. His eyes flew open. Don Gonzalez was squatting over him, his bony hand laid gently over Culver's heart. The shaman studied him in silence.

"You have walked the path of the jaguar people," he said in a low, gruff tone. Removing his hand, he took a wooden bowl and flicked droplets of water over Culver. "You have taken on the power of the jaguar. It is very dangerous, but it can bring the rainbow, too. The jaguar is our most powerful spirit guide. Many pursue that power, and most are killed by it. You are a Norte Americano, and you are ignorant of her ways." He nodded and slowly stood as he continued to sprinkle the water.

The water cooled Culver, and his heartbeat began to slow and grow steady again. His breathing went from rasping gasps to deeper lungfuls as he felt himself return to the here and now, no longer caught up in the vision vine's storm.

"You will discover the power of the jaguar, my son. Once you know it, it will be up to you to integrate it into yourself." Don Gonzalez set the bowl aside and came and squatted once more by his side. "It is female energy—the most powerful on Mother Earth. We are her children. All of us." He waved his finger at him. "You will meet a woman who is a jaguar priestess to our people. If you love her, you will become her."

Stunned, Culver lay, still caught up in the remnants of the winds of ayahuasca. What was real? What was not? His body vibrated with the memory of what he'd experienced, with the jaguar and then with the beautiful, virginal maiden.

"And if I don't love her?" he croaked to the shaman.

Don Gonzalez smiled benignly. "No man can resist the offer of jaguar medicine. She embodies all of the positive and negative of the feminine, my son. She is part seductress, part destroyer. You will experience both. The question is will you survive? And if you do, what then, I wonder?" His smile increased knowingly. "I have seen shaman apprentices actively hunt jaguar medicine, only to be killed by a jaguar in the jungle. They are found, torn apart and partially eaten." With a shake of his head, he murmured, "You come by the medicine honestly. Those apprentices who pursue her are in search of egotistical power, not the integration of the power to create a more-balanced human being." His eyes sparkled. "You achieved that state, that integration. Now that you know this feeling of wholeness, you will search for her, and when you find her, you will mate with her as you did in your vision. Then—" he opened his hands and looked to the sky above "—only the Great Mother will know your destiny."

Culver felt cleaner and lighter. Despite the many times he had vomited, then felt caught in a dizzying inner tornado, he felt amazingly good—almost buoyant. "And can I integrate this power?"

With a shrug, Don Gonzalez said, "If the jaguar came to you, yes."

Culver looked deep into the man's dark eyes. Somehow, he knew Don Gonzalez already had knowledge of his eventual success or failure, but the old man wouldn't reveal what he knew. "And if I don't?"

"Then the jaguar goddess will destroy you." He touched his own chest, where a necklace of colorful macaw feathers rested. Tapping his heart, he said, "Jaguar medicine is about integrating the female energy within yourself. It is an inner marriage. It is also the journey to the fullest opening of your heart. No other medicine tests you this strongly. It asks that you open your heart fully, with trust. You must stand completely naked and vulnerable to the jaguar. If you do not, you cannot accept the unconditional love she will offer you. There is no chance for he who hesitates, my friend. Trust. Stay receptive. Remain vulnerable. This priestess is still far away. You will meet her in the summer—a year from now, north of Lima. She will save your life."

Culver shook his head sharply, emerging from his powerful memory into the bright sunlight of Pilar's village. At the time of his vision-vine experience, he had silently laughed at the shaman's prediction. However, when he'd met Pilar, it had been at exactly the time and place the old man had predicted. But Culver hadn't had any idea Pilar was destined to become a jaguar priestess until just now, when Don Alvaro had mentioned it. He absently continued assembling the radio, scowling. "Does Pilar know she's a priestess?"

"Of course. That is why she wears her spirit guardian's hair in the medicine bag around her neck. It is a sign of her destiny."

Pilar came up to her grandfather smiling in greeting. Leaning over, she kissed the old man's parchment-thin cheek. "I see you have met Culver?"

"Yes," the patriarch said, gesturing for her to sit in another rocking chair not far from his own. "Sit, *mi nieta,*" he said, using the Spanish words for "my granddaughter."

Pilar saw the scowl on Culver's brow increase. Should she sit? Or should she disappear and leave them alone? Don Alvaro's long, strong fingers wrapped around her wrist, tugging her toward the rocker. Hesitantly, Pilar sat. Rane beamed at her.

"Mama, look! Culver said I could help him. Look at these radios! I've never seen anything like them."

Pilar held her daughter's light brown gaze, and her heart ached at the sight of her sitting so close to Culver. If he minded her daughter's presence, he didn't show it. She saw him look at Rane, his features softening. A vague hint of a smile played at the corners of his compressed lips. A fierce longing for Culver swept through Pilar, and an odd ache centered in her womb.

"Culver knows a great deal about mechanical things," she told Rane softly. Pulling the towel off her shoulders, she carefully folded it and placed it on the fallen log beside her rocking chair.

"He has been showing me so many things!"

Pilar caught Culver's gaze. He seemed amused by Rane's spontaneity, but how could anyone not be swayed by her daughter's sunbeam beauty and loving nature? No one could remain impervious to Rane's heart-centered love. But then, Pilar reminded herself, Rane had been created out of the heat and passion of the greatest love in her life, so it was not surprising.

"Perhaps," Don Alvaro said to Pilar with great seriousness, "we should have a ceremony before you leave to attack Don Ramirez's fortress in the jungle?"

She nodded. "Yes, I would like to receive the blessing of you and Grandmother Aurelia before I leave." She glanced at Culver. "Do you want to partake of a *ayahuasca* ceremony?"

He shook his head. "No way. Once was enough."

"You have tasted the winds of *ayahuasca?*" she asked, surprised.

"Yes. A long time ago," he said rather abruptly.

Pilar studied him in the intervening silence, feeling the tension radiating around him. "You don't have to take the drink with me. You can take it alone, if you don't want me around. I understand."

Culver's head snapped up, his eyes narrowing on her. "It has nothing to do with you being there or not."

"Do not push him, *mi nieta.*" Don Alvaro patted her arm gently. "You leave tomorrow morning, no?"

Culver's mouth tightened, and he glared at Pilar. "Just how much have you told them about our mission? We're on a strictly need-to-know basis, in case you didn't realize it." He knew he was snapping unnecessarily, and he hated himself for sounding so petulant. He saw Pilar's face mirror hurt from his verbal assault.

"I've told them nothing, Culver."

He stared at her. "Sure," he said mockingly. This was the first time Pilar had lied to him so openly. Usually her lies were subtle as a jaguar noiselessly stalking her prey through the jungle. Her blatancy angered him.

Her lips parting, Pilar stared at Culver, then at her grandfather. "Listen to me, Culver," she said in a low, firm tone. "My grandfather is a shaman. So is my grandmother. You have lived in Peru long enough to know that they possess a knowing far beyond our own. My grandmother told me last night when we arrived that they had been expecting us. They travel in the other dimensions, the worlds of the past and future. They know what is happening around us."

"Really?" he said condescendingly. "Then ask them the outcome of our little jungle hike. Is Morgan alive? Will we successfully rescue him?" He snorted. "Better yet, ask the old man if either of us will survive. On second thought, I can answer those questions myself. Do you know what the likelihood of survival is on our mission? About ten percent. Which means we've got a ninety-percent chance of buying the farm. I don't need a shaman or an *ayahuasca* ceremony where I heave my guts to find out that answer."

"Don't you dare make fun of my grandparents! Just because they're shamans from a culture you don't accept or believe in doesn't take away from what they know!"

Rane got up and moved away from Culver. She slid into Pilar's lap and linked her long, slim arms around her mother's neck as she rested her head against her shoulder. Pilar tried to control the feelings in her voice, aware that their argument was upsetting Rane. "For your information, people who drink *ayahuasca* during a ceremony for a valid reason do not have to heave their guts out. The cleaner a person is inside, the less vomiting he or she experiences."

"I see," he growled, placing the radio back in its protective plastic. "So I'm not clean inside. Well—" he looked straight at her "—you're the jaguar priestess around here. Go ahead and go to your grandparents' ceremony. I'm staying out of it."

Tabling her anger, Pilar gaped at him. "Jaguar priestess? What are you talking about?"

"Oh, come on," he drawled acidly as he leaned over and picked up a revolver, preparing to check it over and clean it, "You know damn well what I'm talking about."

"No, I don't!"

"Pilar, you keep surprising me, you know that?" Culver pulled the safety off the Beretta and studied the weapon critically. "Here you are a jaguar priestess for your people, and you never told me. In fact, you said so little about your real parentage—"

"At the time, it wasn't important," she snapped. No, at the time, she thought ruefully, they'd fallen into each other's arms, loving hotly, without regret or apology.

Culver's mouth twisted into an ugly line as he broke down the revolver piece by piece to begin oiling it against the jungle's humidity. "A hell of a lot of things weren't important except surviving."

Stung, Pilar held Rane more tightly, feeling her daughter tremble at the amount of anger in their exchange. She stroked her long, dark hair, flowing loose around her shoulders. All her life, Pilar had worked to keep her daughter from the violence of the world. Rane sighed and closed her eyes, nestling her face in the curve of her mother's neck. She relaxed, and Pilar was grateful. Too bad her touch didn't have the same mollifying effect on Culver; but too much bad blood had passed between them, Pilar admitted. She could hardly blame him.

"My grandparents have been telling me for as long as I can remember that I had a special responsibility to fulfill with my life," she explained in a low, controlled tone. "But I wasn't aware until you just told me that it was as a jaguar priestess." She glanced at her attentive grandfather, who she knew was listening with his heart. He didn't know much English, but from experience, Pilar knew that the revered shaman could understand on another level exactly what was being said. "That is something I will have to speak to them about now, on top of everything else that is going on."

Culver gave her a questioning look but said nothing. Out of long habit, he began applying oil to the gun's dark metal. Pilar sounded so convincing. If he hadn't learned so painfully, firsthand, of her ability to deceive, he would have believed her statement. She looked sincere and a little in awe of the information he'd given her. Hell, she was just good at lying, he told himself angrily.

"We've got enough to worry about right now," he snapped. When he saw Rane flinch at the tone of his voice, he softened his words. "You do whatever you want to prepare for our little hike tomorrow morning. But I know that vision vine is hallucinogenic, and you'd damn well better not meet me tomorrow in a drugged state."

Glaring at him, Pilar whispered tightly, "I would never jeopardize your life like that and you know it!"

"Really?" Culver allowed the sarcasm to drip from his voice. "You've got a funny way of looking at things, then."

"What are you talking about?"

"You've already killed me in a hundred different ways."

Stunned, Pilar drew in a sharp breath, pain shooting through her hammering heart. She felt Don Alvaro's fingers move in a caressing motion on her arm.

"Mi nieta," he murmured, "there is much to do before you go. Leave Rane here with Culver. You will come with me, eh?"

Blinded by agony, Pilar nodded. Easing her daughter from her lap, she set her in the chair and asked her to stay behind. Rane nodded and curled up in the chair, rocking it slightly with one slim leg. Unable to look at Culver, Pilar helped her grandfather to his feet. He took the twisted, dried jungle vine he used as a cane and leaned heavily on it.

As they walked slowly through the sprawling village, protected beneath the trees' stretching limbs, Pilar tried to steady her breathing. Her heart ached without relief, and as she gently steadied Don Alvaro with a hand around his upper arm, she said unevenly, "I don't know why this happened, Grandfather."

"What?" he inquired, looking down at her kindly.

"My being teamed up with Culver again. I—I thought he was out of my life—forever. I never expected him to walk back into it." She rubbed her heart with her hand. Combating tears, she whispered brokenly, "I still love him so much. I've hurt him so badly...."

"*Niña,* child, you carry both his and your own burden in your heart. It is very hard to carry one's own grief, much less another's anger and hurt, eh?"

Sniffing, Pilar fought back tears and pressed her head against his thin shoulder as he slowly wound his arm around her and drew her against him. "Y-yes, it is, Grandfather."

"Perhaps," he said, looking toward the hut where he'd lived all his life, "when you drink of the ceremonial cup this evening, the winds of *ayahuasca* will speak to you in a vision that will make the way more clear. Perhaps—" he smiled at her gently "—your heart will be healed of the many burdens it has carried alone for so long. The secrets you carry are heavy, *mi niña.*"

Pilar stared up at her grandfather for a heartbeat. Her grandparents were wise, and she allowed her panicked soul to find peace in his liquid, brown gaze, a soothing of the violent ache in her heart. Shamans were wonderful healers, she reminded herself.

Pilar recalled one of the many stories her grandparents had told her when she was a child sitting in the hut at night, about how one had to undergo a near-death experience before receiving the calling to become an apprentice shaman. Since shamans traversed all the dimensions, they could not be afraid of such travels. Only those who had died could be admitted to these other worlds, and shamans were able to make such journeys and live to tell about it—because they themselves had died and returned to life.

Don Alvaro brought Pilar into the hut where Aurelia was kneeling, grinding corn on a heavy, flat stone. Nearby, a small fire of coals was ready to cook the tortillas she was preparing for them. "Pilar knows of her path as a jaguar priestess," he said as he sat down in his favorite rocking chair, crafted from scraps of mahogany.

Aurelia stopped her grinding. "Eh?" She looked at Pilar, who took a seat at the rough-hewn table. Light from the four windows filtered in, accentuating the shadows. "Well," she said busily, returning to her grinding, "we knew she would learn of it soon, anyway."

Pilar ran her fingertips across the table's worn surface. "Why didn't you tell me?"

Aurelia sighed, sifting the corn flour into a small pottery jar. Wiping her hands on her colorful red-and-black skirt, she slowly rose from her arthritic knees. "In order to become a priestess, you must almost die." Aurelia halted in the middle of the hut and stared at her granddaughter. "You have not had that experience—yet."

"Once you had lived through the experience—passed to the other world and returned—" Don Alvaro added softly, "we would have told you. Then you would already have understood the death experience, and what we do as shamans." Opening his hands, he said, "The journey you and Culver take tomorrow will place you in a life-and-death situation. You will have many choices along the way, *mi niña*. We pray for you. And for him. We pray that you return to us alive, but we can not yet know if that will happen."

Aurelia came over and patted Pilar's slumped shoulder. "*Mi niña*, the life path of a jaguar priestess is the hardest of all." She smiled a little and touched her large, ample breast. "I serve the jaguar goddess myself. The first half of my life was filled with tests involving life and death—my own and others'. By the jaguar's grace, I passed them and lived to work in her service as a *shamanka*," she said, using the term for a female shaman. Her worn, plump fingers rested against Pilar's hair. "Your heart carries many burdens, my little one. We ache for you as you do yourself. But a *shamanka* cannot heal others unless she knows what it is like to suffer in many areas as a human being. How can she understand another's pain if she has not traversed that path herself? So you see, it is necessary, this painful process we undergo, to become worthy of the jaguar goddess's attention.''

Shaking her head, Pilar looked up into her grandmother's round, brown face. She felt such peace and love radiating from the old woman that she opened her arms and slid them around her grandmother's ample waist. Closing her eyes, she buried her face against Aurelia's softness. The feel of her grandmother's still-strong arms encircling her gave her courage and dissolved some of the lingering agony in her heart. ''I'm so scared,'' she whispered. ''I've hurt Culver so much. I don't know how I'll get through this mission with him. Being around him is like holding my hand in a fire. I hurt all the time, Grandmother. Sometimes I hurt so much I can barely breathe.'' Looking up, her eyes bathed in tears, she said brokenly, ''Sometimes I wonder whether, if I quit breathing, the hurt would finally go away....''

''Ah, *mi niña*,'' Aurelia scolded softly, framing Pilar's face with her work-worn hands. She leaned over, her features bare inches from Pilar's as she held her granddaughter's gaze. ''The jaguar goddess is hard on us, I know. And the love you carry in your heart for this *Norte Americano* is a blessing and also a curse to you. Is that not what being a *shamanka* is all about? You stand with one foot in this world, your other foot in the many other worlds. How can you know pain if you do not know pleasure? How can you know love if you have never loved fully? Your heart and soul were given to Culver. We do not question his love for you, nor yours for him.''

With her thick, callused thumbs, Aurelia caressed Pilar's smooth cheeks. ''*Mi niña*, this is your final test before you can approach the jaguar goddess and ask her blessing to become an apprentice. This mission will be a test for you in every way.'' Her voice dropped to almost a growl as she said, ''Whatever you do, my little one, you must walk with an open heart. Do you hear me? Do you understand? Even though this man throws arrows of anger and hurt, you must not close your heart to him or anything around you. To do so is to fail this test. Be receptive. Continue to love without anger, guilt or shame."

Pilar's eyes widened at those words. Looking into the wise, velvety depths of her grandmother's eyes, Pilar knew the old woman was aware of the shameful secret she'd carried eight years. Choking on sudden tears of gratitude, Pilar whispered, "I understand, Grandmother."

Aurelia smiled, her entire face radiating with a loving glow. "Tonight, we will hold an *ayahuasca* ceremony for you, to beseech the jaguar goddess on your behalf to protect and watch over you and this *Norte Americano.*"

"Thank you," Pilar whispered. "I want to pray for Morgan Trayhern, too, Grandmother. If anyone needs prayers, it is that brave man, not me."

Chuckling indulgently, Aurelia released Pilar and planted a swift kiss on her brow. "You make the jaguar spirit happy with such unselfish love for another, *mi niña*. That is why I pray strongly that your walk with death will not be final, that you can place your feet on the rainbow bridge, but also come back from it—back to your people. That you can give your heart again, without the clouding of the past as before."

Surrounded by the comfort of her grandparents' love, Pilar felt her burden easing. They had been her nurturing support for so many years—since the deaths of her parents. She realized that she hadn't visited them often enough or long enough in the past eight years. Her stays had generally been limited to weekends, two or three times a year, and Rane always cried when they had to fly back to Lima. Well, didn't she want to cry at the thought of leaving, also? Looking around the simple thatched hut, and at the kind

intelligence in the faces of her grandparents, Pilar felt a new
stirring in her heart.

"If I survive this mission," she said in a tremulous tone,
"I want to come home. I want to come back here and live
with you. I've missed family so much—more than I've realized until now. And Rane needs the love and support you
have for her. She needs to know her people, the source of
her soul and blood."

Aurelia glowed in approval as she stood in the doorway.
"We pray it will be so, *mi niña*. Nothing would give us more
happiness than to have you here at the village with us. You
will begin to apprentice with me and learn the ways of the
shamanka."

Sadly, Pilar whispered, "I've been so blind, Grandmother. You were here all along. Why didn't I realize that?
Why did I have to spend two years in Lima alone after Fernando died, trying to raise Rane by myself? I've suffered so
much by doing that. You know how our society looks down
on a woman and child without a man. I have endured name-
calling and accusing looks, as if I should apologize for living when my husband is dead. They insisted I should re-
marry, but my heart belongs to just one man... and I can
never have him again...."

"Be patient, *mi niña*," Aurelia soothed. "Though the
spirit of the jaguar is harsh upon us, she is also bountiful in
rewarding those who pass the trials she sets before us. Be
patient. Perhaps all your dreams can be fulfilled."

Pilar got up, smiling brokenly. "I have no more dreams,
Grandmother. They died when Culver almost died—for me.
I don't live for myself. I live because of Rane. She deserves
a mother, someone who loves her fully. I don't want to be
yanked out of her life as my mother and father were from
mine."

Frowning, Aurelia murmured, "We must pray very hard
tonight."

Pilar left the hut, following her grandmother down the mountain. Aurelia was in her early eighties, spry despite her weight and age. The trees became thicker as they got farther from the village. Pilar knew without being told that her grandmother was going to a special spot where the *ayahuasca* vine grew wild. The day was warm, the sun shining brightly through wisps of clouds.

Pilar knew that her grandparents had seen death many times. Ramirez and his men had slaughtered more than thirty people from their farming village in the past twenty years, and there wasn't a family in the region completely unaffected by his atrocities. She also knew the chances of surviving the mission were small, as Culver had so coldly pointed out. As the breeze playfully lifted and twisted strands of her hair around her face, Pilar regretted so much.

Chapter Seven

It took every vestige of Pilar's control to hide her tears when Rane stretched her slim arms up around Culver's neck. As he bent to say farewell to her, her daughter's eyes were wet with tears. Culver had crouched and taken her into his arms, holding her tightly against him. He wore a heavy pack on his back and had to balance it during Rane's unexpected embrace.

"Keep Mama safe," the little girl sobbed against his neck, her face pressed against him. "Don't let her get hurt. I love her. She's all I have left. Take care of her, Culver."

Culver patted Rane's narrow shoulder tenderly. Unexpectedly, tears dampened his own eyes as he held her small form to him. This morning when he'd gotten up from the hut where he'd slept alone, he'd been in a foul humor. He'd grimly expected Pilar to be late for their agreed-upon 0600 meeting at the edge of the village. And he hadn't expected Rane to be waiting at her side, gripping her hand as if letting go would be releasing her to her death. The look on the child's usually joyous face softened his feelings, melting away the angry defenses he'd erected in his heart earlier this morning.

Rane's hair was soft and smelled freshly washed, hanging loose all the way to her narrow hips. She had placed a small pink orchid in her hair, attaching it awkwardly with a bobby pin, the delicate flower accentuating her innocent loveliness. Placing his hands on her shaking shoulders, Culver eased her a few inches away from him. The child sniffled and, with trembling hands, tried bravely to scrub her eyes free of tears as she looked up at him. Such emotion showed in her light brown eyes that he managed a small smile for her benefit.

"It's going to be all right," he said, defying his own hard-and-fast rule about not underplaying the danger of any given mission. Gently taming errant strands of hair back from Rane's damp cheek, he placed them behind her tiny ear. At seven-and-a-half, she wore petite diamond earrings that made her look even more feminine.

"M-Mama says you're a w-warrior from long ago," Rane stammered between sobs. "She s-says you saved her life once before."

Culver's gaze flicked to Pilar, standing a few feet away. Another lie. "Well..." he hedged, "our lives were saved because we worked together like a good team." Actually, Pilar had saved his miserable hide. That was the truth of the matter. Still, deep within himself, Culver could understand why Pilar had turned that particular fact around to offer her fearful daughter solace. He saw tears glittering in Pilar's own eyes, her hand pressed to her mouth as if to stop a sob struggling to break free.

Culver leaned over and kissed Rane's damp, pale cheek. Throwing caution and his conservative training to the wind, he said, "Listen, your mama underwent a sacred ceremony last night and it will give her protection. She's going to be all right, Rane." He hoped to God his words would prove true.

Hiccuping through her tears, Rane reached out and touched his recently shaven cheek. "Y-you promise?"

Culver hung his head, avoiding the child's innocent eyes. How the hell could he promise such a thing? Her small hand, so delicate and soft, rested against his cheek, holding the same kind of warmth he'd always noted in Pilar's. Pilar came from a family of healers, and he'd guessed that was behind the heat radiating from her hands, so he wasn't surprised Rane possessed the same warm touch. *Oh, what the hell.* "Yeah, Rane, I promise I'll bring your mama home alive. How's that?"

Instantly, Culver saw Rane's expression change. She was like a chameleon, in a sense—just as Pilar was. Culver knew Peruvian *shamankas* were known as "shape-shifters," able to turn themselves not only into animals, but into other human forms as well. Rane obviously possessed the rudiments of that ability, he thought, as he watched her small face lighten, her eyes glow brightly with relief and hope.

"Oh," she cried, flinging herself back into his arms and wrapping her own as tightly as she could around his neck, "thank you, Culver. Thank you!" Excitedly, she tore from his grasp, touched the orchid resting in her hair, then worked for several moments to free it. "Here, I want you to take this with you. Grandmother says I have orchid medicine. She says that if I give a person an orchid, he will be healed and protected. I want you to be safe, too...." Rane became somber as she leaned over and eased the small bloom into Culver's left shirt pocket, which she studiously buttoned so the flower couldn't be lost on their trek.

"There," she said seriously. "I will go to my altar that Grandmother helped me set up in our *casa,* and I will pray for you, too."

Reaching out, Culver caressed Rane's hair. "Now I do feel safe," he said her in a husky tone. The love shining in the child's eyes rocked him. Rane tilted her head, watching as he straightened and rearranged the heavy pack straps pulling at his shoulders.

"It's time to go," Pilar called gently. She caressed Rane's hair, leaning down one last time to hug her daughter tightly, before releasing her. Out of nowhere, her grandparents appeared. Though they were both old, their features worn by life, Pilar saw the gentleness glowing in their weathered faces. A fog hung just above the jungle, and the humidity was high. She fought tears again as Rane ran to stand between the aged couple. A ragged breath escaped her as she gazed at her family. Chances were good that she would never see any of them again.

Her heart nearly broke with grief. What would happen to Rane? As Pilar looked over at Culver, she saw that his expression remained tender from the child's unexpected attention. Rane had magic in her touch, but then, her heart was pure and she was innocent, and Pilar knew how easily Culver responded to that combination. Once, she had been like that.

"Come on," he rasped gruffly as he passed her on the well-beaten trail leading down the slope toward the jungle.

Raising her hand, Pilar tried to smile at Rane, but didn't succeed. Turning quickly, she fought back tears and blindly followed Culver's huge, striding form down the trail. Some of her anguish eased as they left the upper world of sunlight, clouds and villagers and entered the darkened labyrinth of the jungle. The heavy humidity enveloped Pilar, and instantly she began to perspire as she struggled to maintain her balance with the heavy pack jostling against palms, vines and other encroaching plant life. It almost seemed as if the plants were wishing them well, patting them, reaching out in their own way as the two humans trod ever deeper into the jungle. A blessing of sorts for a successful journey, Pilar hoped.

Hurrying to keep up with Culver, Pilar sensed how upset he was. Because of Rane's unexpected request? Probably. She certainly knew that he didn't want to be here with her. The trail continued to descend along the slope of the hill, and here and there, Pilar could hear droplets tapping from one leaf to another as the thick fog condensed. Above her, the opaque white mist floated like a billowy canopy over the entire region. But it was usual for fog to embrace the jungle until about ten each morning.

About a mile into the jungle, the trail widened enough to allow two people to walk easily side by side. Culver turned and looked expectantly at Pilar. Her skin had a sheen of moisture on it, and her eyes were dark and focused. He saw the stubborn set to her mouth and instantly wanted to kiss her—kiss her until she melted against him. The errant thought was an unwelcome interruption to his own focused attention, and he scowled as she drew to a halt a few feet from him.

"Are you doing okay?" he asked. The packs they wore would provide everything they needed for the next four days. Ramirez's jungle fortress was a two-day trek deep into the heart of Amazonia.

She smiled briefly and wiped the perspiration from her brow with a red kerchief she took from around her neck. "Yes."

"You're not acclimated to this."

"Neither of us are," Pilar said, looking around in admiration at the towering trees, draped everywhere with dark green vines thick as cables. In a way, they reminded her of giant, beautiful spiderwebs. The screeching howls of monkeys preceded them, warnings to friends of human trespassers in their environs. "I'm glad I have Incan blood. I can feel my body shifting, rebalancing to this heat and humidity."

Culver nodded and placed his hands on his hips. "I hate the jungle."

"Why?"

"It's hot and uncomfortable—and I feel like I can't breathe."

She smiled softly. "We have always said that the jungle is the womb of Mother Earth. The moist darkness is fertile. Everything lives and grows here, just as a baby grows inside a woman's body."

Culver was struck by the symbolic beauty in Pilar's words. "I've never thought of it in those terms." He wiped the sweat from his face with the back of his hand. On his hip, he wore a holster and the black Beretta he'd cleaned yesterday. Pilar wore no obvious weapons. Her cover, after all, was that of a *shamanka* guide for a U.S. botanist. Her hair, pulled back into a single, thick braid that curved across her shoulder, was wavier than usual from the jungle's moisture. How clean and clear her golden skin looked, Culver thought. How shining her eyes, with their hints of an inner, secret joy.

"What are you so happy about?" he demanded abruptly as he gazed around them.

"I had forgotten how much I love the jungle." Pilar gestured overhead to an old, thick rubber tree. In its distorted, twisted limbs hung a huge purple-and-white orchid. "Look above you, Culver."

He twisted to look in the direction she indicated. The orchid, one of a string of blooms, hung within his reach. Lifting his hand he gently broke the stem and captured seven blossoms at once. Lifting them, he inhaled their heady fragrance.

"Here," he muttered, handing them to her. "A string of jungle pearls for your neck."

Shocked at his unexpected gift, Pilar reached out and took the slender, bending stem, heavy with flowers. She saw the burning look in Culver's eyes and felt as if he'd reached out and touched her. Cradling the orchids in her hands, she stared up at him. "Thank you...."

Culver gave her a cutting smile. "You always reminded me of an orchid," he grudgingly admitted. *Open, vulnerable, giving and feminine.* "Wear them. You can really play the part of guide to this ignorant *Norte Americano* plant specialist." Turning on his heel, he continued along the now-level floor of the jungle.

Quickly stringing the orchids around her neck, where they rested between her pack's straps and her chin, Pilar inhaled their aromatic fragrance. Dizzied by this surprising gift, she hurried to catch up. For every stride Culver took, Pilar had to take two. But she managed to move to his side. She felt him look down at her, felt his scowl. Too bad if he didn't want her at his shoulder. Still, she noticed he checked his stride slightly for her sake. Puffing a little, she twisted to look up at him.

"In my next lifetime, I'm going to be born tall, with long legs like yours," she teased.

Culver gave a slight smile. Glancing over, he saw that the color of her eyes had lightened. Pilar was happy. The realization struck directly at the heart he was so desperately trying to protect from her dazzling smile, soft voice and tender looks. "Short people do have their problems," he admitted. Right now, they should be safely out of range, for the most part, of Ramirez's men. Because the fortress was hidden so deeply in the jungle, Culver knew from experience that Ramirez didn't post many guards. But several hit men frequently took on the guise of villagers from the small settlements that ringed the fortress. He and Pilar couldn't know for certain if a villager was friend or foe. He did know that it was safer to speak in English, because many of the

Indians and some of Ramirez's men didn't know the language.

Chuckling, Pilar nodded. "Small but mighty. Look at Grandmother Aurelia. She is barely five feet tall, yet she's one of Peru's most powerful *shamankas*."

"Speaking of that, how did the ceremony go last night?" He eyed Pilar and saw her face suddenly close up. Her lips, once parted, became compressed, and Culver sensed a dread in her. In spite of himself, he worried about the vision of the future she might have received and its potential accuracy. He watched as she pushed hair from her forehead—another sign of nervousness.

"It will be," she said carefully, "a difficult mission."

"Difficult being another word for disastrous?"

Pilar opened her hands. "My death is near."

Culver jerked to a halt. He stared down at her. "Death?" His voice came out strangulated, filled with disbelief. How could Pilar stand there, calmly accepting such a thing? Then he remembered how shamans had to traverse between life and death for their patients in order to heal them. Death for them was not the fearful experience that the Western World saw.

Combatting tears, Pilar smiled brokenly at Culver. Gone was the flinty look in his eyes. She saw his sudden anguish on her behalf. "I feel that is why Rane was so upset this morning. Even though she wasn't at the ceremony, she knows...." With a sigh, Pilar whispered, "I don't want to leave Rane, Culver. My parents died early, and I know the pain of it. I don't want Rane to experience that." She shrugged out of her pack and laid it aside. As she rubbed her shoulders, she said, "After the ceremony, early this morning, I talked with my grandparents about my vision. They agree that I could die a physical death. It's part of my final test to take on the spirit of the jaguar. Anyone who is invited to the jaguar medicine must have a near-death experience. Whether I survive depends on many things, some of them outside of myself."

Cursing softly, Culver lowered his pack to the ground in turn and sat next to Pilar on a damp log near the trail. She was only inches away. It was inconceivable to him that she could die, yet he knew that going up against Ramirez could easily guarantee both their deaths. Was he prepared to die also? Staring at Pilar's serene face, Culver knew the answer was a defiant no. Maybe she was already lost to him in some ways, and they could never recapture what they'd had, but he couldn't stick his head in the sand about the lethal possibilities of this mission. As angry and hurt as he was by Pilar's actions in the past, he emphatically didn't want her to die. The admission softened his attitude toward her.

"I know enough about the vision-vine ceremony," he began stiltedly, "to know it's not just a bunch of hallucinations."

Pilar nodded and sighed. "That's why I undertook the ceremony." She clasped her sweaty hands together. "When you nearly kissed me the other morning, I thought I was dreaming," she continued softly, unable to look at him. "I wanted you to kiss me. I felt like a parched plant on the high desert plateau of the Andes, with your kiss like life-giving moisture." She felt a flush rise from her neck into her face at the admission. Culver's intense inspection felt like the heat of a fire upon her.

"Last night, I saw so very much. I saw Morgan...." She lifted her head and gazed at him. "Ramirez has been torturing him brutally. They have given him drugs to drain information from him. He is like a robot, from what I can see. He is alive, but not in his body. Do you know what I mean?"

"Drugs disconnect you, Pilar," Culver agreed harshly. "Damn. I knew Ramirez would do that to him. But you say he's alive?"

"Yes, I saw in my vision where he is. They no longer guard him within the compound. Morgan sits on a small bunk in a tiny room on the second floor of the *casa*. He sits staring into space, unmoving. I saw his shadow—the part that is invisible yet gives us life in this physical body—lying beside him on the floor."

"What does that mean?"

"That he is slowly dying."

"He's probably been drugged so many times that he's toxic," Culver muttered. "That son of a bitch!" He tightened his hands into fists as he referred to Ramirez.

Sadly, Pilar touched her necklace of orchids. "He may not survive, either. My vision—" she waved her hand in the air "—became murky, and I saw us dead. In another phase of it, I saw Morgan alive, but I was dead. In another, we both barely survived the mission."

"How do you interpret that?" Culver knew that shamans under the influence of an altered state created by the vision vine often saw the future broken down into different paths a person could take. One thing he'd learned from shamans in Peru—alternate realities represented choices. What the person chose would manifest physically. Desperately he wondered which choice Pilar would opt for. In his heart, he knew she would struggle toward life, for Rane. But bullets didn't choose who they would kill, and Ramirez would murder them without a second thought.

"Choices," she whispered brokenly. "I'll have the choice to live or die." Rubbing her hands on the thighs of her jeans, she said, "I want to live, but I don't know if that's enough to ensure it."

"What can make the difference between you living and dying?"

Pilar held his agitated stare. "Love."

Her reply haunted Culver. He twisted around on the log, placing his long legs on either side of Pilar, unable to stand the suffering in her face any longer. Driven by hunger and need, he raised his hands and framed her face. How soft and pliant her skin was. Looking deeply into her now-golden eyes, he saw her lips part. The invitation was there. He felt her suddenly tense, and with his thumbs, he caressed her high cheekbones.

"Mi querida," he whispered thickly as he leaned down. For an instant, Pilar tried to pull from his grasp, but then, miraculously, he felt her surrender to him. His heart soared with that knowledge as he closed his eyes just as their mouths touched. How long he had been without her! The tentative grazing of her lips sent a sheet of fire raging through him, from his heart downward. He tasted the saltiness of her lips, and then she opened to him, like the fragrant orchids grazing his cheek as he took her mouth more deeply.

The jungle's humid heat swirled around him as he tasted the nectar of Pilar's lips. When she fearlessly returned his searching, tentative kiss, fire jagged through him, and he felt rather than heard her moan of surrender as she leaned forward, her breasts brushing against his chest. Her arms lifted and moved across his shoulders, and her fingers slid up his neck into his hair. Her touch was as fiery and beautiful as he remembered.

Hungrily, he slid his mouth against her wet, full lips. She was a thick, waxy orchid, opening to him, presenting him her natural, heady fragrance and offering him her nectar as a woman. Her ragged breath fanned his cheek. Her mouth was pliant even as it plundered his own questing lips. He couldn't get enough of her, and his fingers tightened on her face, drawing her more deeply against him. The feel of her breasts was enticing as her fingers ranged over his head, then slid across his face, as if rememorizing every detail.

Culver wanted more. Much more. Tilting her head, he dove his tongue deeply into her mouth, where it tangled with hers in a sliding, molten heat, spiraling crazily toward that door deep within him that he'd kept carefully barred and locked ever since that day Pilar had left him so abruptly. Her moan was like a jaguar's purr, and his pleasure at the sound thrummed through him as if he were a drum being played by her honest need. Her fingers explored his craggy features, outlining his thick eyebrows, caressing his eyelids as softly as butterflies, then moving tenderly down his cheekbones to stroke the hard granite of his jaw.

How much he'd missed all of this. As he dragged Pilar into his arms, Culver pressed her tightly against him, one large hand cradling her back, holding her as close as he could without actually entering her. Volcanic heat exploded through him as her small hand moved downward, sliding beneath his shirt and over his collarbone. As their hurried breathing mingled, Culver's heart thudded without relief. He tunneled his fingers urgently through her bound hair, rewarded by the feel of it loosening beneath his insistence. The ribbon holding the thick, luxurious mass eased, and the strands came cascading down over his hand and arm. The orchids' fragrance combined with her natural, earthy scent. Culver had never felt more alive than when she was in his arms, making exquisite love to her. He'd never felt the devastating, numbing—death of the soul as he had when she'd left him.

In some dim corner of his now barely functioning mind, he began to understand on a new level the concept of the worlds a shaman traverses in his or her inner journeys. Pilar was his life and death. As her mouth crushed against his and they clung wildly to each other, he felt reborn, as if all his dying grief had been transformed in that instant when she had surrendered willingly to him once again. He cared about nothing at this point except Pilar, and the dreaded possibility that she might be torn from him again—this time, by one of Ramirez's bullets.

The jungle's heat, the slickness of their caressing hands reminded him of the giving of life. Pilar had been right—the jungle was the womb of Mother Earth. And Pilar was *his* life. His destiny. Culver realized he had known it on some inner level all along, but had been too bitterly afraid to admit it even to himself. Now she was here in his arms, exchanging intimacies he had only dreamed of.

Thunder rumbled warningly overhead. Vaguely, Culver acknowledged it and knew that pouring rain soon would strike the jungle canopy with fury. Tearing his mouth from Pilar's, he stared down into her golden eyes. His fingers trembled as they tunneled into her hair on either side of her precious face. The words, *I love you,* nearly burst from him, but Culver stopped himself. He knew the folly of opening the depths of his emotions to Pilar. Last time, she'd abandoned him at his darkest hour of need.

Wrestling to contain the feelings rumbling through him like the approaching thunderstorm, Culver gripped Pilar's shoulders and rested his brow against hers. He felt her hands flatten against his chest, felt their burning warmth seem to sear through the damp cotton of his shirt. Though aching as never before to love her fully, completely, he forced himself to release her—and saw a matching desire for him in her eyes.

Pilar's long-ago rejection had left him believing she would never want him again. The discovery that she did was bittersweet. Nothing could come of him giving her his heart again. He simply wasn't willing to risk it. The pain was too great for him to endure a second time. It would kill him.

"It's going to rain," Culver muttered thickly, pushing himself to his feet. Stumbling like a drunken man toward his pack, he absorbed all of his reeling emotions. He felt as if he'd consumed the fury of the coming storm: an incredible tension raged between the longing to lose his soul to Pilar again and the need to prevent that very tragedy. Thunder rumbled again. The storm was within three miles, the rain less than fifteen minutes away.

As they resettled their packs on their shoulders and headed more deeply into the jungle, Pilar struggled with the gamut of emotions Culver had released with his powerful, unexpected kisses. Though sunlight overhead was dispersed by the canopy of trees, occasionally an actual beam of light would find its way to the damp, leaf-strewn jungle floor. Most of the time, the light was dappled and in constant motion, like the patterns of light reflected off a mirrored ball hanging above a dance floor. Clouds were moving in, though, and Pilar watched as shadows began to encroach on the sun-speckled jungle. The storm was approaching, but it was nothing to match the storm she was experiencing within her. Her lower body ached with a burning memory she couldn't seem to banish, of Culver, deep inside her, moving with her, showering life into her just as the rain sated the thirsty jungle.

Pilar walked silently at his shoulder, and a rush of relief flowed through her. Thank God Culver had broken their kiss. He had more sense than her errant body did. She knew all too well the supreme danger of giving herself to him. At this point, without an exploration of the full truth of what had happened, it could only cause him pain.

No, Pilar told herself, shaken by the thought, she wasn't willing to risk the possible consequences of opening herself up to him and telling him everything. She just couldn't. She had too much to lose.

"It's funny," Culver muttered eventually, the sound of his voice instantly deadened by the thick vegetation around them, "I thought I knew what dying was all about when you left me. I grieved as if you were dead. Now you tell me you might die, and I'm feeling it all over again, only worse."

Pilar didn't dare look at Culver. She heard the uncertainty in his roughened tone, and without thinking, she reached out and blindly wrapped her fingers around his big, thickly callused hand. It was a hand that had loved her to oblivion, to a special world of love and light she had never experienced before—or since. He halted abruptly at her touch, and she tightened her grip on his hand as she turned to face him. The expression on his face was heartrending. Instantly, Pilar released his hand, afraid of invoking more pain by her presence.

"I owe you an apology, Culver," she began, her voice unsteady. "I—I...my world was pulled out from under me when you were wounded. You were so close to death. I didn't think I'd reach help in time to save you. I know it happened eight years ago, but at times, it seems like yesterday." Pilar touched her damp, white cotton blouse. The thunder sounded another warning, much closer this time, the jungle vibrating with the booming rumbles. She looked up at the canopy and then back at him. "I can still feel how I felt then. The terror. The grief."

Culver looked at her strangely. Why was she telling him this? "But you didn't have to leave me, Pilar. Why did you run? I remember you at the hospital, holding my hand, crying and praying out loud for me. But when I regained consciousness, you were gone. The doctors didn't know where you were. The nurses didn't know—" His voice cracked. "I wanted to die when you didn't return. I couldn't understand why you left me. You saved my life, then just disappeared. Why?"

Biting down on her lower lip, Pilar looked away. "*Dios,* Culver, I—I wish I could tell you, but I cannot." Abruptly, she remembered hearing him say casually, not long after they met, "Oh, sure, I love kids." They had stopped to help a small girl crying outside a village, she recalled. "But I'm a long way from being ready to settle down with children of my own."

"Hector said you were pulled undercover again," he was saying now, his mouth flattened. "A Q-clearance mission. I knew from CIA experience that if someone goes Q-clearance, I might as well ask a brick wall for information. Hector refused to tell me anything more. Two weeks in that hospital, and I was transferred by plane back to the States. I tried," he said, frustration ringing in his voice, "through Hector to reach you. But he gave me nothing."

Wincing, Pilar nodded and closed her eyes, unable to stand the anguish in Culver's gaze. *"Mi querido,"* she whispered faintly, "I didn't want to leave you, but something...came up. Something only I was able to handle." She opened her eyes, Culver's rugged features blurring before her. "I'm so sorry, Culver. I didn't mean to wound you that way. I had no intention..." She opened her hands helplessly. "I wish I could heal your pain. I see you still carry the injury in your heart, the grief and anger toward me." Her voice broke, she was so close to tears. "Can you ever forgive me, Culver? If I am going to die, I need to know you will forgive me for abandoning you at the moment of your greatest need. Can you?"

Culver's throat constricted. Reaching out, he cupped her cheek. How soft and firm her skin was beneath his fingertips as he grazed that velvety slope. She'd called him "my darling." The sweetness of the words soothed him like a healing salve, easing the ache in his heart. He saw tears swimming in Pilar's eyes, saw her valiant attempt to force them back. The girl he remembered from so long ago would have burst easily into uncontrollable tears, and he would have pulled her into his arms, rocking her as she cried, soothing her tiny kisses and caresses.

How badly Culver wanted to do just that. For the first time, he began to understand the depth of Pilar's own anguish over abandoning him. He had thought she didn't care, but he'd been wrong. So very, stupidly wrong. Now he continued to stroke her cheek with his thumb, seeing the magic of his touch as her large, cat's eyes changed to glorious gold. Joy coursed through him, sharp and breathtaking, avalanching his old grief, which at long last began to dissolve.

All he had to do was take one step forward, drop his arms around her small form and pull her against him. He saw the unmistakable need in Pilar's eyes. Yet, as she held herself rigidly, he knew just as surely that she didn't want his embrace. Before, a simple kiss, a loving touch would have eased her pain. But back then, life had been simple between them. Joyous. Bitterly, Culver dropped his hand from her cheek and sighed.

"I forgive you, Pilar. I guess I had already forgiven you a long time ago, if you want the truth." He felt an immediate lightening in his chest, as if merely speaking those words freed him of so much of the ugliness he'd carried. Anxiously, he watched Pilar's face, to see if his words would have an equally healing effect on her. Never had he wanted anything more for her.

Pilar took in a deep, cleansing breath. "*Dios,* thank you...thank you...." She stepped away from Culver, feeling suddenly dizzy—and at the same time an uncontrollable need of more contact with him. But she didn't dare give in to it. He'd wanted to kiss her again—she'd seen it so clearly in his eyes. And she'd wanted him to. Breathing raggedly, Pilar turned and began walking as fast as she could down the trail. *Culver forgave her.* She'd seen the sincerity in his darkened eyes. Heard it in the grave tone of his unsteady voice. So much of her guilt and shame was miraculously dissolving around her as she moved swiftly through the jungle.

Raindrops heralding the approaching storm began to plunk loudly against the highest canopy of leaves more than a hundred feet above them. The three levels of trees in the jungle's distinctive canopy would absorb most of the storm's fury, Pilar knew. Still, the gentler droplets cascading off the leaves of the lowest trees would soak them thoroughly soon enough. Where was Culver? Pilar slowed and partially turned, to see him walking a good hundred feet behind her, his features alert, his gaze constantly shifting like personal all-terrain radar, on the lookout for trouble.

The many shadows had lengthened as the sunlight was doused by dark gray clouds, which were illuminated occasionally by brilliant bolts of lightning. By dusk, the combination of darkness and fog would make this storm-ridden scene seem bright. They had about four more hours of daylight, Pilar figured. She turned and resumed walking, this time at a more reasonable pace. Rain continued to explode against the upper canopy, and lightning zigzagged above them, creating sudden, eerie shadows. As she'd known it would, water began to drip steadily, quickly soaking her hair, face and clothing. Eventually, as the trail twisted and turned, Culver was again at her side, and Pilar gathered the courage to steal a quick glance at him. His mouth was no longer pursed, as if to stop a wave of pain, and the look in his eyes, though sharpened, no longer had the frozen quality that had so dismayed her.

Somehow, a small miracle of healing had occurred between them, she realized humbly. The kiss they'd shared had broken open the old, infected wound. And her reaching out to touch him and ask his forgiveness had somehow allowed him to find that forgiveness in his heart. A new light shone in his eyes, and his very gait had changed. Pilar couldn't define it exactly, though she sensed a great weight had lifted from his too-long-weary shoulders. She bit her bottom lip. If only she had the courage to tell him the whole truth of what had happened eight years ago.

Chapter Eight

Culver prodded the small fire with a twig. Near dusk, they'd made a lean-to of huge, thick palm leaves. He'd dug a deep hole, and Pilar had started a fire. Luckily, a snake had slithered across their path earlier, and he'd killed it, so chunks of meat were now roasting in the flickering flames, slowly turned by Pilar. The two of them had been soaked to the skin by the thunderstorm, and though the rain had long since stopped, Culver knew their clothes would never completely dry in the perpetually high humidity.

They sat close together, as the lean-to's tiny dimensions dictated. After adding a few more still-damp twigs to the fire, Culver glanced at Pilar. Her hair was in mild disarray about her face, framing her haunting, jaguar's eyes—eyes that had communicated to the depths of his soul with just one look. The taste of her kiss still lingered hotly in his memory. Her cheeks were high with color, and he sensed she hadn't forgotten it, either.

Darkness was falling. Culver watched as the thin smoke rose and caught in the palm-leaf roof above them, swirling and separating until only slight wisps escaped the shelter. No one should be able to detect their presence—at least for tonight. Tomorrow, Culver knew grimly, was another situation altogether. Tomorrow, by nightfall, they would reach Ramirez's fortress. With every mile closer, the danger to them increased exponentially.

"Did you ever marry?" Pilar asked softly. She looked up from the skewer of meat she held over the fire. Culver's eyes sharpened on her, his expression quizzical, and she realized he probably hadn't expected her to ask personal questions of him. Yet, to salve her own conscience, she needed to know. If she died, she wanted to know what had happened to Culver in these intervening years.

He gave a one-shouldered shrug and prodded the fire with a stick. "No. You married," he added, his voice flat, filled with resentment.

"Yes, I married Fernando."

"Were you . . . happy?"

Unable to bear his burning gaze, Pilar looked down at the fire, continuing to slowly turn the meat. "Fernando was a dear friend," she whispered tremulously. "He . . . was generous."

"Rich?" Culver didn't mean for his voice to sound hard. He wanted to know of Pilar's past. He saw how his spat-out query had struck her. She winced, unable to look up at him.

"Yes, Fernando was rich." With obvious effort, she lifted her chin and eventually met his gaze. "He was rich from the heart, too, and that was why—well, why I agreed to marry him."

It wasn't unusual in this culture, Culver knew, for an old man to take a young wife. He was sure Fernando had been more than satisfied in the bargain. Too, marriages here were often arranged, though he had a hard time picturing that for

Pilar, with her independence. His mouth compressing, he asked, "Was Fernando a friend of your father's?"

"Yes, he worked at the Spanish consulate as assistant to my father. They were the closest of friends."

"I see." So it had been an arranged marriage. Culver stared down at the dark brown leaves and twigs that covered the ground beneath them. Pilar's father had undoubtedly betrothed Pilar to Fernando when she was a young girl of ten or eleven. The agreement would have been that when she reached a certain age, they would marry. Had that age been twenty-one?

His mind raced with these potential new answers to his old questions. By South American custom, Pilar would have had to give up her independence and marry Fernando whether she wanted to or not. Culver had crashed into her life when she was twenty-two. And he'd taken her virginity, no question of that. Virginity was a virtue highly prized by South American men.

Perhaps Fernando had demanded Pilar's hand in marriage when she'd come off their mission. Though Pilar was independent by the standards of a South American woman, her Quechua blood also made her a product of her culture. She couldn't operate completely outside it and survive. Her fling with him had been exactly that—a wild, untrammeled instant out of time. Her opportunity to explore her curiosity about a man's touch. Maybe Pilar hadn't meant to give him her virginity. Maybe she'd been as carried away by the moment as he had—to her later regret.

Culver wasn't sure if Pilar had ever loved him. She had been young and naive. He'd had enough women over the years to know that that much hadn't been an act. And she definitely had been a virgin when she'd come into his embrace. Perhaps Pilar had fallen in love with him—the sort of girlish, romantic love that was lucky to last beyond two or three months.

He knew his own feelings had been deep and real, more than a passing infatuation. Though, to give her credit, he'd been so overwhelmed by the intensity of his emotions at the time that he hadn't stopped to think about long-range plans. He'd felt then as if life stretched out forever before them. Serious decisions had seemed miles away, so he hadn't talked of love and marriage. As he glanced at Pilar's sad features now, his heart twinged with that old, never-forgotten love. Pilar's fault in this might have been nothing more than youthful ignorance, he realized now. He'd been the sorry fool to love her honestly, to the depths of his soul. Pilar hadn't had the experience to recognize what he was giving her—and what it meant to him. How could she? Fernando might have gotten her body, but had he touched her soul? Culver knew that when he and Pilar had kissed back there on the trail, he had tapped into her soul as surely as he had eight years ago.

Now she was a widow with a child, but far too young in South American society to get the usual widow's respect. And men of this hemisphere probably were threatened by her independence, money and full-time career.

"Where did you go after you went home to North America?" Pilar asked, breaking the thoughtful silence that lay between them. Around them, monkeys were howling and screaming to one another. As the insects of the night began their songs, it were as if a musical surrounded them, soft and nonintrusive to the web of good feelings spinning between them as they huddled in the shelter of the lean-to.

"I recuperated in Bethesda, Maryland," Culver said slowly, rolling a twig between his thumb and forefinger, studying it critically in the coming darkness. "After that, I was sent to Europe to work undercover in Spain."

Pilar smiled softly. "My father's home."

"Yes. I was stationed in Madrid."

Sighing, Pilar met and held his tender gaze. "I have always wanted to go to Spain, to see my father's hacienda, to visit where he was born. I heard so many stories, growing up, about how he used to escape from his nanny and ride the countryside around Madrid on his Andalusian gelding. His nanny, who was in her fifties, was poor at riding and would take him out only occasionally."

"So you have your father's love of horses." Culver suddenly felt aware of how much he didn't know about Pilar. Their time together eight years earlier had been concentrated, passionate and dangerous, leaving little time for talking or in-depth exploration. Now he savored this moment more than he'd ever have thought possible. They were safe. They were alone and without interruption. Stretching out so that his legs curved behind her, his head resting in the palm of his hand, he studied her in the failing light.

Pilar chuckled slightly. "My father said I had the blood of a caballero—a horse person—in me from a very young age."

"Did he take you riding as a child?"

"Often. I loved it. He bought me a Pampas pony from Argentina—a Spanish mustang—and I took lessons at a riding academy in Lima when I was six." Smiling wistfully, Pilar said, "My father made a point of riding with me each Saturday. It was our time together, and I loved it." She sobered, looking out into the grayness. "I loved him so much. I miss him even more now—his counsel, his wisdom...."

Fog was developing at the lowest level of the canopy. Culver watched it disinterestedly as he absorbed the tremor in Pilar's tone. Her eyebrows knitted as she leaned over the fire, tending to the skewer. One of the positives of South American culture, he thought, was the connectedness of families and how close extended families remained, whereas in the U.S., the family unit had, for all intents and purposes, been dissolving rapidly.

"When Fernando died, did you feel alone?"

Pilar twisted to look at him. How peaceful Culver seemed, stretched out like a jaguar at rest. But he was lethal—to her volatile, vulnerable emotional state—as never before. "I felt like a ship without a rudder," she admitted. "I was in Lima, alone. My parents were dead, and I was an only child. The sole family I had left was here in the village—my grandparents. My father's family lives in Spain, and when Fernando died so suddenly, I thought briefly of moving to Madrid to be near them. I . . . I needed someone at that time. . . ."

Pilar didn't tell Culver she'd needed him, though it was true. It would have been cruel to say so. She fully realized what her decision to leave him at the hospital had cost him, and she didn't wish ever to inflict that kind of injury again. From that perspective, had their kiss been good or bad? She wasn't sure. It certainly had opened up a kaleidoscope of memories and yearnings she'd thought she had put to rest over the years. Evidently she hadn't.

"What stopped you from moving to Spain?"

With a shrug, Pilar picked at a rectangular piece of white meat with her fingers, delicately pulling a strip off and tasting it. Their meal was done. Picking up two small palm leaves to serve as plates, Pilar divided the meat between them. As she handed Culver his share, she said, "I cannot ever ignore my Incan blood, my ancestry as an Indian. Moving to Spain would be like dividing my soul from my body." She looked out at the jungle lovingly. "This is my soul, Culver. Here, in the forest, the womb of Mother Earth.

"My grandmother has helped me see the wisdom of staying, in terms of looking deep into my heart and understanding that my power, my strength, comes from the soil I was born on." She pulled a piece of snake meat apart and ate another bite.

"Because you are a *shamanka* jaguar apprentice?" he wondered aloud, chewing a bite of the snake, which tasted like fresh, grilled chicken.

"In part, yes." She smiled a little. "As a *shamanka*, I would always have the capacity to walk in many worlds simultaneously, Grandmother said. Some know me as manager of a horse farm. Others as a competing rider at horse shows. I am a socialite to others, a rich widow, a woman without a husband. Then to others, I am a mestiza—or an undercover agent." She looked up, a smile playing on her lips. "Or a *shamanka* apprentice."

"You wear many hats," Culver agreed. For him, she was a friend, lover and confidante—the woman he wanted to make his wife. The only woman. Pilar would never know that, however, he thought, and an incredible sadness blanketed him.

"Since Fernando's death two years ago, I have tried to come here more often, but I see now it has not been often enough. Rane needs family, and she has no one in Lima or at the rancho. She needs to know the love, support and guiding wisdom of her great-grandparents." Her smile dissolved. "I need them, too," she added in a whisper.

"I imagine," Culver said in a low tone as he finished his portion of the snake meat, "you need them more than ever."

With a little laugh, Pilar said, "I have been seriously thinking of quitting my job as rancho manager and moving to my grandparents' village."

Culver's eyes narrowed on her. Pilar had been educated in the U.S., at Harvard, sent abroad to get the best possible education, as was common for the children of rich families in Lima. She had a degree in economics, and her father had once planned for her to go into the family business in Spain, a manufacturing concern. But with his early death, none of that had transpired.

"What would you do in a village with no electricity? No modern conveniences?"

Laughing gently, Pilar finished her meal and plucked some of the damp leaves just outside the lean-to, using them to wash her fingers. "You may be shocked to hear that I prefer the light of the sun and moon to electricity. So what if we have no indoor plumbing? We have a spring-fed pond where I can wash at the end of each day, in pure water, without chemicals, unspoiled by the hand of man. The vegetables my grandparents raise are healthful, grown without pesticides in rich, composted soil." She shook her head gravely. "No, Culver, I find life in my grandparents' village calling me strongly. Rane would have a family there—and I could be with her, guiding and teaching her in so many ways that haven't been possible in Lima. City life deadens one's heart, disconnecting us from the sacred unseen that lives and breathes around us." She held his dark, thoughtful gaze. "I know you understand what I am saying."

"I feel it," he agreed in a roughened tone. "And I don't disagree. City life is a big disconnect from the country—from so many things. I never thought I'd hear myself say it, but I could actually see myself living in a village like your grandparents'. I'm ready to give up my high-risk merc life. Maybe it's going to extremes, but I'd like to experiment with something simple in a way that's not available in the U.S. anymore."

Pilar absorbed his words, heartened by his obvious love for the village life that was so important to her. She shivered. "I was never so glad to leave Lima as right after Fernando's death, when I went to visit my grandparents. I hated the hypocritical aristocrats who, once Fernando wasn't there to protect me, again looked at me as if I were less than them because I was mestiza."

"Your mestiza blood is the royal blood of Incan kings," Culver said. "It's nothing to be ashamed of. It's something to be proud of."

Pilar opened her hands in a helpless gesture. "It's one more reason to get Rane back to the village. I want her to reconnect with her Incan roots. I didn't have that choice, growing up, and I see the struggles I've had, reaching back to that deep instinctive part of who I really am. I want Rane to dig her small fingers into the rich, black soil. I want her to laugh in a thunderstorm and feel the cool drops of water refreshing her. I want her to lose herself in the beauty of the Andes and the caressing moisture of our beloved jungle." She stopped, realizing she was babbling. "I want so much for her...." she whispered.

"You want for Rane what was denied you," Culver said gently. He saw tears glittering in Pilar's eyes, and in that moment realized how alone she had been all her life. It was true, her father was a powerful and rich Spanish diplomat, but her blood was in the Incan soil of Peru. And because Pilar's mother had been trapped in a society that did not honor women or their needs, he was sure Pilar hadn't been allowed to go home—to the spiritual home that he knew her grandparents' village was for her.

"Yes," Pilar murmured, feeling tired and very old. She sifted some of the dark, moist soil through her fingers, using it to douse their fire in its deep pit. "Rane is the light of my heart, my only future," she began, her voice raw with emotion. "I do not want her family ripped away from her as mine was. I want her to know the love of a man and a woman. If she can't have a father, at least she can have a grandfather." She squeezed her eyes shut, fighting back tears. "Rane reminds me of myself so long ago. I felt so lost growing up, but now I know why. Something deep within me is driving me to leave Lima and come back here, to my roots."

Culver nodded and stretched out, using his arm as a pillow. He could no longer see anything beyond Pilar's silhouette, but that didn't matter. He reached out, his fingers coming to rest on her bent, tense back. "Come on, lie down here beside me," he entreated huskily. "You're tired. You've been through a lot in the past couple of days...."

Dashing the tears from her eyes, Pilar acquiesced. Culver's hand felt steadying. If she was going to die on this mission, for her last night on earth, like a greedy miser, she wanted to gather to her as much as she could of that thing that was most important to her—time with the only man she had ever loved. Culver made it so easy for her to lie down beside him and stretch her length against him. Her back fit against his chest, and where their hips met, she felt an instant ache.

But it could not be. She dared not love him—even if it was for the last time. Exhausted emotionally, she felt Culver place his arm beneath her head.

"Here," Culver whispered thickly, positioning his hand against her hair and guiding her head to his shoulder, "lie on me." A sigh escaped him as Pilar fitted her head and shoulder against him. They were far enough apart to allow the humid breeze to move between them. It was simply too hot to lie pressed together, though that was exactly what Culver wanted with every fiber of his being. He wanted to tear the clothes off her small, beautiful body and press into her until they breathed each breath together, and their hearts thundered in that mystical, powerful union he so ached to experience again.

The terror that Pilar might die filled him as he felt her tired body surrender to him. He sensed a fine tension running through her as he placed his hand protectively on her upper arm. The night beings—crickets and frogs—sang to them as he closed his eyes and inhaled Pilar's unique fragrance. Little by little, she began to truly relax, as if sinking not only into his light embrace, but into the arms of Mother Earth herself.

Somewhere in the distance, Culver heard thunder rumbling as if to warn him of the coming daylight—and the coming danger Pilar would be in. Was there any other plan possible, rather than sending her into Ramirez's fortress? Culver racked his brain as the night deepened around them and a vague fog shrouded them, muting the night creatures' sounds. One thing was certain: if he were to walk into Ramirez's fortress, they'd blast him out of existence in a hail of submachine-gun fire.

Pilar's soft breath caressed his outstretched arm, which she lay on like a pillow. The heavy strands of her ebony hair were silky against it, and the velvet of her cheek was soothing. Stabilizing...

Culver jerked awake. He must have fallen asleep, but he didn't remember doing so, because his mind had been crawling with possibilities of how to keep Pilar safe. Somewhere above the canopy, a full moon shone, and as he looked over her small form, the jungle around them appeared luminescent and otherworldly. Fingers of fog drifted among the dark shapes of a huge variety of leaves. He shifted his awareness to Pilar. Sometime during the night she had turned over, and her face now pressed into the hollow of his shoulder, her limp arm curved across his torso. Her small breasts moved with each slow breath she took.

Culver's eyes filled with tears as he pulled away just enough to gaze down at her sleeping features. Her lips were parted, her lashes dark fans against her cheekbones. Innocence radiated from her. Her hair was curling from the humidity, curving around her oval face. How could he ever have been angry with her? Culver felt he understood better now why Pilar had left him. He could accept her explanation, knowing the cultural bounds she had to survive within.

With his finger, Culver lightly traced the winged arch of her eyebrow, following it down the slender curve of her jawline to her neck. Her skin was damp from the humidity, and he felt the slow, constant pulse at the side of her neck. What a brave, courageous heart she had, Culver thought. For no apparent reason, the image of Rane's face hovered before him. The child had her mother's oval face and Incan features, from her large, slightly slanted eyes to the voluptuous, bowlike mouth. Yet Culver saw her father in her, too—a mouth that was more set, more stubborn than Pilar's, and her eyebrows weren't wing-shaped. He saw other differences, too. Her skin tone was lighter than her mother's. Culver hadn't thought about that much, because many Castilian Spanish were light skinned.

Rane's eyes were much lighter brown than Pilar's, though they possessed the same jaguar gold in their depths. He smiled a little. That kid was going to break many a young man's heart when she grew up. Yes, she was a heartbreaker just like her mother, though she'd be taller and more sturdily built than Pilar. He recalled the photo of Fernando, and how slender and light framed the man had been. Where did Rane get her build? he wondered. Pilar's bone structure had always seemed fragile as a bird's despite her strength and tenacity.

Perhaps Rane had gotten genes from some long-ago relative on Fernando's family tree, someone who had been larger and more broad shouldered, as she was. Judging from her height now, Culver guessed she would be five-eight or five-ten by the time she was a young woman, and those proud shoulders and that erect carriage would work in her favor.

Pilar whimpered in her sleep, pulling Culver out of his thoughts. The sound wasn't loud—more like the soft, frightened cry of a child left alone in the dark. Gently, he caressed her hair, shoulders and back to soothe away what-

ever was scaring her. Within moments, the small wrinkles
that had gathered on her broad forehead disappeared.

How easy it was to love her. Culver smiled tenderly. Just
one touch took away her fear. And God knew, she had reason to fear. Worriedly, he lifted his head and stared out at
foggy, moonlit landscape. His mind again touched on the
possibility of Pilar dying, and instantly he recoiled from the
thought. He'd just found her again. He couldn't lose her so
soon. Then he laughed harshly at himself. Pilar wasn't his
to have, any more than he could reach out into the nebu-
lous moonlight and capture those ethereal strands of fog.

Too much from the past still stood in the way. Pilar
hadn't said she wanted him back, and Culver knew her well
enough to realize she would have said it if it were true. No,
her destiny was elsewhere; he wasn't part of her life's picture. Oddly, the realization didn't pain him as much as before. The kiss they'd shared had been as much healing as it
had been a sensuous reminder of their shared past.

Culver sensed it was near dawn—perhaps another hour
till daylight. Their night in each other's arms was nearly
over. Their only night. An ache centered in his chest. He
could die today, too. They both could. As he lay on his side,
absorbing every detail of her lovely face into his heart, he
wished for so much.

When he'd met Pilar at that embassy ball, she'd stood
there in a white silk gown that lovingly outlined every con-
tour of her body, and the powerful urge had struck him to
take her, love her and plant the seeds of children in her—
that this could be the woman to settle down and raise a
family with. Never had Culver entertained such thoughts
before meeting—Pilar. Gently, he caressed the crown of her
hair, knowing she was a true earth mother. Though she was
small, her hips were naturally wide, and he knew she'd be
able to carry babies well. Many babies. Their babies. Slowly,

unwillingly, he began to recall that first time they'd made love, a month after their embassy meeting. . . .

"I want to bathe," Pilar said. She stood on a grassy bank by a shallow green pool they'd discovered. Above her, a narrow waterfall splashed into the pool with a constant, soothing sound.

Culver nodded and studied the area. "I think we're safe here," he told her gruffly. Pilar wore a short-sleeved, khaki blouse and slacks, with a brown leather belt cinching her slender waist. Though her clothing was masculine by South American standards, it took nothing away from her powerful femininity. That shined through, Culver decided, whether she was in a clinging white silk gown at an embassy ball, as when they'd met, or dressed for this dangerous mission, where they played a deadly tag with cocaine growers in the mountains north of Lima.

Culver saw the relief in Pilar's face and allowed a partial smile to form on his mouth. They were both hot, dirty and stressed to the limit. For a week, they'd been chased by Ramirez's soldiers. But now it looked as if they'd gone deep enough into the jungle to lose them. Culver knew the respite was temporary, but they desperately needed time out for a good night's sleep and a chance to recoup.

"Turn around," Pilar ordered, her lips curving in a shy smile.

Reluctantly, he did so. His loins ached with need. Being around Pilar was an exquisite torture he could barely endure. At twenty-five, he'd thought he knew everything about the wiles and ways of women from his CIA travels around the world, but he'd been so very wrong. Pilar's sultry golden gaze made him feel like a wildfire out of control.

Hearing a splash, he turned automatically, an unconscious agent's reaction to the slightest sound after a month on the run from men who would kill them without hesitation.

Too late. Pilar stood in the center of the emerald pool, her wet hair gleaming in the afternoon sunlight that dappled the sparkling surface. His mouth went dry and his heart started a slow pounding that this time wasn't due to fear.

Pilar was naked, her lithe golden body gleaming with the water that ran off it in rivulets as she lifted her hands to slick back her nearly waist length hair. When her lashes lifted and her gaze met his, she froze, standing like a statue, her hands still in her hair. Her lips parted. Culver groaned, the sound coming out in an animal-like growl. Somewhere in his spinning senses, as he devoured her with his gaze, he recalled the old shaman telling him he'd meet a jaguar priestess north of Lima who would steal his heart. Well, right now, Culver would gladly sell his soul to the devil himself to have her.

Though everything in his training forbade it, it was as if an invisible force was pushing him forward. He held Pilar's startled gaze as, piece by piece, he dropped his clothing on the bank. It was as if some strange spell had come over him. Was it her huge golden eyes rimmed with sable brown that held him captive? Culver no longer cared. All he knew in that suspended moment out of time was that Pilar was his; they belonged together. She was his mate, his destiny.

Culver heard a splash and realized he'd stepped into the cool water of the pool. White sand glowed beneath his feet as he waded toward Pilar, their eyes still fixed upon each other. This time, he knew, he was helpless to stop himself. A new and urgent desire to make Pilar his once and for all overwhelmed him. The water deepened as the sand sloped gently downward. Pilar stood in waist-deep water, her small, uplifted breasts taut, the nipples full and hardened.

Slowly, very slowly, she allowed her fingers to ease from her hair. Culver's eyes narrowed and he felt his body respond powerfully to her femininity. Culver was young, and *strong and handsome as he walked toward her. With each step he took, he was mesmerized by the flow of her thick black hair rippling around her shoulders and breasts. His heart pounded wildly in his chest, and he saw her lift one hand and barely touch the top of her breast as she waited breathlessly for him.*

It seemed so right to him—her waiting as he waded slowly toward her. He saw the intent in her golden eyes, which captured and held him prisoner. Oh, how many times had he ached to kiss her? As the dappled light moved across his tight, hard body, Pilar's lips parted in anticipation. Yes, this was right. So very, very right. No longer did Culver allow years of training to whisper that loving this woman was forbidden. From the moment he'd met her at the ball, he'd known Pilar was destined to hold a special place in his life.

Culver knew that Pilar lived in two worlds: Quechua and Spanish. And between two religions—Catholic and shamanic. Perhaps that was why this felt so right. She was South American; he, North American. All her life, Pilar had experienced opposing life-styles and philosophies. It seemed fitting that her first time loving would be with a man who was not of her world.

As Culver halted mere inches from her and reached out with his right hand, Pilar closed her eyes and waited. He knew she didn't know how to love a man—only whatever she might have heard from other girls on her university campus. It didn't matter. Now she waited for his touch—for that coming together he'd dreamed of since their fated meeting in Lima.

As his palm grazed her wet hair, a small gasp escaped her lips. Culver's fingers tremble imperceptibly as they ranged downward toward her shoulder, where the thick, ebony mass lay, then curved across her left breast.

"I'll be gentle...."

His growled words seemed to ease the fear of the un-known he'd seen banked in her eyes. His touch proved gal-vanizing, provocative. Pilar swayed, seeming dizzied by the feel of his lingering fingers on her sensitive skin. Barely opening her eyes, she looked at him. Despite her inno-cence, he could see a kind of knowing in her gaze—proba-bly due to her shamanic upbringing, he realized.

Without thinking, for being around Pilar seemed to erase his conscious mind and open his heart, he reached out and took her small hand, placing it on his chest. His skin tight-ened instantly at her touch, and he froze momentarily as Pilar boldly allowed her gaze to move upward, to meet the need he knew must be burning in his own eyes. He was barely aware of the light splashing of the waterfall behind them, of the melodic call of the birds and monkeys. All that existed in his world at this moment was Pilar.

He was going to kiss her. She was a novice at the ways of men and women, and Culver saw momentary anxiety in her eyes, as if she was afraid she might disappoint him. As her other hand came forward and touched his skin, her fingers automatically ranged upward, and Culver felt as if the sun itself was touching him. A new level of understanding seemed to come to life in her expression. He dipped his head to take her mouth, to ask her to surrender to something beautiful within her, and suddenly all the anxiety disap-peared from her eyes. In its place, he saw a wonderful look of primal, heated desire, so essential that Culver groaned. Pilar raised up on her tiptoes and lifted her chin to meet him halfway.

As Culver's mouth settled on hers, he felt her tremble. In one smooth motion, he lifted her off her feet and up into his arms. Their mouths clung together as she lay warmly against his bulk. She'd closed her eyes, her arms automatically wrapping around the thick column of his neck as he waded back out of the pool with her. Culver lay Pilar on the soft carpet of grass, aware only of the natural way her supple body settled next to his. She was on her back, and he moved above her, his callused hands framing her face as he began in earnest to teach her how to kiss him.

He kept his mouth tender and cajoling, and her lips parted beneath his gentle assault. He tasted her power as she tasted him, the ragged moisture of her breath flowing across his face as he eagerly returned her tentative, exploring kiss. Her nipples tautened against him as the wall of his chest met her rounded breasts. He sank more heavily against her, and as he deepened the kiss, Culver's senses spun out of control. A low moan, like the throaty growl of a jaguar, reverberated in Pilar's chest as Culver's hand captured and followed the curve of her breast. Automatically, she strained upward, and Culver realized hazily that while she might not know exactly what she was asking for, her body knew.

He encircled her breast with his fingers and felt her skin tighten deliciously. Tearing his mouth from hers, he allowed his lips to settle on that hard, straining peak. Pilar uttered a small cry of surprise and pleasure. Automatically, she threw back her head and pressed herself against him. Her fingers opened and closed spasmodically against his thickly bunched shoulders as he suckled her, and a white-hot sensation bolted downward through him. Reaching out to her, he slid his fingers between her ripe, curved thighs, which parted willingly to him.

The world ceased to exist for Culver. He knew only the feel of Pilar's untutored mouth on his, the softness of her inner thighs. His breath became ragged, and he felt a silent plea from her as he slowly began to ease his fingers into the velvety inner folds of her womanhood. Oh! The pleasure was golden, hot sunlight falling wonderfully upon him. Her thighs parted farther, of their own accord, and Culver felt the depth of her need. No longer did he worry about taking her virginity or what her future husband might think. She

*had captured his soul and willingly offered herself to him in
return.*

*Each stroking sensation of his fingers brought another
shattering cry of pleasure from Pilar. As she moaned and
twisted in his arms, pressing herself wantonly against him,
a pressure began building like the power of a volcano within
him. He heard her cry out his name, felt the reverberation
of her voice move through him like the deep tone of a shamanic drumbeat. Moisture and warmth combined, and
moments later Culver heard Pilar utter a small cry of surprise, felt her whole body tighten in an exquisite trembling
that moved him to awe. He growled her name, but saw that
her world in those moments consisted only of heat, light,
intense pleasure and her gasping breaths. She clung to him,
her form bowed tightly against his, hungrily absorbing the
continued pleasuring of his fingers as he brought her to an
exquisite fulfillment she'd never known before.*

*Moments later, Pilar opened her eyes and looked daz-
edly up at him. Culver's face was mere inches from hers,
and at the sated, dazed expression in her luminous gaze, he
felt alive as never before, all his senses intensified. He
breathed in her exquisitely feminine scent, his body trembling as if the last of his control was disintegrating.*

*"You're like those orchids," he rasped, leaning down and
caressing her lips. "A beautiful, opening orchid." He
stroked her again, and she moaned, her lips—more sure
now—needy upon his. Smiling to himself, Culver was
thankful he'd had enough control to allow her the gentle
discovery of her first orgasm. She was trembling with
pleasure, and he felt her thighs open again in silent invitation. There was only one way to do this, to welcome her into
the world of a man loving his woman. In one sure motion,
he rolled onto his back, moving Pilar on top of him, positioning her legs across him so that the moist wetness of her
womanhood made direct contact with him. He groaned as*

he felt her featherlike weight settle provocatively upon him. Gripping her arms tightly, he felt his lips draw away from his clenched teeth as her womanly heat bathed him.

The sultry look on Pilar's face as she settled upon him included surprise and joy. Culver watched her expression closely as he gripped her slim hips and slowly began to ease her back and forth across his hardened member. Her lips parted, and he saw her eyes go gold again with utter pleasure. "Enjoy me," he growled. "Take me into you as much as you want...." This way, he knew, he would not hurt her. This way, she'd have a chance to adjust to him naturally, as her own desire dictated. He continued to rock her back and forth, feeling her hands move of their own accord across his torso and chest. She seemed lost in a world of intense pleasure, and Culver felt the hot explosion within his knotted loins moving closer. He didn't know how much longer he could control himself.

When Pilar leaned forward then eased back, Culver growled. Her silken depths were hot and tight. He felt her hesitate, felt her body begin to accommodate him—felt the veil within her that told him unequivocally that she was a virgin. Moving his hands upward, he caressed her straining breasts and captured her nipples between his thumbs and forefingers. Instantly, she gasped, and her hips moved in a primitive knowing. Culver increased the intensity of his contact, pressing up against that wall within her. He knew she was feeling pressure as well as some pain. Stretching upward, he put one hand on her back and brought her forward, his lips capturing one of her nipples.

As he suckled her, he felt her melt against him. He curved his other hand along her lower back and hips and drew her close, feeling the veil break within her. A small cry escaped her lips and he teethed her nipple, transferring her attention from the discomfort below to the pleasure above. Pilar had frozen momentarily as he'd pierced her virginity, but as *his lips and tongue continued their ardent attention at her taut nipple, she sighed like a contented jaguar and lowered her head till her forehead rested against his hair. Realizing her pain was gone, he released her nipple and, sitting up, brought her legs around him so that she could sit on him. The look in her eyes was one of cloudy pleasure, the last remnants of pain quickly dissolving as he moved his hips to bring that pleasure full circle.*

Framing her face, he took her mouth, deeply. Irrevocably. Thrusting his tongue into her hot, liquid depths, he allowed it to tangle with hers. Her hands clenched at his shoulders and she surged forward like butter melting upon him. He felt her body accepting him, and to his great joy and intense pleasure, she began to move her hips in a rocking motion, her movements so evocative that at last they snapped his massive control. The tantalizing friction within her hot tight confines was too much for even him to bear. Groaning deeply, he helped her move against him and heard her gasp, this time with the luxury of pleasure.

The scent of orchids teased his flared nostrils, heavy and fragrant even as the velvet of her body encircled him, holding him a willing prisoner. With each rhythmic movement, Culver felt himself hurtling toward an explosion he could no longer contain. He gripped her hips hard and felt the volcanic release surge through him and into her. She cried out, and he growled her name, his arms wrapped tightly around her slender form. He felt as if he became a jaguar in that moment, and she, his eternal mate.

Culver's eyes closed, and all he could do was hold her tightly, rigid with such a white-hot pleasure such as he had never tasted before. The oneness with her that spun through him at that moment was unlike anything he'd experienced in his life. They were no longer man and woman. They were one being of light and energy, and Culver understood for the first time in his life what love really meant. It meant losing

himself completely in his mate—a giving over, a wonderful
surrendering of not only his physical body, but of his heart
and soul as well. In those split seconds after his release, he
felt two things. One was that he wanted Pilar to be preg-
nant with his child—a child created out of their intense
coupling and the love he held for her. The second was that
Pilar was his mate for life. No other woman could ever hold
his heart as she now held it, gently within the confines of her
own heart and body. No one....

As he picked up a strand of her hair and tested its pliancy
between his thumb and index finger, Culver shook his head.
If Pilar had known how many times he'd almost broached
the subject of marriage, she'd no doubt have laughed at his
foolishness. Always before, Culver had taken his time with
a woman, set his own pace. And never before or since Pilar
had he been so smitten. They'd made love three more times
in those long-ago, dangerous days. And although he'd loved
her, he'd never said the words. But this time he had a chance
to make unerringly clear exactly how he felt about her.

Yes, they could have made some beautiful children between them, and God knew, these children would have been
well loved. He'd been willing to give up his traveling for
her—for them. Raised in a loving household of eight, Culver knew the strength of the family unit. His parents had
loved him and his siblings well and continuously, and he'd
wanted to experience that with Pilar through children created out of the fires of their own love.

Now that idea—once so certain—was a dust-covered
dream, buried deep in the vault of his heart, with no chance
of resurrection. But dammit, he wanted—no, demanded—
a second chance. Culver laid the strand of hair gently on the
side of Pilar's face and watched it bend to the contours of
her bone structure. He didn't dare think of the future—or
the past. Only the present was alive now. Very possibly, they

had no future at all, beyond this day and evening. By nightfall, they would have arrived at the fortress. From then on, each breath they took might be their last.

A gut-wrenching cry started deep within Culver as he continued to stroke Pilar's cheek. Life was so unfair. Of all the people who deserved to live, Pilar was foremost. She wasn't a bad person, just a woman caught in a culture that didn't respect her as a human being. They could have had so much together had she not run back to Fernando to fulfill her marriage obligation.

The fire in Culver's loins throbbed like a pulsating drumbeat begging to be released—by her. Pilar knew she might not survive this day. She had already kissed him. Might she consent to make love to him? His heart beat hard at the errant thought. As he laid his hand on her shoulder, his fingers lightly kneading the flesh beneath her blouse, he decided he was going to find out.

Chapter Nine

Just as Culver leaned forward to place his mouth tenderly against Pilar's, he heard the heavy whapping of helicopter blades moving rapidly in their direction. Instantly, he gripped Pilar's shoulder and shook her awake.

"Let's get out of here," he rasped, practically dragging her out of the shelter and into his arms. He saw the confusion in her sleep-ridden eyes as she gripped his shoulders to steady herself.

"What?" she asked thickly.

It was still dark, but Culver's eyes had long since adjusted to the gloom. "A helicopter," he said in a harsh whisper, pulling her away from the lean-to and into the jungle's cover. He put his arm around her waist holding her close beside him as they crashed through a tangle of vines and over brush.

Fear gushed through Pilar as she clung to Culver for balance. He was like a bulldozer, knocking down small trees and plants as he lunged forward. In her barely functioning mind, she knew the helicopter could be one of Ramirez's. Keying her hearing, she tried to shake away the hand of slumber. She had been sleeping deeply, better than she could recall in a very long time—but then, she'd been in Culver's arms. She'd felt safe. Protected.

Even now as she stumbled along, sometimes tripping over exposed roots in the darkness, she felt protected. Culver wasn't wearing his shirt, and she felt the power of his muscles as she hugged his waist.

The helicopter drew closer, the *whap, whap, whap* of its blades punctuating the dense fog still lying like a blanket over the treetops.

"Here," Culver grunted.

Pilar felt herself being hauled up beside a huge rubber tree. He flattened her against the tree's smooth bark and moved protectively in front of her, shielding her with his body. Her face was pressed against his naked chest, the hair tickling her nose. She heard the powerful pumping of his heart, felt the strength and warmth of his body as he leaned forward to completely shield her from any possible view as the helicopter moved ever closer.

Pilar wanted to struggle, but it was useless. Culver was looking upward, his eyes narrowed, his eyebrows drawn in concentration. Now she was experiencing the warrior side of him, a side she'd known so well eight years ago. By shielding her with his body, he was making himself a potential target. Her mouth went dry as the sound of the helicopter continued to reverberate through the jungle. While the fog absorbed some of it, the humidity accentuated the vibration, so that Pilar could feel the resonation through the trunk of the tree she was pressed against.

Fear mingled with concern for Culver. If it was one of Ramirez's helicopters—and who else besides the Peruvian army had them out here?—it could mean a team of drug runners was being flown in. Or the aircraft could be intending to land at the fortress and take millions of dollars worth of the white powder known as cocaine to some distant drop point.

Pilar's hands rested tautly against Culver's waist. Perspiration made her palms slick against his skin. She looked up as the vibration and noise heightened, and Culver automatically pressed her more closely against the tree. What if Ramirez's pilots saw them? Did the aircraft possess the infrared technology necessary to detect them by their body heat alone? Real fear choked Pilar, and she struggled to breathe.

The helicopter roared overhead, probably two or three hundred feet above the canopy, skimming the edge of the fog. Culver let out a ragged sigh of relief as the chopper continued its trajectory toward the east. Easing away from the trunk of the tree, he could barely make out Pilar's stricken features in the growing light of dawn. Terror showed in her eyes and in her parted lips. Her hair lay in disarray around her face, and automatically he smoothed several strands away from her eyes.

"It's okay," he rasped unsteadily. Stepping away from the tree, he kept his hand on her arm, because she seemed as if she might fall. Pilar touched her brow and gave him a grateful look as he guided her away from the tangled roots of the tree to a flatter area.

"I never expected a helicopter," she confided breathlessly.

Culver frowned. "Makes two of us." Shaking his head, he added, "I got too relaxed. I should have been expecting something like this. Though we're on the periphery of Ramirez's fiefdom, I should have been more alert."

"No," Pilar whispered as she turned and faced him, her hands resting on his forearms. "You couldn't have known, Culver."

"Maybe not." He absorbed Pilar's upturned features. Her clothes were wrinkled, clinging to her curves in the humidity. How hauntingly beautiful she looked. His mouth twisted tenderly as he reached out and caressed her hair. "You look so beautiful...."

Where had that come from? Culver cursed himself for allowing the intimacy to escape. For an instant, he thought he saw Pilar's dark, fear-filled eyes turn tender with longing—for him. But just as quickly, she hid her reaction to his words, to his touch. Bitterly, he forced his hand back to his side.

"Come on," he growled, "we've got to get packed up and go. We're going to have to be careful today. Really careful."

Still trembling from his unexpected caress, Pilar had to force herself not to step closer to Culver. Right now, she wanted to kiss him—and love him. Her heart bled with the truth—that he could never want her as she needed him. Culver might have forgiven her, but Pilar knew that the past now lay buried permanently between them. Not even a man of Culver's generous heart could be expected to forgive her for the dark secret she carried.

Following him back to the lean-to, Pilar gently put to rest her heart's overwhelming longing for him—for a future together. After all, today could well be the last day of her life. She was going to absorb each moment with Culver and enjoy him on every level she could. And he wouldn't even have to know.

"We'll stop here," Culver said. It was midday, and in about three hours they would reach Ramirez's fortress. The jungle was thick around them, and the path they followed had probably been made by wild pigs. More than once, Culver had spotted jaguar spoor along the trail. The big cats probably waited patiently in the twisted, gnarled limbs of a rubber tree over the path, then dropped silently down upon whatever unfortunate pig or other animal passed by below.

Pilar shrugged out of her pack and placed it beside a fallen log, which she gratefully used as a seat. Culver joined her, sitting about six inches away. They hadn't spoken much today. They knew that small villages were situated all around them, and hunters could be out combing the jungle for meat, or women might be looking for roots and berries nearby. The jungle was so thick that unless one knew exactly what to look and listen for, a person could easily pass within ten feet of another and not be noticed. Consequently, they had kept verbal communications to a bare minimum, relying on hand signals when necessary.

After taking a refreshing drink of water, Pilar passed her canteen to Culver. She watched as the container nearly disappeared within his huge, callused grasp, and he tipped his head back to drink. His neck was thick and strong, his Adam's apple bobbing with each gulp. His face was bathed in a sheen of sweat that accentuated his rugged features, and dark strands of hair lay plastered against his brow. As he finished drinking, he looked directly at her, and Pilar felt herself melting inwardly beneath his pale blue gaze as he studied her in the intervening silence. A tingle spread deliciously through her as his careful look seemed to caress her face, lingering on her mouth, then moving down to embrace her breasts. But he turned away abruptly, frowning, and capped the canteen.

Wiping his mouth with the back of his hand, Culver reached inside his knapsack. Drawing out a holstered pistol, he strapped it about his waist. The time was upon them. He eased his leg over the log, straddling it so that he faced Pilar. Tension was evident in the set of her full lips and the worry she couldn't hide in her expressive eyes.

Taking her hand and easing her around so that she, too, straddled the log facing him, Culver gave her an intense look. "From here on out, things are going to get dicey," he said softly.

"I know," Pilar whispered, her voice barely audible. She tightened her fingers around Culver's strong hand. He seemed so confident, she thought, and she felt so helpless.

"I may not get to say too much from here on out," he murmured in a low voice. He lifted his head and surveyed the jungle around them critically. Swinging his gaze back to Pilar, he continued in a roughened tone, "Dammit, I wish this wasn't going down. I would much rather walk into Ramirez's snake pit than send you. I know it's not possible, but that's what I wish, Pilar." His hand tightened on her slender one. "Whatever you do, don't take chances." He stared at her hard. "I want you alive. Do you hear me? *Alive.*"

Looking away, Culver fought the tears that pricked the backs of his eyes. When he spoke again, his voice was raw with undisguised emotions. "I know there's a lot of pain and hurt between us. Eight years ago everything seemed so simple. We met, we...loved each other." He wanted to say, "We fell in love with each other," but he didn't. He had no idea any longer whether Pilar had seen him as her only fling before submitting to a marriage cast for her since childhood, or if she had truly loved him as he had her. The point was moot now anyway, wasn't it?

"I just want to say I'm sorry I took my anger out on you, Pilar. I understand better why you left me. I can even accept it...." His mouth flattened and he gazed into her luminous, tear-filled eyes. "You've got a beautiful little girl. Rane's the spitting image of you. I guess the main thing I hope for out of this is that you survive to live your dream of taking Rane back to your grandparents' village to grow up."

Pilar wanted to sob. She could see glittering moisture in Culver's eyes. Understanding just how hard it was for him to say these things nearly ripped her heart in two. But she didn't have the time to discuss things as she might want to.

How could Culver ever really know why she'd left him? Just talking out loud was a risk to their lives right now, and she knew it.

Gripping his hands in hers, Pilar leaned forward, her voice soft and trembling. "Promise me one thing, Culver. I swear I'll never ask anything of you again—only this."

Shaken by her quiet intensity, he stared at her. "What is it?"

Swallowing against a lump forming in her throat, Pilar whispered, "Promise me that if I die, you will take care of Rane. Care for her as if she was your child.... *Dios,* this means so much to me. Take her back to the village and live with her and my grandparents. I know what I'm asking of you, but you're the only one I can trust with this. Love Rane and be her father in my absence. She needs a father." Her voice cracked with desperation as she said, "Promise me you'll do this, Culver? For Rane, if not for me?"

Anxiously, Pilar searched his stoic expression and saw the tears gathering in his eyes. Up until this moment, she'd had no idea how much sway she still had with Culver, but she saw it now. His expression grew vulnerable at her pleading, and she was thankful. Nothing was more important than this last request. Pilar knew she might have ruined her own chances, but Rane had a whole life stretching out in front of her. With Culver's guiding hand, beneath his care and nurturing her daughter would blossom.

Looking away, Culver fought the tears. He'd never cried in front of anyone before. For some unknown reason, Pilar's request touched his aching heart as nothing else ever had. He felt her fingers gripping his, sensed her anxious gaze on his face as she waited for his answer. Agreeing could mean leaving his job as a mercenary and living in the village for at least a decade of his life. His gut wrenched, and he felt a powerful attachment toward Rane coming to life within him. He had no explanation for the feeling, but it was undeniably there, vibrant and alive. As alive as his love for Pilar.

Culver's heart twisted in his chest. Part of him wanted to go into denial and tell himself that of course Pilar would survive this mission and fulfill her dream for her daughter on her own. Another part of him—the hardened realist—recognized that she could very easily die. Meeting Pilar's gaze once more, he saw pain, love and hope burning in her guileless, golden eyes. How could he deny her anything? Even this?

"All right," he rasped, "I promise."

All the tension bled out of her, and she sank back, her shoulders sagging. "*Dios!* Thank you, *mi querido*. Thank you...."

"There's a possibility I'll get killed, too, you know."

Pilar nodded. Battling her tears, she covered her face with her hands momentarily. "I know," she rattled hoarsely. Allowing her hands to drop from her face, she looked up and absorbed Culver's vulnerable expression. How could she ever have doubted that he would fulfill her last request? Blindly reaching out, she wrapped her arms around his massive shoulders and pressed her cheek against his. "Th-thank you, *mi querido.* I will never forget your love for me. I...I promise you that." Swiftly, she kissed his lips, tearing her mouth from his and moving away before he could react. The burning desire that flamed instantly in Culver's eyes made her tremble. Pilar wanted nothing more than to love him fully. Completely. But their time was up.

"We must go," she said unsteadily as she stood. "It is time...."

Ramirez's fortress was large. Culver hunkered down beside Pilar as they watched the movements of the guards at the wrought-iron gate to the hacienda-style home, situated in a clearing in the jungle. The pale pink stucco seemed out of place amidst the greenery. A dirt road, rutted deeply with the tracks of four-wheel-drive vehicles, led to the fortress, connecting it to surrounding villages.

Dusk was upon them. Night would fall within half an hour. They had been crouching here for the past two hours, timing the guards, noting the vehicles that come and went. Several men, dressed like farmers, wore bandoliers of ammunition across their chests and carried submachine guns.

During the hours of waiting, Pilar's heart had settled down. The fear that had swept her like an ocean tide had eased a bit. She had changed into the costume of a village woman—a dark blue, cotton skirt hanging to her ankles, a white blouse and bare feet. She had braided her hair and put on several native necklaces. To anyone passing by, she was simply another Indian from one of the nearby villages.

Pilar wasn't sure how well Ramirez's guards knew the villagers. It would be impossible to recognize them all, she hoped; she would be taking that chance when she walked up to the gate. Though only the guards and Ramirez's staff lived within the fortress, food and water were supplied daily by villagers. She hoped the guards would see her as just another housekeeper come to fulfill part of her village's expected duty to Ramirez.

If they did doubt her, she could be taken prisoner at that point and interrogated—just as Morgan had been. But then their mission would fail.... No, she had to get into the fortress, confirm that Morgan was alive and make her way back to Culver, who would alert his contact, Major Mike Houston.

The Peruvian Special Forces helicopters would come flying in like the cavalry when Culver called. But first Pilar had to get back into the fortress at three in the morning, when the guards were at their least alert, and the household would be sleeping as well. It would be up to her to free Morgan and lead him out of the enclosure.

The plan had many ifs, Pilar acknowledged, but it was their only chance of saving Morgan. Well, first things first. She had to get inside the fortress. Nervously, she adjusted her blouse and looked up at Culver. Wordlessly, he gripped her and swept her into his arms. The breath escaped her in a near gasp of surprise as she felt herself pressed against his hard, male body. Tilting her chin, Pilar parted her lips and knew he was going to kiss her one last time.

Her eyelashes drifted closed as she felt Culver's breath wash across her face. She ached for contact and wasn't disappointed. His lips brushed hers with a demanding force. This kiss, she realized, was one of claiming, telling her how much he loved her—still. Lifting her arms, she slid them around Culver's neck, pressing herself wantonly against him as his mouth plundered hers and she drowned in the resulting splendor. His lips branded hers and she felt his tongue enter her, stroking her, letting her know she was the only woman for him.

Their breathing grew ragged as Pilar offered herself upon the altar of love. Culver tasted male, the saltiness of perspiration mingling with the sweetness of a mango he'd recently eaten. Hungrily, Pilar returned his ardor, and wanting to leave him indelibly touched by her lips, as proof of her unspoken love for him. Finally, tearing her mouth from his, she gripped his arms to steady herself. Her knees felt like jelly, and she was gasping for air as she met the full intensity of his narrowed, predatory gaze.

"I must go...." Abruptly she turned, hurrying away from him, because if she didn't leave that instant, she knew she'd burst into tears of grief, of loss. Oh, if only she could turn the clock back those eight long years and have a second chance at her tragic decisions. But, it was too late. Shifting her focus to the danger that lay ahead, she hurried through the jungle, moving swiftly and silently toward the edge of the clearing that held the fortress.

She did not look back. She didn't dare. Gripping her skirt, she raised the material above her knees and leapt to avoid small roots blocking the path before her. Her heart was pounding with fear as she saw a large, meaty guard moving lazily back and forth in front of the main gate. She prayed to the spirit of the jaguar to give her the cunning she needed to gain entrance.

Culver crouched, well hidden by the jungle. His mouth still tingled wildly in the wake of Pilar's heated response to his kiss. His body throbbing with unsated desire, he watched her approach the guard. It was so dark now that he couldn't see more than their silhouettes. Whatever Pilar was saying, the guard did not lower his deadly submachine gun from his shoulder. Blinking sweat out of his eyes, Culver held his breath. Would the man let her by?

They'd noticed a lot of activity—frequent comings and goings of villagers as night approached. Culver wondered if Ramirez was having some sort of feast or celebration. He'd also heard some singing, guitar playing and shouts coming from inside the compound. Now he saw Pilar lift her skirt and twirl in front of the guard. Despite his anxiety, Culver noted the elegant grace of her movement. At last the sentry lifted his arm and pointed, and Pilar disappeared through the wrought-iron gates.

Swallowing hard, Culver looked down at his watch. It was nine o'clock. Relief swept through him; she had been given access to the fortress. But she still had so many barriers to clear. Would she find Morgan? Would someone blow her cover? Keying his hearing, he heard several shouts, followed by laughter, the sounds happy and celebratory rather than threatening. Several jeeps drove up carrying armed guards. More of Ramirez's goons, Culver thought as he watched them being waved through.

His mouth dry with worry, Culver eased his bulk down until his knees sank into the damp carpet of decaying leaves near the huge rubber tree where he hid. He had no way to know if Pilar got in trouble. Though they'd brought state-of-the-art technology with them, she couldn't chance wearing a mike and radio. She must do nothing to rouse the curiosity of the guards. Never had Culver prayed more than he did now—for Pilar. He was relatively safe in comparison. If she was discovered, she'd be taken immediately to Ramirez.... Culver shuddered, unable to follow that devastating line of thought.

Still, his mind veered this way and that, filled with terrible fear for Pilar. Dammit, he should be protecting her. She shouldn't have to enter that pit by herself. Yet he knew she was an excellent undercover agent with an uncanny ability to camouflage herself, blending easily into her surroundings. She had jaguar medicine, he reminded himself as he rested his hands on the taut fabric covering his thighs. Jaguars moved like shadows in the jungle—undetected until the moment they revealed themselves to freeze their victim with a mesmerizing stare. Then and only then would they pounce.

Wiping his mouth with the back of his hand, Culver tried to keep his nervousness at bay. His mind swung to safety measures he could institute if, God forbid, Pilar should be taken prisoner. Unfortunately, he had very few options. If the Special Forces came in, blasting away, Ramirez would counter with his army of loyal followers, and the fortress bristled with equal, if not better, firepower. Besides, Ramirez would likely put a gun to Pilar's head and blow her brains out even if they were able to breach his defenses.

Rane's face flashed before him—her delicate features and huge, light brown eyes with their look of innocence. Shaking his head, Culver wondered what in the hell that was all about, but he didn't have time to think it through. Pilar's life was on the line. How brave she was—courageous in a way few would ever be. Because Morgan had helped her and her people, she had boldly taken this mission—even knowing Culver would be her partner. That decision alone took guts, he admitted grimly. And he hadn't been kind to Pilar, either. Yet she'd braved his withering anger and had magically turned his fury back into burning desire. Her jaguar medicine again, Culver thought with a slight smile.

The Indians believed that jaguars could shape-shift into different forms, human and animal. Well, Pilar would need all of those talents and more to get to Morgan. So much could go wrong. What if Morgan was dead? Or so ill he was unable to leave the compound under his own power? Pilar could hardly carry him out on her own. Suddenly, Culver remembered Pilar's vision-vine ceremony. She had seen Morgan—like a robot, but able to move about. And without guards? Culver found it very hard to believe.

But he'd lived in Peru for five years, and he knew better than to laugh at mystical visions. Rubbing his jaw, his eyes narrowed, he continued staring at the entrance, praying for Pilar to hurry up and come out. Come out with good news of Morgan Trayhern.

Chapter Ten

Pilar released a ragged breath of relief. Her vision-vine experience hadn't been wrong. She stood on the second floor of the hacienda, at the western corner, which was dark and hidden from the lights of the celebration taking place down in the courtyard below. Peeking through a small, barred window in a heavy door, she saw Morgan Trayhern sitting on a narrow cot.

Pressing herself back against the stucco of the hallway, Pilar gulped, her heart pounding. Risking a second look, she watched Morgan for several moments, hardly daring to believe it was really him. Because of a huge shipment of cocaine successfully delivered to the United States, she'd been able to gather, Ramirez had ordered a party for his soldiers and the many people of the surrounding villages who collected and grew coca leaves for him.

It had been relatively easy to slip past the guard at the gate, who had looked at her with lascivious eyes. She'd told him she was one of the dancers for the celebration, and he'd easily accepted her explanation. Having memorized the blueprint of the fortress, Pilar had headed straight for the area where she believed Morgan was being held. Now she watched Morgan closely. His face was unshaven, his unkempt black beard slightly streaked with gray. He sat on the cot, his elbows on this thighs, his hands loosely clasped between his legs. His hair was long, unwashed and uncut, giving him a wild look. Obviously they had not allowed him to shower.

His clothes were threadbare and of the type a peasant farmer would wear. What bothered Pilar most, though, was the blank look in Morgan's usually intelligent gray eyes. His pupils appeared dilated, and she wondered if he was drugged. He sat motionless, staring into space, his face slack.

Suddenly she heard footsteps approaching up the stairs at the rear of the hacienda. It was one of the guards! The man wore a white cotton shirt with two bandoliers across his wide chest, a submachine gun resting on his left hip as he slowly climbed upward. Her heart pounding, Pilar realized she would be discovered. The black iron railing that enclosed the balcony leading to the second-floor rooms curved to an end a hundred feet away. Only one stairway reached it, and the sentry was on it.

Desperate, Pilar moved quickly to Morgan's door. Sliding her fingers over the knob, she twisted savagely. It opened! Not daring to believe her luck, she shoved the door open and slipped inside, praying Morgan would remember her, or at least realize she was friend, not foe. She knew drugs could distort a person's senses. Pilar had seen people turn paranoid—even against their loved ones.

She quietly shut the door and whirled to face Morgan. The window was open, and she could hear the guard's boots scuffing lazily against the red-tiled floor as he came closer.

Morgan didn't move. Pilar stared at him in utter disbelief, but he didn't so much as bat an eyelash at her unexpected presence. The guard drew closer. Pilar swallowed hard, her mouth dry, her heart pounding heavily in her chest. What if he came in to check on Morgan? She had nowhere to hide. The tiny room had no closets or bathroom.

Pilar didn't want to die. The feeling struck her so hard that a ragged breath tore from between her compressed lips. Her hearing keyed to the shuffling gait of the guard, and she pressed herself flat against the wall, out of view of the window. A sudden sound of metal striking the iron bars made her jump.

"Hey, gringo!" the guard snarled in Spanish. "Pig. You stink! Look at you. *Big Norte Americano* pig! You're filthy!"

Pilar's eyes widened tremendously as the guard ran what she thought must be the barrel of his weapon against the bars. She watched Morgan closely as he lifted his head at the sound. He stared at the iron bars, his face still completely blank.

The guard laughed loudly. "Gringo pig! You not only stink like one that has rolled in garbage, you look like one!"

Pilar's breath snagged. The guard cursed Morgan richly for another moment. Would he test the door? Rigid with fear, she waited.

The guard moved on, shuffling slowly on down the hall. Pilar sagged back against the wall, her knees limp with relief. Breathing raggedly, she waited again. The guard came back, racked the window bars once more with his weapon and left. Oddly, Morgan remained staring at the window, as if transfixed by it.

Anxiously, Pilar craned her neck and studied the window. Thin yellow curtains hung on either side of it. They were dirty, with holes here and there, but they could be drawn across the aperture. How long did she have until the guard came back? She wondered.

Moving slowly so as not to startle Morgan, she lifted her hand and carefully pulled the curtains across the window. There, it was covered. Breathing a small sigh of relief, Pilar moved over to Morgan and knelt in front of him.

"Morgan?" she whispered, her voice unsteady. She watched his eyes. It took nearly a full minute for him to respond to the sound of his name. First, she saw his pupils contract slightly. Then, very slowly, he shifted his stare from the now-curtained window to her.

Pilar sat quietly, hardly daring to breath beneath his cloudy gaze. Taking a risk, she followed her instincts and slowly placed her hand on his clasped ones, still hanging loosely between his thighs.

"Morgan? Do you remember me? I'm Pilar Martinez. You met me three years ago at the American consulate in Lima. Morgan?"

Pilar kept her voice low, and she saw him struggle with her words, as if he wasn't absorbing all of them. His face was an expressionless mask, as if he were more dead than alive. Pilar saw the lurid red spots running up and down the insides of his arms, from his wrists up to the raggedly cut off sleeve of his shirt—needle tracks indicating he'd been repeatedly drugged.

Worse, as she studied him more closely, she saw that his nose had been broken and had not been reset. It was swollen, with yellow-green bruises visible beneath his eyes. His mouth, which Pilar recalled as such a strong feature, was split at least four places on the lower lip, suggesting frequent beatings. She wanted to cry for him—for the pain he'd experienced at Ramirez's hands. The odor of his unwashed body assailed her nostrils, and she forced herself not to react as Morgan continued to stare blankly at her.

Pilar tightened her fingers around his scraped and bruised hands. His knuckles were puffy. Wincing, she saw that his fingernails were missing.

"Oh, *Dios,*" she whispered, stricken. On the heels of her shock came the anger. She hated Ramirez. She hated his delight in inflicting intolerable pain. Pressing her brow against Morgan's knuckles, she fought her tears.

Choking back a sob, Pilar lifted her head and gently framed his bearded face with her hands. "Morgan?" She spoke slowly, in clear English. "Morgan, can you hear me? If you can, nod your head."

His head moved fractionally.

Pilar's smile was filled with relief. "Do you recognize me? Nod if you do."

He continued to stare at her, as if transfixed.

"Morgan, I've come to help you escape. Do you understand me?" The look in his eyes didn't change. Pilar tightened her hands on his face. "Morgan?"

With an effort, he pulled out of her imprisoning hands. "Who—is Morgan?"

Pilar's heart slammed into her ribs, and her mouth fell open as she stared at him in shock. "*Dios . . .* oh, *Dios. . . .*" He didn't even know his name! The drugs had taken everything from him, she realized as she knelt in front of him—even his identity. Trembling, she touched his knees, barely covered by the threadbare fabric.

"*You* are Morgan," she said firmly. "I am Pilar, your friend." She spoke the words clearly and slowly and was rewarded by seeing his pupils contract slightly again. Pilar sensed a reaction in Morgan, but was unsure exactly what it was. Her mind whirled with options. With agony. No wonder the guards didn't bother to lock his door. He was more vegetable than human. This was Ramirez's way of getting even. She rose unsteadily to her feet.

Looking around, she realized she must leave. Memorizing the layout of the small, smelly room, she leaned over. Did she dare tell Morgan they would rescue him later tonight? Would he slip and say something to his captors, thereby putting them in jeopardy? Under the circumstances, Pilar sensed she should say little. She placed her hands lightly on Morgan's slumped shoulders, feeling huge, thick welts on his skin beneath the shirt. Looking more closely in the feeble light provided by the sole dim bulb hanging from the center of the ceiling, Pilar saw that his entire back was matted with yellow lymph fluid—the results of lashings he'd received probably a week or two earlier. Here and there, his shirt clung to the fluid.

Overwrought at the thought of his pain, Pilar whispered, "Morgan, I will be back. Do you hear me? Nod if you do."

He inclined his head slightly, his stare fixed on the window again. It was as if he couldn't see her, though she stood directly in his line of vision. Uttering a prayer, Pilar turned and carefully pulled open the curtains. Everything must be left as it had been before her visit so as not to arouse the guards' curiosity.

Listening intently, she heard the guitar music, brassy horns and jangling tambourines from below. The merriment was proceeding nonstop, and the drunken shouts of the men and women would provide good cover for her escape. Moving to the door, Pilar opened it a crack and looked both ways. No one was in sight. Giving Morgan a final glance she felt her heart plummet. He was staring at the window, unmoving.

Slipping outside, she quietly closed the door and made her way swiftly down the darkened staircase. The fortress was surrounded by a ten-foot-high stucco wall. Thorny bougainvillea in many colors climbed the wall, providing an additional barrier. Pilar prayed she could find another way out of this place besides the main gate, though none was indicated on the blueprint. She needed to explore the possibility. Switching to the internal instincts that her Grandmother Aurelia called her "jaguar sense," Pilar left the staircase and became a shadow in the night.

Culver was chafing from inactivity and worry. Nearly an hour had passed and Pilar still hadn't returned. His mind spun with possibilities—all of them frightening—as the music continued to float out into the night around the fortress. Cars and jeeps came and went in an almost ceaseless stream of partygoers now. The guards at the gate were lax. At least he could be grateful for that.

Angrily wiping the sweat off his brow, Culver narrowed his eyes against the light emanating from the fortress and wondered what had happened to Pilar. A slight sound from behind him, so vague and indistinct that he nearly missed it, caught his attention. The night insects stopped their busy chirping and singing, and instantly, Culver went on guard, his pistol raised and ready.

To his disbelief, he saw Pilar emerge from the jungle's dark embrace to appear, almost magically, at his side. Was she a figment of his overwrought imagination? Stunned by her stealth, Culver wasn't sure. Reaching out, he wrapped his fingers powerfully around her extended hand and saw her wince as he crushed it in his to prove to himself that she was real. As he relaxed his grip, a gasp slipped from his tightened lips.

"You scared the hell out of me," he snarled softly as she knelt down beside him. "I almost blew your head off. I thought you were the enemy."

Gulping, Pilar nodded, then reached out and gripped Culver's left arm. He uttered her name, and she felt herself being dragged against him. Her body met his, and his arms swept around her. With a moan, she surrendered to his anxiety on her behalf, understanding his need to embrace her.

"God," he rasped thickly, his lips near her ear, "I thought you'd been captured." Culver crushed Pilar hard against him, until he could feel the birdlike beat of her heart against his chest. Breathing raggedly, he felt the words *I love you* threatening to escape from his lips, but now was not the time or place to speak of such things. Still, Pilar felt so warm and alive in his arms. He buried his face in her hair, never wanting to let her go, but knowing he must. But the fact that her arms had slid around his waist and she'd returned his viselike embrace told him much.

Reluctantly, he eased her away from him and looked down into her distraught eyes, seeing terror there.

"What happened?" he rasped, unwilling to release her completely.

"Listen to me," Pilar whispered as she held his hands in hers. "Morgan is heavily drugged." Trying to steady her own frayed emotions, she sat close to him, her head bent near his ear to give him the information. For the next ten minutes, she went over every aspect of her foray into the fortress. Culver's face tightened more with each passing moment. When Pilar detailed Ramirez's torture methods, he cursed under his breath.

Pilar divided her attention between their hiding place and the front gate of the fortress as she talked. "One good thing, though," she went on breathlessly. "I found a small wooden door on the west side of the hacienda. It was covered with bougainvillea." She held up her arms, marked with bloody scratches from easing her way through the thorny plants that nearly covered the entrance. "I broke the branches, but left them in place in case someone checks that area. I didn't see a path to it, so I know it's not used. The bougainvillea has grown over it, and the lock was rusty. I had to find a rock the size of my hand and hit it several times to get it open."

Gently, Culver skimmed his hand over her torn, bleeding arm. What a pity to mar her beautiful golden skin, like warm velvet beneath his fingertips. He examined her fingers in the darkness and realized the rock had cut them, too.

"Can we use the door?" he asked, encapsulating her hand between his.

Pilar nodded. Then, frowning, she studied the fortress. "There are at least two hundred people in there right now, singing, dancing and very drunk."

"That's good," Culver muttered. "I'm sure the guards would rather be partying than making their rounds."

"To a degree, they do make their rounds," Pilar said, feeling the healing heat of Culver's hand over hers. She saw the worry in his eyes at her small injuries—negligible in comparison to Morgan Trayhern's horrible wounds. "We should go in about three. By then, everyone will be drunk and exhausted. If they aren't asleep—"

"They'll be making love," Culver finished grimly. Ramirez's men were well known for their lusty capture of young women from the villages to satisfy their sexual appetites.

Pilar nodded. "I worry about Morgan. I don't know if he'll come with us, Culver."

"He'll come if I have to knock him out and carry him on my shoulders."

"You may have to."

"They're probably shooting him up with a mind-altering drug every six hours or so. That's why he looks like a robot," he said. "Maybe, if we get lucky, the drug will be wearing off by three." He glanced at his watch. It was one-thirty. "Morgan was probably injected shortly before you found him."

"Which would explain why he was so glazed and unresponsive."

Culver's mouth twitched. "Exactly." He reached for his pack. "I'm going to contact Major Houston now and start setting up the time frame for their landing after we get Morgan out of there."

Pilar sat back, suddenly drained by the danger she'd escaped. At any point, she could have been snatched by one of Ramirez's guards. Leaning against a rubber tree, she felt the dull ache of her arms from the many scratches the bougainvillea had inflicted. Closing her eyes, she honed in on Culver's deep voice as he made the necessary radio contact.

She drew her knees up, wrapped her arms around them and tried to relax. But her mind swam with the trials still to come. So much still could go wrong.

Just listening to Culver's voice soothed Pilar's taut nerves. Going into the fortress once had devastated her, and she felt overwhelmed by the thought of doing it again. But she had to—for Morgan's sake. In her mind's eye, she pictured Rane's small, oval face, and her heart wrung with terror. A suffocating feeling threatened to overcome her, and she felt death stalking her.

Forcing her eyes open, Pilar sat up. Culver's knee barely grazed her hip from where he was sitting. To a degree, the physical contact ameliorated the terror she felt not at the idea of dying, but at leaving Rane, who so badly needed a mother—and a father. She stole a look at Culver's hard, sweating features as he continued to trade information with Houston. He looked so capable, and strong—as if he could survive anything life threw at him.

Yet when his gaze rose from the map laid out between his legs to meet her eyes, Pilar felt a trembling heat feather through her and her fear dissolved. She stared back at Culver, not daring to believe what she saw. Love? But how could he still love her? Hope sprang powerfully in her heart, flowing through her like a rainbow appearing after the dark of a storm.

Pilar's emotions felt battered. Being around Culver had aroused a whirlwind combination of guilt, shame and agony. She hated to hurt anyone—it went against her nature. And to hurt the only man she'd ever loved was the greatest of all crosses to bear. Culver broke eye contact and focused again on the map as he answered Houston. Pilar felt bereft. Culver's kisses meant more than she'd realized, she thought as she sat absorbing the very special look he'd given her.

Or, she wondered as she felt an ache center deep in her body, had it been merely her imagination working overtime because she smelled the presence of death? She hung her head, closed her eyes and blamed herself for the lack of healing between her and Culver—a healing that could never occur until she told him the truth. The *real* truth. But how could she? She feared that he would instantly reject her, and therefore reject Rane. Or he might try to take Rane away from her, which would be even worse. No man would stand still and accept what she'd done. It was beyond her to hope that Culver could be so much different. She sighed deeply. It was an impossible, heartbreaking situation. If she had to, she would go to her death with acceptance, and with one sincere regret—that she'd withheld the truth from Culver.

Vaguely, Pilar heard Culver sign off. She lifted her head and studied his shadowed expression. She saw an aggression in the depths of his eyes that she knew must involve their coming plans. "What will happen?" she asked softly.

Culver put the radio away. It was 2:15 a.m. In half an hour they would attempt to rescue Morgan. Handing Pilar the black nylon harness she would wear, he said, "They're winding up the birds right now. Two gunships will be coming in, fully loaded with weapons and a squad of Peruvian soldiers. Major Houston is the advisor to the group. He can't actively participate, but he'll stay with the choppers and direct them by radio, if needed." After putting on an armored vest beneath his shirt, he slipped his own harness across his shoulders. Hand grenades were snapped to it, as well as extra clips of ammo stored in special pockets. He strapped on the hearing device that curved around his ear; a black collar fit snugly around his throat so that as he adjusted the pencil-thin microphone against his lips, Pilar could hear him no matter how softly he spoke, and vice versa.

To his right calf, he strapped a large, wicked-looking knife in a black nylon scabbard. Looking up, he saw Pilar hesitating over putting on her own harness. She'd donned the armored vest over her white blouse; it would help camouflage her.

"I'm not wearing this," she said, allowing the harness to drop. Pilar saw the expression in Culver's eyes harden. "I can't kill, Culver. I—I never could...."

"What if we need extra grenades? Or more clips of ammo?"

Helplessly, she opened her hand. "I know you're right...."

"Wear it...just in case," he muttered. "If there's any killing to be done, I'll do it." His eyes narrowed speculatively on her. "I don't want you in the line of fire. Understand, Pilar?"

Shaken by his roughened tone, she swallowed against the lump forming in her throat. "I—I'm sorry, Culver. You deserve someone who can protect you as well as you can protect me...."

His smile was mirthless as he checked his Beretta, then holstered it beneath his left arm. "You've never been able to hurt a fly, Pilar. Don't look so guilty, okay? I know you can't fire that weapon."

Tears gathered in Pilar's eyes, and she nearly blurted, "I've hurt you more than you'll ever know, *mi querido*." Bitterness galled her as she watched Culver blacken his face, arms and hands. With no need for such camouflage because of her naturally dark skin, Pilar stood. Time was of the essence now. They were on a schedule. The helicopters would be in the air shortly, speeding toward them from an unknown point.

Pilar fitted the ear- and mouthpiece over her head, making sure the collar was snug enough not to slip. The tiny microphones would be their only means of communication. Licking her dry lips, she took the lead; she would show Culver the way to the rear of the fortress.

Damp leaves from the low bushes swatted her skirt and legs as she tried to focus and steady herself. She had to become the jaguar again—stalking silently through the jungle. Jaguars owned the night. They were the night in all its aspects. To become one with the jungle, the plants, the animals, the insects, the very ground her bare feet trod upon, was the challenge.

Pilar's need to focus began to override her aching heart and worries about Culver—and Rane. As she melted into the darkness around her, she felt a subtle shift in her consciousness that heightened her hearing, sharpened her vision and enlarged upon her ability to sift one odor from another. She was now the jaguar. Unerringly, she wove silently closer to Ramirez's fortress.

Soon they were on the western side of the complex. As Pilar slowed, reached out and encountered the rough, wooden door, she felt another subtle shift. What replaced her heightened senses was more emotionally devastating. She felt Culver nearby, the aura of protection bristling from him. People still sang and strummed guitars in the courtyard—not half as many as before, but enough to cover any slight sound they might make slipping into the fortress.

As Pilar turned and looked up into Culver's face, she had a wild desire to reach up and kiss him one last time. Oh, she would give anything to feel his masterful mouth against her, guiding her, consuming her until she became one with him again. It was a ridiculous urge, and she sadly turned away, knowing full well she didn't deserve such a final, parting gift from him. Instead, she draped her fingers across the old, rusty latch and gently pushed down. She heard a distinct click, and the door creaked open.

Chapter Eleven

Culver didn't know what to expect when they slipped undetected into Morgan's room. The chamber was dark, except for what little light danced into it from the huge bonfire still blazing below in the courtyard, and it stank of urine and vomit. At least a hundred of the harder-core celebrants were still going strong, and Culver and Pilar had managed to sneak up to the second floor of the hacienda undetected.

Pilar closed the door and quickly pulled the thin curtains across the barred window. Culver crossed the room, his gaze pinned on Morgan, who was lying down. Was he asleep? As he closed the distance, he saw the man slowly lift his head. Leaning over Morgan, Culver gripped the man's shoulder and whispered, "We're friends, Morgan. Don't make a sound. We're going to get you out of here."

Pilar pulled Morgan into an upright position. Every second counted. If they didn't get away from the fortress fast enough, the guards would hear the helicopters and realize something was wrong. She saw puzzlement on Morgan's bearded features as she crouched before him to study his eyes, her hands on his knees.

"Morgan? It's Pilar. Remember me? I was here a little while ago." Her voice was low and breathless, her heart pounding unremittingly. She saw confusion come to his cloudy gaze. He looked at her, then twisted to look up at Culver, who stood over him.

"No," he mumbled. "Who are you?"

Crestfallen, Pilar said to Culver, "His eyes are the same. He's no better or worse than the last time I saw him."

With a nod, Culver came around and knelt at Morgan's side. "Do you remember me? Culver Lachlan?"

Morgan stared at him. "No..."

"That son of a bitch...." Culver rasped as he straightened. Ramirez had wiped out Morgan's memory completely with some drug. Fury sizzled through him, but Culver quickly clamped down on it and gestured sharply to Morgan. "Come on, we're springing you from this pigsty. It's time to go home."

"Home?"

Pilar panicked. "Morgan, your home is in Washington, D.C."

"It is?"

"Oh, no," she whispered. "You're married to Laura. You remember Laura, don't you?"

Morgan shook his shaggy head. "I...don't know any of you." Forlornly, he looked around the room and then back at Pilar. "Who is Laura?"

Rising, Pilar bit back a cry of sadness. "You have two children, Morgan. A boy and a girl. Do you remember their names?"

Rubbing his brow with his filthy, bloodied hand, Morgan whispered, "I don't have any children...."

"Enough," Culver snapped roughly. "Pilar, check the door to make sure the guards aren't around. I'm going to get him on his feet."

Instantly, Pilar responded. Morgan was a big man, but Culver, built like a huge, powerful bull, was larger, and Morgan was pathetically thin, a mere shadow of his former self. Culver pulled his arm across his own shoulder and hefted him to his feet. With a groan, Morgan sagged against his rescuer's tall frame, his knees buckling.

"Try to stand," Culver ordered gently, steadying him. The drugs they'd given him had not only made mush of his brain, they'd affected his entire nervous system. Morgan was weak and uncoordinated.

"It's clear," Pilar whispered. She stepped out the door and opened it wide. Moving ahead, she heard the scraping of Morgan's bare feet on the tiles. Her heart pounding, she hurried to the stairs. Shadows from the firelight danced along the walls. Shouts and loud laughter drifted up to her, and guitar music provided more dissonance as she carefully made her way down the darkened steps to the ground below.

Turning, Pilar watched the corner of the hacienda and the men's progress. Morgan was only semiconscious, leaning heavily against Culver, who was practically dragging him down the stairs. Breathing hard, Culver tottered beneath his load, added to the weight of the equipment he wore. Anxiously, Pilar looked on, her palms growing sweaty. She had no weapon. If someone came around the corner unexpectedly, she could do nothing. Culver wouldn't be able to get to his own weapon because he was helping Morgan.

The drugged man groaned as Culver guided him toward the west wall and the small wooden door. Pilar brought up the rear, constantly on guard. Morgan's knees kept giving out on him, despite his pitiful attempts to walk.

"Pilar!"

She spun around at Culver's rasping command. Understanding that he wanted her to open the door for them, she hurried ahead. The bougainvillea scraped and cut at her arms as she waded into it. Breathing through her mouth so she wouldn't make too much noise, she groped about until her fingertips met the rough wooden door. She heard Culver's heavy breathing through the earpiece she wore. Scrabbling to find the rusty lock, she wished for more light.

"Hurry!" Culver snapped.

Pilar heard the crunch of branches behind her. Morgan groaned again, the sound one of raw pain. She was sure those whiplash wounds that covered his back were being opened. Frantically, she moved her hands over the door's surface. There! She jerked it open and the rusty hinges gave a loud creak of protest. It took all of Pilar's weight to open the door far enough for Culver and Morgan to pass through.

Once outside Culver propped Morgan against the now-open door. "Hold him."

She nodded and pressed her hands against Morgan's chest to steady him. She watched as Culver removed his submachine gun.

"Take it," he ordered. "Cover our escape."

Nodding jerkily, Pilar stepped aside and took the safety off the weapon. The steel felt cold in her trembling hands. She hated violence of any kind. In her undercover work, although it had been dangerous, she'd refused to carry a weapon.

Dividing her attention, she saw Culver heft Morgan under his arms and drag him away from the wall.

¡Hola!

Sucking in a sharp breath, Pilar whirled around. Her eyes widened. A guard stood tensely at the corner, his face etched with surprise.

"*¡Altoi!* Stop!" he yelled, and jerked the submachine gun off his shoulder.

No! Pilar backed up and slammed into the wall. She saw the guard's face turn ugly as he lowered the weapon, pointing it toward her. Culver was gone!

"You there! Stop!"

Whirling around, she lunged for the open door, hearing the instant spat of the weapon as she did so. Bullets whined around her as she reached the entrance, and wood exploded in splinters to her right. Stucco flew past her. With a small cry, she dropped to her knees and tried to get out the door, but a vine caught her foot and she tripped forward. *Dios,* no! Panicked, Pilar scrambled on hands and knees through the doorway.

A siren started to wail behind her. Gasping, she struggled to her feet. Ahead of her, Culver had put Morgan in a fireman's carry over his shoulder and was lumbering quickly into the jungle, she saw. Time. Culver had to have time to get far enough into the jungle that Ramirez's men couldn't find them. Jerking around, Pilar dropped the weapon and reached for the rusty latch. She heard more startled cries from the guards. They were coming her way.

Wrapping her fingers around the latch, she yanked the wooden door closed. Then, picking up the submachine gun, she sprinted across the small clearing toward the wall of darkened jungle that stretched in front of her. It represented safety. She'd lost sight of Culver, but she knew from their game plan which direction he would go. Besides, with Morgan on his shoulders, he'd be making noise and moving slowly.

Breathing hard, her bare feet digging into the moist leaves and sandy soil, Pilar ran as hard as she could, the cries of the guards ringing out behind her. They sounded so close! Not daring to turn around and look, she lengthened her stride. Part of her wished she was taller, with longer legs to carry her away from the pursuing enemy more quickly.

"Stop!"

The command rippled through her, and Pilar winced at the fury in the male voice behind her. They were going to kill her, she knew. Running hard, gasping as she went, she dove into the jungle. Safe! At last she was safe!

Pilar didn't break stride. As if her feet had eyes, she felt each step across the lumpy ground. She keyed her ears to the crashing of foliage ahead that heralded Culver's awkward progress. Would he make it to the landing zone in time? Pilar knew Major Houston would wait there only five minutes. If he didn't see them, he'd have to order the two helicopters to lift off. To remain on the ground too long in Ramirez's backyard was folly. A single guard could shoot a helicopter to oblivion.

Bullets whined around her. Vines snapped; bark flew. Pilar hunched over and ran harder, her mind racing even faster. In another minute or so she would catch up with Culver. But he and Morgan needed protection, someone to stay behind and create a diversion to ensure their escape.

Increasing her precarious speed, she was struggling to catch up when she heard someone fall. Then Culver grunted. Her eyes narrowing, Pilar saw Morgan sprawled on the ground, with Culver nearby, rising onto his hands and knees. Rasping for breath, she sped to his side.

"They're after us!" she gasped as she helped him stand. Culver had fallen over a thick, exposed root. Anxiously, she turned to Morgan, who was slowly sitting up, a dazed expression on his shadowed features.

Culver grimly swung around. "It isn't far," he growled.

"I'll create a diversion."

"No!" He whirled, his eyes thundercloud black.

"Don't argue!" Pilar cried. Reaching out, she grabbed his arm. "*Mi querido,* whatever happens, take care of Rane for us, please...."

Culver opened his mouth to protest. Before he could say a word, Pilar had disappeared back into a jungle, like a jaguar on the hunt. Shaken, he got Morgan back up and across his shoulders. Groaning under the other man's weight, he could do nothing but head forward again. He heard the yelps of the guards, like bloodthirsty dogs, then a sudden spate of gunfire. Swinging around, Culver dove onward, toward the landing zone. He wanted to stop, to turn around and help Pilar. She was right, he thought bitterly; a diversion had to be created or the guards would recapture Morgan.

More gunfire sounded, off to Culver's left. Pilar was leading them on a wild-goose chase, and they were following her. Breathing heavily, his muscles aching from the load he carried, Culver forced himself into a dogtrot toward the clearing he knew was ahead of them, but his heart and mind spun back to Pilar. She was risking her life for them. Again. As she had before, long ago. She was so small and delicate, yet she possessed such incredible courage.

More gunfire erupted—heavier and more concentrated. Stray bullets whined past them, and Culver automatically cringed, tightening his grip on Morgan. They could just as easily be killed by ricocheting bullets. His heart ached with unadulterated fear for Pilar's life. *Oh, God, please protect her. I love her. I love her.* It no longer mattered that she'd run out on him. He needed her, even as he needed each breath of air he forced into his heaving, burning lungs.

Suddenly, the *whap, whap, whap* of helicopter blades caught his frantic attention. Honing in on the sound, Culver realized with a sinking sensation that they were behind schedule. *Five minutes.* That's all they had before Houston lifted off without them, thinking that mission a failure. His heart pounding, Culver lengthened his stride. Leaves swatted heavily at them, branches slapping his face, cutting and jabbing at him. Still, his mind swung to Pilar. Behind him and to the left, he could hear the gunfire, almost nonstop. What if she was wounded? Dead? The thought nearly paralyzed him midstride. Shaking his head, Culver hunched forward, the weight of Morgan nearly unbearable despite the man's emaciated condition. Culver's muscles screamed in protest. His knees ached with each footfall.

Morgan groaned.

"Hang on," he panted. "Just hang on."

Morgan's life for Pilar's. The thought was startling. Horrifying. Culver breathed heavily through his mouth. No. No. Pilar couldn't be dead—or worse, captured. She would catch up with them. She would be waiting in the clearing, signaling the helicopters. She had to be!

His thoughts skewing wildly, Culver lifted his booted feet higher, hoping to avoid the lethal tangle of roots. Each step felt as if he were lifting a thousand pounds of weight. Burning pain flowed up from his cramping calves, affecting his thigh muscles and shortening his stride. Clenching his teeth against the searing pain, he crashed on through the foliage. The sound of the helicopters was growing louder. At any moment, they would land. How far away was the clearing?

Sweat poured into his eyes, blurring his vision. Shaking his head in a bullish motion, Culver suddenly found himself at the edge of the huge, open space. The sky was just turning gray with dawn and he saw the black, silhouetted shapes of the choppers appear out of the night sky. Breathing raggedly, Culver turned around. Where was Pilar? Damn! Where was she? Anxiously, he scanned the jungle.

The helicopters would arrive within the minute. Culver shoved off on cramping legs toward the center of the clearing, where they would land. Morgan hung limply over his shoulders now, unconscious. The soil here was soft, and Culver struggled to keep his balance with his heavy load. Somewhere in the distance, above the powerful beating of the helicopter blades, another spate of gunfire broke the dawn. Pilar? Was she coming? She knew the timetable. She knew five minutes was between landing and lift-off.

The helicopters set down, their blades still whirling at full power. Culver saw the nearest chopper door slide open. The aircraft had no landing lights—nothing to give it away to the enemy. Tottering, his knees like jelly beneath the weight, Culver moved forward again and saw a man in tiger fatigues running toward him full tilt. It had to be Mike Houston. Culver felt his strength draining with each step he took. As the man neared, Culver recognized his old friend from Army Special Forces. Houston's square face was painted in green, yellow and black stripes, his expression hard and set as he reached out toward Morgan.

"Let's go!" Houston yelled above the roar of the aircraft. He hauled Morgan off Culver's shoulders.

Culver staggered as the weight was taken away. Two Peruvian soldiers grabbed Morgan and hauled him quickly toward the first helicopter. Culver felt Houston's steadying grip on his arm. Turning, he met the grim-faced major, who was near his own age.

"Mike, Pilar isn't here. She decoyed for us," he panted.

Houston turned on his booted heel and lifted a pair of infrared binoculars to his eyes. "I don't see her, Lachlan."

"Damn!"

Every muscle in Culver's body ached, but nothing more so than his heart. "She shouldn't have done it!" He swore loudly. Glancing past the major, he saw that Morgan was now safely stowed on board the chopper.

Lowering the binoculars, Houston faced him. "We've got three minutes."

Frustration ate at Culver. He couldn't argue with Mike. If they waited for her, they could all be killed. Ramirez's men had powerful weapons capable of putting the helicopters out of commission. Compressing his lips, he gazed at the dark line of the jungle. "She's in trouble."

"What?" Mike shouted, leaning forward.

Culver cupped his hands around his mouth. "I said Pilar is in trouble. I feel it."

Houston straightened. He glanced at his watch. "It's time to go, Lachlin."

Culver reached over and took the submachine gun that hung from Houston's shoulder. "No. I'm staying. I've got to find her."

Houston eyed him. "That's stupid. Ramirez's men are crawling all over this place."

Terror gripped Culver. "I'm staying behind, Mike. You've got Trayhern. Take off."

"Dammit, Lachlan—"

Culver waved him away. "Somehow, we'll make it out of here—together."

"You're crazy!"

"Maybe."

Houston traded looks with him. Rubbing his jaw, he said, "All right, if you can find her, contact me on the same radio frequency. I can't promise anything, but I'll try to talk the Peruvian government into giving us a chopper to come in and pick you up—wherever you are."

Gripping Houston's hand, Culver nodded. "Thanks, Mike."

"Just be damn careful," Houston warned, then he turned and trotted back to the waiting aircraft.

Culver moved quickly back into the jungle's cover. He knew the sound of the helicopters would bring Ramirez's men running. He had to take some swift tactical action to get out of the immediate area. When things quieted, and dawn broke, he would try to track down Pilar.

His stomach turned with nausea. Pilar was either dead, wounded or captured. Tears burned in his eyes, but he fought them. Moving swiftly, his legs aching in protest, he headed away from the clearing, but parallel to the fortress, which was at least a mile away. His hunting and tracking instincts moved to the fore. He would need every ounce of jungle skill he possessed to avoid capture. In the distance, he heard the helicopters already growing fainter as they headed out of danger.

Pilar? His heart lurched with dread. Sweat covered him. The foliage was damp from the night's fog, stealing silently around him, just above his head. His hearing keyed, Culver caught the sound of several men talking in excited Spanish to his right. Crouching down, he became invisible, swallowed up by the thick bushes. He listened carefully but, heard no mention of Pilar. They were crashing through the jungle toward the clearing where the helicopters had been. Good.

The moment they'd passed him, Culver eased to his feet and moved in the opposite direction. His mind spun. What had Pilar meant by "Take care of Rane for us"? *Us?* A strange word to use and he'd already promised, so why had she repeated it like that? Stymied, his terror for her very real, Culver pushed on. He consulted his compass every now and then in the dim gray light. Mentally fixing in his mind where the fortress was and which direction Pilar had headed, Culver kept his eyes trained to the ground.

Lucky for him, his father had been a hunter in the Rocky Mountains and had taught him tracking skills as a very young boy. Culver had developed the skill to an art form over the years, though these days his quarry tended to be two-legged enemies rather than some hapless deer or elk. As the sun rose and the light improved, he began watching for other signs—the telltale broken leaf or twig indicating someone had passed hurriedly through an area.

Was Pilar hiding in the jungle? Was she hurt? Bleeding? The image made him wince. It was only then that Culver realized they should still be in radio contact. Kneeling, hidden by the foliage, he pressed his fingers against his throat, where the communication device lay.

"Pilar? Pilar, this is Culver. Come in."

He waited, his breath suspended. He knew that the state-of-the-art headsets they wore were waterproof. Capable of working under the ocean if they had to.

"Pilar, if you can hear me, say something. Anything..."

Slowly scanning the area, Culver waited tensely. Nothing. His mind ticked off the possibilities. Pilar could be dead, her body hidden by the jungle. She could be unconscious and unable to respond. Or—his heart instantly rejected the final possibility just as strongly—Ramirez's men had found her, stripped her of her military gear and taken her back to the fortress.

Wiping his smarting eyes, he digested the situation. Day was breaking and the fog was thinning. Lifting his head, Culver spotted a swath of jungle that had obviously been disturbed. Getting up, he eased in that direction, his gaze moving to the soft, moist earth.

His heart slammed into his ribs. He halted. There. Everywhere he looked, the foliage had been torn up, leaves bruised and twigs broken. The soil was marked by numerous bootprints. Bending down, Culver looked closer. His mouth went dry as he saw a small, partial imprint of a bare foot. Pilar. A fight had taken place here, no doubt about it. Looking around, he searched the underbrush for other signs that would confirm Pilar had been here.

Several bullets had gouged into the smooth, gray surface of a thick rubber tree. As Culver eased toward it, something dark on one large, exposed root caught his eye. Stymied, he knelt down, unable to identify the substance in the dim light. Reaching out, he carefully touched it, then lifted his fingers to his nostrils. The metallic odor was distinctive and unmistakable. Blood. His heart started a slow hammering as he bent down and continued to search around the roots. They had caught Pilar, he was certain. But was it her blood or someone else's?

Getting down on his hands and knees, Culver searched frantically for any other sign that might confirm whether Pilar had been truly captured. Running his fingers beneath some large, broken-off leaves, Culver struck something. Lifting the leaves away, he felt his eyes widened with dismay. It was the black throat collar of the communications device Pilar had worn. Sitting back on his heels, he picked it up and studied it grimly. And then his gaze caught something else. His lips parted as he stared at it for a long moment in disbelief. A sizzling arc of pain moved through his chest as he leaned down and retrieved it.

The small, dark brown bag on a leather thong dangled from his fingers. Pilar's medicine bag. He would recognize it anywhere. As he slowly turned it over, his breath snagged, and his eyes bulged. The rear of the bag dripped—with blood.

Chapter Twelve

Forty-eight hours had passed—the most hellish hours in Culver's entire life. For a long time the jungle had crawled with Ramirez's men, combing and recombing the area for evidence of more enemies. At least six helicopters had come and gone as Culver lay buried beneath leaves in the hole he'd dug under the roots of a particularly large rubber tree.

He overheard passing guards say that Ramirez had left the fortress and flown to Bogota, Colombia, until things settled down. But what of Pilar? What had he done with her? Culver's gut felt like he'd swallowed acid, and his heart wanted to explode with frustration and grief. He couldn't even be certain if Pilar had been wounded. One of the guards could have torn the medicine bag from her neck and let it land in someone else's blood. What he did know was that this waiting was slowly killing him.

Finally Culver got a lead, though the news was not what he wanted to hear. Some guards walked within fifty feet of his hiding spot and he heard them say that Pilar was wounded and being held in the fortress's small dispensary. Culver didn't know how badly she was wounded, but it was enough information for him to proceed with. A blueprint of the fortress was branded in his mind, so he knew the dispensary was next to the guards' barracks along the north wall.

At three in the morning, Culver made his move. By luck, he'd also heard two guards talking about an entrance to the fortress on the north side of the compound. His heart pounded with fear. If he were caught—if they were caught— it would mean death for both of them, and Culver couldn't stand the thought of seeing Pilar tortured. His mouth compressed into a thin line. No, if they caught him, too, he'd pull out his pistol and put a bullet in Pilar's head before turning the weapon on himself and doing the same. They weren't going to be carrion for Ramirez. Not if he could help it.

Pilar moved her head slowly back and forth on the perspiration-soaked pillow as she moved in and out of consciousness, the fever sucking away at her strength, at her desire to live. Culver's dark, hard face appeared before her. So close. So real. Pilar blinked to clear the stinging from her eyes. Oh, how many times had she thought of him? Slowly, the tragic events of eight years ago began to unfold in her hazy mind like an old black-and-white film.

"You are pregnant, Señorita Martinez," Dr. Sanchez said heavily, his brows drawn down in disfavor.

Pilar sat on the gurney, dressed only in a light blue gown. Her thigh where the bullet had grazed her, had taken ten stitches and was throbbing like fire itself. But the pain that gripped her heart as the meaning of his words washed over her erased the ache of the injury.

"What?" she whispered.

He nodded his graying head. *"You are two months pregnant. You did not know?"*

Oh, Dios! Pilar hung her head in shame as she saw the doctor look significantly at her left hand, where no wedding ring encircled her finger. She saw the accusation in his eyes. She had committed an unpardonable sin as a South American woman, not protecting her virginity for marriage.

"I suggest," the doctor said abruptly, *"that you tell the father of your child and get something done about it legally, señorita."*

With those parting words, Dr. Sanchez turned on his heel, leaving her alone in the coolness of the hospital room. Covering her face, Pilar tried to think. The baby was Culver's. They had made love only four times in the past two months—moments stolen out of time.

A sob tore from her as she lifted her head and looked toward the door. Culver was in surgery. He could die. He had taken a bullet for her, and she'd watched him go down like a felled ox. Had it not been for the American army advisor with them, Culver would have died in her arms on that damp jungle floor. Instead, they'd called in a helicopter and flown him directly to Lima, fifty miles away.

She loved Culver! She loved him so much that the ache in her heart nearly overwhelmed her. Now, she was pregnant—with his child. Pilar knew he didn't want children right now. He'd made that clear on several occasions. What was she to do? Pilar couldn't bear the idea of taking a life that lived within her. As a shamanka in training, her whole focus was on helping people to live.

But what could she do? Even if Culver lived, how could she tell him she was pregnant?

The door to her room opened and closed quietly, and she looked up to see her father's oldest and dearest friend, Fer-

nando. He was in his sixties, his hair silver. His dark brown eyes traveled to hers.

"Hector Ruiz called me, Pilar. How are you doing, my child? He said you were hurt." *Fernando walked forward with a limp, leaning heavily on his gold-encrusted cane, his hand outstretched, his smile filled with concern.*

Pilar hung her head. "Oh, Fernando, I am all right...." *She began to sob.*

"I talked to Dr. Sanchez in the hall," *he said, gently patting her slumped shoulders.* "He said your leg is injured. Is it bad?"

Tears blinded Pilar as Fernando took her into his arms and very carefully held her. Resting her head wearily against his shoulder, she began to tell him what had happened. Her words came out in torn gasps, until the ugly truth about her pregnancy had been revealed. Fernando, older than her father, had been like a kindly grandfather during her growing-up years. He'd been her father's inseparable friend, and since his own wife had died in childbirth long ago, he'd made Pilar part of his extended family. As she told him the horrible truth of her condition, Pilar eased out of his arms, trying to scrub the tears from her lashes.

"I don't know what to do, Fernando," *she quavered.* "I am with child. Culver's child. I—I love him, but I know he's not interested in having children—and we've never talked of marriage."

Gently, Fernando touched her hair, taming it to one side. "Does he love you?"

Sniffing, Pilar turned her head away. "We have been very close, but he has never said those words to me."

"Never?"

It hurt to say in a choked voice, "No."

"I see...." *Fernando sighed.*

Pilar felt the terrible weight of responsibility on her shoulders. "I will be castigated, Fernando. Lima society will *ostracize me. I will be worse than a mestiza to them now. They will call me a whore. The whore of a* Norte Americano." *She shut her eyes tightly.* "Oh, Dios, Fernando, *I did not mean to get pregnant. I—it just happened. I'm so sorry. . . ."* She hid her face in her hands and began to cry in earnest.

"Hush, hush, my child," Fernando soothed as he patted her shoulder. "I have a plan. It is a good one. Stop crying and listen to me."

Pilar tried valiantly to stem her tears. Lifting her chin, she looked into Fernando's kindly, weatherbeaten face. Although he was of the Castilian aristocracy and a millionaire, he acted neither part. He'd always been a quiet, kindly shadow in her life, loving her as the daughter he'd never had.

"Wh-what?" she asked in a whisper.

He smiled paternally. "I will marry you, Pilar. You will have my name and my protection. It is the least I can do for your father. He was my best friend, and I know he would feel shame upon his family name if this secret got out. He was a good man. And you are still a child. I do not fault you for what you did. I know how youth can be." He smiled a little and caressed her hair. "How far along are you?"

"Dr. Sanchez said two months."

"Ah, good. That is not too far."

"You would marry me?" she asked, stunned.

"To protect you, your baby and your father's good name, my child."

"B-but—"

"You know that I love you as a daughter, Pilar. I will care for you and your child. I will ensure your baby has a name." He shrugged a little and gave her a gentle smile. "I know I am not long for this world with this old, leaky heart of mine. If I can do this for you, no matter how little time I have left on this earth, then I consider it an honor. I have never told *you, but you filled a large hole in my heart by allowing me to be close to you. You loved me as if I were part of your family. This is the least I can do for you.''*

Pilar's mind spun. Her emotions reeled. If only Culver wanted her! But he could die on the operating table. And even if he lived, he no doubt would reject her outright. Fernando's kind face blurred before her eyes as she struggled with the problem. "I—I have made such a mess of things,'' she whispered brokenly. "I love Culver so much, Fernando. He's lying on the operating table, gravely wounded by a bullet that should have killed me. I know he loves me— he must.''

"But he is Norte Americano, Pilar, and a government agent. He may not survive this operation. What then? You have said he doesn't want children. He's never told you he loves you. Those are not good signs, my child. If we marry today, we can still convince people the baby is two months early when it is born seven months from now. But we don't have much time. No one will suspect your child belongs to Culver, Pilar. He does not need to know.''

Pilar's heart felt as if it was shattering with pain. Hot tears blinded her. "I have failed so many people,'' she sobbed. "I love him, Fernando. He's the only man I will ever love! I know in my soul he is for me. I saw it in his eyes, in the way he loved me.''

"My child,'' Fernando said heavily, "I'm sure Culver cares deeply for you. How could he not? But enough to accept that you are pregnant? Do you think he will marry you in this condition? Even if he lives, he will not want you. What will his family think? Think clearly now, Pilar. You are a South American woman. His family are Norte Americanos. Would they accept you?''

Miserably, Pilar shook her head. "I have sinned so badly, Fernando. Even God will not forgive me for what I have done.'' She lifted her head and sniffed. ''I do not deserve what you offer me.''

''Your life has been hard, Pilar. I saw you struggle as a young girl growing up. Your mestiza blood has caused you much pain and hardship. I do not wish you to stain your family's name before the rich and powerful of Lima. Let me marry you. I will never ask for a husband's rights. You will be a daughter to me, not a wife. My heart has room only for my dear Angelica, who died in childbirth with our baby girl. But I can be your friend. Let me help you....''

Fernando had married her that very evening in front of a priest at his church. And he had saved her family name and made good on his promise to treat her as his beloved daughter. Pilar knew he had done it for her father, and she was grateful. When Fernando passed on, he'd left a half-million-dollar estate and his name to continue his powerful protection. And no one, outside of Dr. Sanchez, who had never breathed a word and her grandparents, knew the truth.

Pilar tried again to force her eyes open. How many times in her feverish state had she hallucinated that Culver was here to rescue her? She knew the infection of her bullet wound was creating the dream—mingled with her deep longing to see Culver again.

A cooling hand settled on her brow. She opened her eyes. This physical sensation wasn't a fevered hallucination. The hand—Culver's large hand—moved caressingly from her sweaty brow to her cheek.

Her dry, cracked lips parting, Pilar watched as Culver leaned closer. His face was smeared with mud to camouflage his white skin. He put a finger to his lips in caution. Pilar gulped and nodded that she understood. How had he gotten here? Her mind gyrated wildly with questions, then suddenly blanked out from the fever. She wanted to laugh hysterically and sob with relief. Sudden fear gutted her: if Culver was here, he was in great danger.

"Pilar," Culver rasped close to her ear as he crouched down by the cot, his arm moving protectively across her, "I'm going to carry you out of here. Whatever you do, don't cry out. Just hang on. You hear me? I'll get you to safety."

His eyes glittered with a feral quality she'd never seen before. And she saw tears in his eyes, along with blazing anger. Since her capture, Pilar had received no medical attention for the bullet lodged in her left shoulder. Ramirez's last order before he'd boarded a helicopter for Bogota was to let her lie without antibiotics or medical intervention until she told what she knew of the raid. Pilar had refused to talk, but in some ways felt thankful for her injury. There were many worse ways to die at Ramirez's hands. So she had lain here, preparing to die....

Culver left her side and she heard him rummaging around. Then she heard glass breaking, and he was back at her side. He scrubbed the inside of her right arm with an alcohol swab, then she felt the jab of a needle.

"Antibiotics," he rasped.

Sighing, Pilar felt relief flowing through her. Culver had accurately read the situation. For the first time in days, she allowed herself some hope that she might not die. She closed her eyes.

Pilar felt Culver's hands sliding beneath her body. She still wore her same clothes, now mud caked and foul smelling. She felt Culver lift her as if she were a feather. Instantly, pain ripped through her shoulder, and Pilar stiffened in his arms. This definitely was no dream. Biting down hard on her lower lip to keep from crying out, she squeezed her eyes shut.

Her head lolled against his shoulder, and her face pressed into the side of his neck as he carried her to the door. Pilar wanted to help him somehow, but weakness flooded her.

Struggling to keep a hold on consciousness, she focused on remaining quiet. The guards had said she was dying and then had laughed at her. They had stopped coming to check on her, saying that in another twenty-four hours they would carry her out in a body bag.

Now Pilar felt the powerful beat of Culver's heart against her side. The warm jungle air flowed across her, a welcome contrast to the antiseptic odors of the dispensary. Pilar knew they were still in serious danger of being discovered, but she couldn't think about it. The last of her reserves had to go toward fighting to maintain a thread of consciousness and to not cry out in pain. Each soundless step Culver took tore at her wound. Pilar heard insects singing. Opening her eyes, she looked up. For once, the fog hadn't formed above the jungle. Miraculously, she saw stars shining softly in the ebony sky.

Just as quickly, they disappeared as Culver eased her through a door and back into the jungle's dense foliage. Her energy was leaking away with each step he took, and she felt his sharp, punctuated breath as he moved deeper into the leafy darkness. They still weren't safe, and Pilar knew it. But with Culver's arms holding her tightly, she felt beautifully protected, even as the last vestiges of her practical mind told her it was an exaggerated sense of safety.

At one point, Culver stopped and laid her gently against a tree trunk. Pilar watched him through blurred vision as he called Major Houston and asked for a helicopter to meet them at certain coordinates. Pilar struggled to speak, but couldn't form words.

"Hold still," Culver ordered gruffly as he pulled the stained and bloody blouse away from her left shoulder. His eyes narrowed at the sight of her swollen, purplish skin. "Those sons of bitches," he rasped as he gently replaced the material.

Pilar looked dazedly up into his fiery gaze. "Th-they said they would give me medical treatment if I told them everything," she managed to whisper. Her lips pulled into a grimace. "I told them nothing, *mi querido.*"

Culver touched her feverish face. "I know," he whispered thickly. "Hang on, Pilar. Just hang on. We've got an hour's hike to the LZ, where Houston will meet us."

Pilar barely managed to nod her understanding. Then, as Culver picked her back up, she felt herself floating out of her body. No longer was she in pain, and because of her shamanic training, she recognized that she had slipped into an altered state of consciousness. Culver's mouth pressed momentarily to hers as he lifted her against him. Weakly, Pilar tried to respond, but it was impossible. Still, his mouth was natural and strong against her lips, feeding her strength and energy.

Moving in and out of consciousness, Pilar was barely aware of leaves swatting against them, splattering them with dew. At least it was clean water and how she'd longed, at first, for a shower. But, more than anything, she was thirsty. The guards had withheld even water. Her mouth was cottony, and she felt nearly delirious for moisture in any form. As Culver carried her through the dense jungle, droplets of water occasionally splashed on her lips, and she ran her tongue across them to absorb the precious liquid.

A siren began to wail.

"Damn!" Culver muttered, turning briefly back toward the compound. They had come nearly a mile. A guard must have discovered Pilar missing. The hunt was on. His arms tightened around Pilar's light body. Glancing down at her, he saw that she was unconscious again, her head lolling back across his arm.

His heart rate soaring with anxiety, Culver began to trot awkwardly with his load. Pilar moaned softly with each footfall, and he knew the jarring motion was hurting her.

His fingers flexed, holding her even more snugly against him.

If the guards found them, they'd kill them. He increased his stride, lifting his boots higher to avoid tripping over roots. Leaves and branches swatted at him continuously, some of them cutting mercilessly at his face and arms. Pilar might die. The thought terrified him. He knew the bullet was still in her body. What if it was near an artery? This jostling could sever it, and she'd bleed to death in minutes.

The added sound of barking dogs made his skin crawl. Ramirez's men had called in guard dogs to follow their scent through the jungle. Culver increased his speed. He had to run. Despite Pilar's thinness, she still weighed at least a hundred pounds, and the muscles in his back began to protest. Culver knew he had another twenty minutes before they reached the small clearing north of the compound. Would Mike get there in time with the helicopter? If he was late, Ramirez's men and dogs would catch them without question, and Mike, too, would be endangered.

His mind gyrated back to Pilar. He loved her. He loved her more than life. And still he hadn't told her. If she died, what would he do? How could he go on living? Culver hadn't realized how dark his days had been for those years without her, until she'd magically reentered his life, like rays of pure sunlight and fresh breezes filling a room too long closed away. He no longer cared about the past or her reasons for what she'd done. He'd forgiven her. All he wanted now was a second chance, and with each step, he prayed to be given it.

The baying of the dogs grew closer. He and Pilar were ten minutes from the clearing. Culver pressed her head and shoulders tightly against his chest as he ran, covering the ground in long, loping strides. He was grateful she had passed out, so she no longer felt the awful pain of her wound. Then, to his terror, he felt something sticky and warm trickling across his arm. He jerked his head, glancing downward. Pilar's wound was bleeding heavily.

From far in the distance, Culver began to hear the faint sounds of a helicopter speeding toward them. The dogs were closing in. Five minutes. Just five minutes to the clearing. The guards were firing wildly through the trees in a wide arc, though they couldn't yet see him. Bullets whined and gasping for breath, Culver hunched over, using his body to shield Pilar. He heard her moan, then cry out as he leapt over an exposed root.

''Hang on,'' he gasped, tearing through the foliage and brush like a madman. He felt her hand weakly try to grasp his shirt, without success.

Suddenly, Culver burst out into the clearing. He jerked to a halt, panting heavily. The helicopter was close, though he couldn't see it. The dogs were closer, too. Placing Pilar on the ground, he allowed her to lean against his body as he knelt beside her. Pulling out his radio, he contacted Houston.

''Roger, White Raven, our ETA is two minutes. Out,'' Houston said.

Culver shoved the radio back into the web belt around his waist. Anxiously, he looked down at Pilar. She had slumped against his left side, her head sagging wearily on his chest. Culver tried to steady his breathing as he glanced behind them. He pulled out his revolver, knowing that any minute now the dogs would find them. The vicious Dobermans were trained to kill. He'd have no remorse about shooting them.

''Culver...''

He leaned down, struggling to catch his breath as he placed his ear near Pilar's mouth. She was speaking softly, in delirious fragments.

''What is it?'' he rasped, dividing his attention between her, the approaching aircraft and the howling dogs.

"*Mi querido*...you must know..." Pilar used the last of her waning strength to reach up and wrap her fingers into the damp cotton of his shirt. She saw the hard set of his jaw, saw the terror and anger in his eyes. "Listen..." she pleaded faintly.

Culver looked into her dazed eyes, filled with tears. "What is it?"

"Rane..." she forced out the name, feeling the fingers of oblivion pulling at her again, "Promise to take care..."

"Dammit, I told you I would. Now stop this, Pilar. You aren't going to die. I want you to hang on. I love you. You can't die. You have everything to live for."

Culver loved her. Though the words were distorted by her semiconscious state, Pilar clung to them, focused on them. She felt her fingers slipping nervelessly from the fabric of his shirt as she tried to hold his attention. "Rane..." she whispered faintly, "your daughter... Promise to raise her, *mi querido....*"

Thunderstruck, Culver stared down at Pilar as she sagged against him, unconscious. A trail of fresh blood gleamed like a dark river across her left breast and arm. Had he heard right? Rane was *his* daughter? So much was happening that Culver didn't have time to think clearly about it. He saw the dark shapes of two Dobermans hurtling toward them. Without hesitation, he lifted the revolver and fired off two shots. The dogs yelped and dropped dead to the jungle floor.

Holstering his weapon, Culver scooped Pilar into his arms. The helicopter was landing, its whapping blades like thunder pounding through the jungle around them. Bullets whined as Culver sprinted across the clearing, the wind from the blades buffeting him like the blows of a boxer. Any second now the guards would burst into the clearing, firing.

As the helicopter touched down, Culver saw the door slide open. Mike Houston had a submachine gun, and the gunner at the door had an M-60 machine gun. Both began firing over Culver's head into the jungle as he ran. Fifty more feet. Forty feet. Thirty. All he had to do was make it to the helicopter. He dug his toes into the damp jungle floor, smelling the fresh blood from Pilar's wound and the hot oil of the helicopter engine. Smelling death.

His breath tore from him in ragged gulps and his chest burned from exertion as he prayed that they would be allowed to live. His muscles were in spasms of torturous pain, but the anguish in his heart overrode in his physical discomfort. All that was important was Pilar. Just as he reached the helicopter, a spate of bullets peppered it. Ducking, Culver saw a medic just inside the helicopter, his arms outstretched. Mike Houston was on the man's left, the machine gunner on his right. In a supreme effort, Culver lifted Pilar up to the medic.

More bullets exploded around him. With a grunt, Culver leapt into the helicopter and rolled heavily onto the metal deck.

"Lift off! Lift off!" Houston thundered, jerking the door closed.

Culver swore violently as the helicopter broke contact with the earth. He was thrown against the bulkhead as the aircraft made erratic maneuvers to escape, but his attention remained focused on Pilar, who lay sprawled on the deck behind him. He saw the paramedic frantically working over her. Houston pulled Culver upright and handed him a set of earphones plugged into intercabin communication.

"What's her condition?" he demanded.

"Critical," Culver rasped, wiping the sweat off his brow.

"I'm a trained paramedic," Houston barked. "I'll help Sergeant Ernesto, who's a Peruvian army medic. Just stay out of the way."

Culver nodded, feeling helpless. With the two men bent over Pilar, he could see nothing. He sank against the bulkhead as the helicopter strained for higher altitude and safety. Suddenly a faintness flowed into him. His muscles were knotted with cramps in his back, legs and arms, and he was shaking badly—shaking from the fear of losing Pilar. As he tipped his head back, he squeezed his eyes shut, her last words haunting him: Rane was his daughter. Oh, God, now it all made sense. Those four beautiful times they'd made love, he hadn't worn any protection. They'd been unplanned moments between violence and danger, and he and Pilar had come together out of a need to reaffirm the life link between them.

Rubbing his face savagely, Culver felt hot tears prick the backs of his eyes. The helicopters swaying and bobbing had stopped and flew in a straight, steady line toward Tarapoto. Pilar had become pregnant with his child. With beautiful, ethereal Rane, who looked so much like her mother. No wonder the little girl had such light skin and eyes. Now that he thought about, Culver realized Rane's jaw was shaped exactly like his. Picturing her, he began to see other small things in her face and body that spoke of his indelible stamp. She was going to be much taller than Pilar and strongly built, like the men and women in his family.

His lips parted, and he felt tears trickle through the stubble of his beard, squeezing between his fingers, which were pressed hard against his face. Pilar had had to disappear, he realized, once she'd found out she was pregnant with his child. With a jab of pain, he recalled telling her he wasn't ready for a family yet. But in South America it was taboo for a woman to be pregnant and unmarried. It was a sin of the worst kind in this culture, and Culver saw more clearly why Pilar had married Fernando—out of safety for her child and herself. Lifting his head, he saw Houston holding an IV above Pilar's still form. The tears in his eyes blurred his view of the two men working frantically to save her life.

What if Pilar died? Oh, God, no. Not now...

Pilar must have thought he would spurn her—refuse to marry her and give their child his name. They had spent three months on that mission—most of it in danger. The sexual attraction between them had been explosive. Pilar hadn't had a chance to get a real grasp of him as a person, Culver realized.

The vibration of the helicopter moved through him as it flew swiftly through the night toward the small hospital in Tarapoto. Pilar hadn't known him well enough to believe he sure as hell would have married her and insisted on keeping their child.

Culver lifted his face, warm tears streaming from his eyes, no longer caring if anyone saw him. He'd made so many assumptions, all of them negative, and had held his anger against Pilar for all those years.

Agony ripped through him at the look of worry in Houston's eyes as the other man turned to him.

"It isn't good, Lachlan. She's lost too much blood. We're doing what we can to staunch it. Didn't they take the bullet out?"

"No," he croaked. "I gave her a shot of antibiotics back at the compound. Ramirez was going to let her die if she didn't tell him about the mission."

Grimly, Houston nodded. "Her blood pressure is very low, and she could go into cardiac arrest any minute. She needs a transfusion. Surgery."

A cry ripped from Culver as he scrambled from his position on the deck of the aircraft. He made a wild grab for Houston's arm. "You save her life, you hear me?" he yelled, glaring into the other man's haggard face. "Dammit, save her life!"

Chapter Thirteen

"Pilar is in intensive care," Major Mike Houston said tiredly in way of greeting as he gripped Culver's slumped shoulder. "I just talked to the surgeon."

Culver roused himself. He'd been sitting in the hospital waiting room for nearly six hours. In the ambulance, he'd sat with Pilar, her small hand swallowed up by his, and at the emergency room door, he'd made the surgeon promise to allow Pilar to hold her medicine bag in her hand. The surgeon had understood, placing the small object in her limp fingers.

"She's out?" he croaked, his voice thick with exhaustion.

Houston came around the chair and stood in front of him, hands on his narrow hips. "Yeah, I caught up with Dr. Juarez in the scrub room. He'll be out to see you shortly." The officer smiled a little. "You look like hell, Lachlan. Why don't you get a hotel room down the street, take a shower and hit the sack? You can't do anything here for her right now."

Scowling, Culver stood. The Special Forces major still wore his tiger-striped fatigues, and darkness showed beneath his eyes. Houston had stayed with him in the hospital, and Culver was grateful for the American's care and interest. Right now, he felt damned alone. Helpless. He hadn't slept in over sixty hours, and he swayed drunkenly on his feet.

"They got a shower facility here?" he demanded.

"Yeah, in the surgeon's quarters. Why?"

"Can you get me some clean clothes from somewhere?"

Houston gave him an assessing look. "Yes."

Rubbing his bearded jaw, Culver nodded. "Good."

"You're staying." Houston didn't phrase it as a question; it was a realization. With a shrug, he said, "I'll get my aide, Sergeant Javier, to rustle up some civilian clothes."

"Thanks." Culver's vision kept blurring. He had been sitting in that chair sweating for six hours. As badly as he needed sleep, he couldn't rest. His mind raced with thoughts about Pilar, Rane and himself. He so desperately needed to talk to Pilar.

"This woman," Houston began awkwardly. "She means a lot to you, doesn't she?"

Culver nodded wearily as he began to walk down the polished tile hall toward the surgeon's scrub area, Houston falling into step beside him.

"I just got off the phone with Perseus. I thought you'd like to know that their aircraft is on its way to the U.S."

"Anything on Morgan's condition?" Culver asked. His feet felt as if they were weighted with cement.

"They've got him stabilized. They brought a flight surgeon with them, a woman doctor who works for Perseus. Arrangements have already been made to put Morgan in Bethesda Naval Hospital in Maryland."

"Did the flight surgeon say anything about his condition? You saw what he was like—a vegetable, with no memory of anything."

Houston nodded grimly and pursed his lips as they slowed down in front of the surgeon's area. "No...no change, I'm sorry to say."

"And he's got a wife and two kids," Culver muttered. "He either has amnesia or they've permanently wiped out his memory. The poor bastard."

Houston opened the door for him. "I feel for his family."

Culver agreed as he walked through the entrance and saw the surgeon changing out of his green operating clothes. Turning, he held out his hand to Houston. "Thanks—for everything."

Grinning a little, the major gripped his hand and shook it. "I'll be hanging around until things stabilize for you here."

Culver nodded gratefully. First he'd talk with the surgeon, then he'd get a hot shower, shave and put on some clean clothes. After that he'd sit with Pilar. She wouldn't know he was there, but that didn't matter.

Culver awoke instantly when Pilar regained consciousness for the first time. He'd been sitting in an uncomfortable chair next to her bed, his head tipped back against the wall. Major Houston had a lot of power in Tarapoto Hospital, Culver had discovered very quickly. Ordinarily, visitors weren't allowed to stay in intensive care, but Houston had seen to it that he was allowed to sit with Pilar. The beeps and sighs of machines surrounded him as he tried to shake off the grogginess.

Culver had completely lost track of time. He'd nodded off while stroking Pilar's cool, limp hand. The clock on the wall read six p.m., so he must have slept a long time. Blinking away the drowsiness, he focused on Pilar.

She lay with IVs in both arms, her shoulder heavily bandaged beneath a light blue gown. Her hair, once muddy and tangled, had been washed. Though it hadn't been combed very well, the strands lay like shining raven's wings about her pale face. Her once-beautiful lips were badly cracked. Culver had been told that more than anything else, Pilar had been dehydrated. At once he'd realized she must have been denied water since her capture. He wanted to kill Ramirez for his inhumanity. But now the IVs fed her life-giving fluids to help her body fight off the massive infection.

Culver turned to call for a nurse, but she was already there. His attention riveted on Pilar, who had begun to move her head slightly. She closed and opened her mouth, whispering something. Leaning closer until his ear nearly touched her lips, Culver strained to hear her words.

"Rane...Culver..."

Holding her fingers in his, Culver swallowed with difficulty. The nurse, after checking the monitors, seemed satisfied.

"Is she doing okay?" Culver asked.

"*Si, señor.* She is becoming conscious. I will get the doctor."

Relief swept through him. He leaned down and placed a kiss on Pilar's frowning forehead. "Hush, *mi querida,*" he told her. "Everything is fine. You're going to make it. You hear me? You're going to live. Rane is safe, and so am I. Just rest." He watched the wrinkles on her brow ease. Somehow, Pilar had heard him and responded. The knowledge shook him to his soul. Her thick, dark eyelashes stood out in stark contrast to her pale skin.

Lifting his hand, he began to caress her hair with gentle strokes designed to soothe her. Pilar wasn't moving much, but he could feel a shift in energy around her. And then he laughed harshly at himself; he was so deprived of sleep he wasn't sure whether he was dreaming or if this was real. Still, her small, slender fingers in his hand provided a definite connection to reality. As Culver looked down at her, he felt his heart open like a flower. Without thinking, just following his instincts, he leaned forward and gently laid his mouth on hers in a kiss designed to breathe life and strength back into her.

"Eh, Señor Lachlan?" the nurse inquired.

Culver broke the kiss and looked up. The doctor and nurse stood expectantly in the doorway. "Oh...yeah, come and take a look at her, Doc." He flushed a little as he stood up and stepped aside. "I think she's going to make it. What do you think?"

It didn't take the doctor long to make his assessment. He briefly studied the raw, swollen wound briefly and had the nurse apply a new dressing. He nodded his gray head when he took her blood pressure. As he lifted each eyelid to check her pupils with a small light, he even had the ghost of a smile on his mouth.

"You are right, Señor Lachlan," Dr. José murmured as he straightened and looked across the bed at him. "Señora Martinez will live."

Joy swept through Culver, strong and overwhelming. He stared at the tall doctor. "She's going to live?"

He smiled slowly. "*Sí*. You are a tough *hombre*, eh? Maybe it was you being here that made the difference. Your love for her. Your prayers, perhaps? Or—" he pointed to the small medicine bag that Pilar still clutched in one hand "—maybe the power of her jaguar medicine."

Culver struggled to find words as emotions overwhelmed him. Pilar was going to live. Live! Gulping, he rasped, "Or maybe all the above, Doctor?"

Tapping his chest, the doctor smiled wider. "Many times I have seen people hover in the arms of death in this room. I see the families of these patients sitting in the lobby, praying for them. Prayer is very powerful, eh? Especially prayers of a loved one. No, I think your love brought her back to us. I do not take the medicine of the jaguar lightly, for I've seen it work, too. But there is nothing like the heart, eh?" He gestured to the chair. "*Señor,* you still need sleep. She has decided to come back and live with you on this earth. The nurse will show you to a room with a bed. If Señora Martinez awakens, I will have someone come and get you."

Culver studied Pilar, who had sunk into a healing sleep. The bed sounded damned inviting. "Yeah, I'd like that, Doctor. Thanks..."

Culver awoke on his own. Glancing sleepily at his watch, he realized it was six in the morning. Hoisting his feet over the side of the narrow bed, he sat up. A small knock sounded on the door and he looked up.

"Come in."

A nurse poked her head in the door. "Señora Martinez is awake and asking for you, *señor.*"

Instantly, Culver was on his feet. He still hadn't shaved, but at least he'd showered and had clean clothes. The nurse couldn't walk fast enough to keep up with him as he hurried down the hallway toward ICU. Dr. José was standing just outside Pilar's glass-enclosed room, and he smiled as Culver approached.

"She is asking for you, *señor.*"

His heart soared. Yet it pounded with dread, too. As Culver reached the glass enclosure, his gaze swept immediately to Pilar, who was sitting up in bed, propped by many pillows. Her dark eyes looked almost black in her ghostly face. Yet when their eyes met, Culver felt his heart mushroom with joy, leaving him breathless. Entering the room, he closed the door quietly behind him. Someone had brushed Pilar's hair, and it shone like an ebony frame around her oval face. The look she gave him was shy and uncertain. Why?

Reaching her bedside, he took her delicate face between his hands. His eyes filled with tears as he croaked, "Welcome back, *mi querida...*" Culver leaned down and brushed his mouth against Pilar's lips, feeling her soft response to his tender foray. It was all he could ask for. Sensing her weakness, he eased his mouth from hers and allowed her to lean back against the pillows.

Pilar's eyes were luminous with tears as she stared up at him. He saw that she had the medicine bag gripped in her right hand, resting on her blanketed stomach. Retrieving a chair, Culver brought it over and sat down close to her. He laid his hand on her arm and discovered she felt full of life now, not death.

"How are you feeling?" he asked thickly.

Pilar sighed softly and studied him. "Very weak," she said, her voice rough from disuse. "I—I didn't think I would live."

"I know." His fingers tightened briefly on her arm. "A lot of people were praying for you."

Her throat constricted. "You stayed..."

He frowned. "Why wouldn't I?"

Pilar felt a panic cut through the calming effect of the painkilling drugs. "I thought I dreamed it—or maybe I did not...." She gazed at him. Culver's face was shadowed by several days' growth of beard, giving him a dangerous look. His eyes were bloodshot, his features haggard with exhaustion. His hair, too, was uncombed, and she longed for the simple strength to lift her fingers and tame some of those dark strands back into place.

"What are the tears for?" he inquired gently, taking his thumbs and wiping the moisture from her cheeks. "Pilar?"

Closing her eyes, she absorbed his grazing touch. Oh, how strong Culver was. "Did I dream saying it?" she asked brokenly. She felt his fingers drift away from her face and his hand move slowly up and down her arm, as if to soothe her. Pilar had no strength to protect herself from whatever answer he might give her. She thought she'd told him Rane was his child. But had she? Or had it been a fevered hallucination? Wearily, she forced open her lashes and looked up at him. The tenderness burning in his eyes would dissolve when she told him.

Gathering what little courage remained to her, she murmured, "Rane...is your daughter...our child...." She could barely hold his gaze. Trying to steel herself against the coming explosion, Pilar realized she was completely defenseless, with no way left to shield her raw emotions. Had she been brought back from the upper world by the jaguar goddess to tell him the truth? Was that why she had been sent back through the tunnel of light into her body?

Culver's lips parted, and he felt hot tears well into his eyes. He reached over and covered the hand that gripped the medicine bag. "I know, *mi querida*. You told me out in the jungle when you were dying. Don't you remember?"

His voice was rough with emotion and to Pilar's shock, she could detect no recrimination in Culver's eyes—only the tears that had begun to wind down his cheeks, disappearing into the bristles of his dark beard. Short-circuited, her senses spun. She *had* told him! "But...you are still here...." she whispered weakly.

Culver slowly stood, then leaned over and framed her face with his hands. Pilar looked so frightened, so unsure. He understood why. "Listen to me," he said rawly, his voice gruff with emotion, "I love you, Pilar. I love Rane. Nothing matters to me but the two of you. Do you understand?'' He blinked and looked up. ''I didn't want to lose you. When I got you to that chopper, all I could think was that Rane was ours, and that I didn't want you to die.''

Gazing at her, not caring that he was crying, Culver leaned down to caress Pilar's mouth. Her lower lip trembled, and he felt a sob catch in her throat as his lips gently took hers. In that golden moment, all he was aware of was her warmth, her softness and her incredible courage. Easing his mouth from hers, he stared deeply into her tear-filled eyes. ''Nothing matters except you and Rane. Do you understand me, Pilar? The rest of our collective worlds can go to hell. All I want—all I'll ever need—is you. Rane is ours—created out of our love.'' He took a deep, ragged breath. ''And God knows, I loved you all those years. I never stopped loving you.''

Culver didn't approach any other serious topics with Pilar for several days. She had lost consciousness shortly after his admission, and Dr. José was concerned that too much stressful emotion would cost her dearly in terms of surmounting the infection that had nearly taken her life. Culver agreed. Pilar was transferred to a private room, and Culver had a bed brought in for him. He slept nearby, and whenever she awoke, he did, too, as if an invisible cord connected them.

Pilar had a number of nightmares, and Culver was grateful that Dr. José allowed him to stay with her twenty-four hours a day. Culver brought her books and read to her. She hated television, preferring instead to talk with him about many things—but never again did she broach the subject of Rane being his daughter. Sometimes Culver wondered what was going on inside Pilar's head. Had she heard his admission? That he was willing to take responsibility and become

Rane's father? Perhaps she'd been too drugged from the surgery to remember his words.

At times Culver wanted to say something, but recalling Dr. José's warning, he took the man's advice to heart. Pilar, he discovered, had been badly broken by her recent experience. She wasn't as strong and resilient as he'd thought. But then, he ruminated as he walked down the hall toward her private room with a handful of orchids in a vase for her, Pilar had carried a heavy load for eight years by herself. Culver ached to talk to her of all she'd been through, to share with her his understanding of why she'd made the decisions she had.

Maybe today, he hoped. It had to be Pilar's decision, though. As he knocked on the door, he smiled to himself. Every day, Pilar grew a little stronger, and despite everything, it was sheer joy for Culver just to be with her. As he opened the door, he saw to his surprise that she was out of bed. She wore a dark pink cotton robe, her right hand deep in one pocket as she stood with her back to him, looking through the venetian blinds.

When Pilar heard him enter, she slowly turned. Her left arm was in a sling and she managed a small smile of welcome. "You were gone a long time."

Culver grinned roguishly and lifted the vase of purple-and-white orchids so she could inhale their heavy, sweet fragrance. "One of the nurses in ICU told me about this old woman, a jaguar priestess living just outside Tarapoto, who raises the most beautiful orchids in the world." He smiled down at Pilar and watched a rosy flush come to her pale cheeks. "Well? What do you think? Are they half as beautiful as you are?"

Touched, Pilar leaned over and inhaled their heady fragrance. The burning hope in Culver's eyes lifted her depressed spirits. Straightening, she caressed the thick, waxy petals. "They are far more beautiful than I am," she whispered. Pilar had never thought of herself as beautiful, though the way he looked at her made her feel that way.

Snorting, Culver slid his hand around her elbow and guided her to a wooden rocking chair near the window. "Your face could melt the hardest of hearts," he said. Pilar moved slowly, her balance not yet totally restored. As she lowered herself carefully into the rocker, Culver placed the orchids on the table next to her bed.

"It's good for you to get away from here for a while anyway," Pilar said. She loved the rocking chair because it reminded her of being rocked in her mother's arms when she was small. "You are built for the outdoors, not places that close in on you like this." She looked around the sterile room and then back at him. Culver took another chair and brought it over to sit down facing her. How much she enjoyed their quiet moments together. In the past few days he'd talked a great deal about himself and his family. She'd learned so much. He was sharing a side of himself she'd hadn't known, and it left her yearning for him, for his kisses.

Oh, how she'd missed his kisses! She could recall each one with burning clarity. But since she'd been transferred to this room, he'd oddly removed himself in that sense. Although he slept here with her, on his separate bed, and he held her hand or caressed her hair occasionally, he hadn't kissed her again. Pilar's spirit died a little each day, bereft of the feel of his healing mouth upon hers. She was so needy right now, but she didn't expect Culver to understand her physical need for his touch. She was like a battery that had run down, and his kisses recharged the very depths of her spirit, infusing her with light and hope.

Sighing softly, Pilar folded her hands in the lap of the cotton robe. It was time. She felt strong enough now to talk to Culver without sleep overtaking her as it had been doing, suddenly and without warning. The antibiotics had worked their magic, and she had come back from the arms of death, fully back in her body and in the present. Glancing up, she saw Culver watching her with a curious, burning gaze. Her lips parted, and the corners of her mouth lifted slightly.

"I'm afraid," she admitted, opening her hands and giving a weak laugh. "I felt I understood jaguar medicine, but I do not. I felt it was about strength and power. It is more than that. It is about living honestly." Pilar held his caressing gaze. "When I met you, Culver, I felt my heart open and embrace you. I had dreams all during my young life of a man's face, and it was your face. I did not know the gift of the jaguar was to bring visions of the future to me until Grandmother Aurelia told me. It was then I confided my dreams of your face to her.

"She laughed and hugged me. She said that was the man who would hold my heart gently in his hands. I asked her how I could know when I was so young who was going to love me. Grandmother said there are many things we can never explain. But when I saw you, I felt my chest open up, like one huge orchid unfolding all its rich, beautiful petals."

Pilar studied her tightly clasped hands for a long moment, searching for the right words to convey her feelings. The silence stretched out between them, but without tension. Instead, she felt Culver's respect and interest in her words, in how she saw her world—and his. That assurance gave her the courage to go on.

"When you compared me to an orchid, I felt this cord strung between us." She lifted her hand and moved it gracefully from her solar plexus to his. "How could you know of my special love of the orchid people? You seemed to know so much about me, and I felt it was because you remembered coming to me in your dreams. I didn't know how a *Norte Americano* could do such things. In South

America, it is common and accepted, but..." Pilar shook her head and gazed at him in awe. "We had three months together, *mi querido*. I was so young at the time. Young and thinking that my life was endless. I laughed at the danger around us. I jeered at the violence always nearby. And when you loved me that first time by the pool in the jungle where the orchids grew, I felt my spirit fuse with yours. I felt our hearts melt into one. I felt my womb expand with a warm, golden light, and I felt your life within me."

Pilar licked her lower lip and went on in a softer voice. "I did not know it at the time, but I was pregnant with your daughter, our child—Rane. A wonderful, joyous sensation emanated from my womb. I felt the pulse of life in there, and I thought it was because we had become one and loved without regret or shame." She laid her hand across her abdomen and smiled fondly in remembrance. "Each time we made love after that, I felt stronger, more sure of you and of myself."

Pilar touched her forehead and frowned. "And then you were wounded. I was so afraid you were going to die. I didn't know at the time that I'd suffered a small bullet wound in my thigh—it was no more than a stinging sensation. When they took you into surgery in Lima, the doctor examined me thoroughly. I was bleeding." She pointed to her thigh beneath the robe. "That was why he examined me. I thought it was my moon time, though I'd not had one for three months. The doctor said no, the blood between my thighs wasn't moon blood, nor was it from the fleshy wound on my thigh."

Pilar looked up, and her voice grew hoarse. "He told me I was two months pregnant. He said I would lose the baby if I stayed on my feet, that the shock of the mission had started to tear the infant from the wall of my womb." Pilar covered her abdomen and rubbed it gently with her hand. "I had never lain with another man. I knew you were the father of this baby who was fighting to survive. The doctor said I must go home, stay in bed and rest, or I would lose her."

A ragged sigh escaped Pilar's lips as she looked up at the ceiling beyond Culver. "I had no one. My parents were dead. What was I to do? I had only one friend, and that was Fernando. Hector called him, and he came immediately to the hospital. I told him that you did not want children right away, that you were not ready for them. And he asked me if you had said you loved me. I said no. He said it was a bad sign, and I could not disagree. I wanted my baby to have a name, Culver. I did not want her to suffer as I had, with mestiza blood. To be a child out of wedlock is a curse here. She would be called the child of a whore. I couldn't stand it. I wanted Rane to be able to overcome her mestiza blood and hold her head high. She would not have been able to do so with a mother who was pregnant and unmarried. Fernando convinced me you would not want me pregnant." Frowning, Pilar shook her head. "Now I wonder about that. At the time, I believed him. I was so confused that afternoon. I was in shock from your nearly being killed. I was traumatized by my own bullet wound, though it was small in comparison to yours. And to be told I was pregnant..." Her voice wobbled. "It was too much for me to cope with." She rubbed her furrowed brow with trembling fingers, and her voice lowered with feeling. "We were married that evening, so that when Rane was born, I could say she was premature, and no one would suspect she had been conceived out of wedlock."

Opening her hands, feeling drained, Pilar held his tender gaze. "Oh, Culver, I hated leaving you in the hospital. But the doctors told me you would live. Fernando said it would be best never to see you again, but I sobbed myself to sleep for weeks afterward."

Getting up, Culver slowly moved over to crouch in front of Pilar and capture her hand. The stricken look on her face was telling. "I don't know what I could have done at that point, but I would have claimed Rane as my daughter," he said.

Tears shimmered in Pilar's eyes as she studied him. His voice was gruff with emotion, his hands strong and steadying on hers. "You would?"

"Yes," he rasped, "in a heartbeat. I know how people look upon unmarried mothers down here. Your culture is very different from mine. In North America, a woman with a baby out of wedlock isn't such a big deal. Down here—" he scowled "—it's a damned mortal sin. You're shunned by everyone, and the child is an outcast—forever."

Wearily, Pilar rested her brow against his. "Oh, Culver, I wish I had known. I wish . . ."

"It doesn't matter anymore, Pilar," he whispered gently, releasing her hands and framing her face.

Tears streamed down her wan cheeks. "I—I remember you telling me you wanted a family someday, but not at that age. I thought you'd send me away, that you wouldn't want to be told the truth. I sobbed it all out to Fernando, and he felt, under the circumstances, that I should marry him to protect my family's name and my daughter's future."

Culver bowed his head. "I was just blowing smoke at the time, Pilar. I never really meant what I said about not having a family. It just didn't occur to me you'd get pregnant. Everything seemed so natural between us that—that the possibility escaped me. I wasn't being responsible, and that was my fault—not yours. I was older, more experienced, and I should have seen that we took precautions. But I didn't. . . ." He gazed into her swollen eyes. "Fernando married you because he was your friend, and he was giving you and our baby protection from this society."

"Y-yes... We never laid with each other, Culver." Her voice shook with tears. "H-he never touched me. He was like a father to me, very warm, very kind. He loved Rane so much. He treated her as if she were his own child."

Once again Culver wiped away her tears. "I'm just sorry I didn't know, *mi querida*. This isn't all your fault, you know. I bear a heavy responsibility, too."

Sniffing, Pilar said, "I gave up hope at that point. I thought you would be ashamed of me. Of getting me pregnant. I didn't think you wanted me or our baby. As I got older, I began to doubt what I had done, but by then, it was too late. I knew your anger with me would be great if I told you the truth. I was afraid you might want to take Rane away from me if you knew. Oh, *Dios,* how could I ever have left you when you needed me? How could I have been so cruel to keep you and Rane from knowing and loving each other?" She placed her hands over his and held his glistening gaze. "I never loved anyone but you—ever. So many times as Rane grew up I wanted to tell her about you, about our love.... But I did not want to hurt her like that. She was mestiza; that was enough. I did not want her to feel even more different from society by being an outcast, too."

"I understand," Culver said gruffly, leaning over and gently taking her mouth. Pilar tasted of wet, salty tears. He felt her moan, a slight vibration as she hungrily returned his gentling kiss, intended to soothe the pain she still carried in her heart. Easing away from her, he saw the gold flecks deep in her eyes again, for the first time since she'd been wounded. Her cheeks were suffused with pink, and hope thrummed strongly through him.

"I love you, Pilar. I never stopped loving you through all those years."

With a little sob, she sat up, her hand pressed to her lips. "Y-you never stopped loving me?"

Culver crouched, one hand on her thigh, the other on the arm of the rocking chair. "Never."

"I have hurt so many people," Pilar whispered brokenly, and she covered her face with her hand, beginning to weep in earnest.

"Come here," Culver whispered roughly as he drew her out of the rocking chair and into his arms. Careful not to jar her wounded arm, he brought her fully against him and held her. The sounds coming from deep within her reminded him of the cries of a wounded animal. Pilar shook in his arms with each ragged sob. All Culver could do was hold her, rest his cheek against her hair and rock her gently in his arms. He felt the pain of the load she'd carried alone for so long. Guilt ate at him. She shouldn't have borne so much by herself. Culver shook his head. He'd been young, irresponsible and foolish. And look how much it had wounded Pilar—the only woman he'd ever truly loved. Could she forgive him? Could Rane? Bitterness coated his mouth as he held her shaking form.

Little by little, her sobs abated, and finally Pilar leaned against him. He took her full weight and kissed her hair. "I never knew I'd be sent back down here, Pilar, but I'm glad as hell now that I was."

Wiping her cheek with trembling fingers, Pilar said in a wobbly voice, "I was in shock when Hector told me I would be working with you." She eased away just enough to meet his warm gaze. "I was so scared, Culver—afraid you'd realize my secret. I died inside when you first saw Rane. I thought you might see the resemblance and prayed that you wouldn't."

Nodding, he ran his thumb lightly across her arched eyebrow and cupped his hand against her cheek. "You don't have to be afraid any more, *mi querida*. It's no longer a burden you carry alone. I'll help you shoulder the load from now on."

Relief swept through Pilar. The moments spun between them as her mind cartwheeled over so many options. "I'm worried for Rane. She grew up thinking Fernando was her father...."

"Shh, one step at a time, sweetheart," he said huskily, drawing her against him. "First I want you to get your strength back. We'll stay in Tarapoto until then. Then we'll go back to the village. Rane is old enough to understand some things, Pilar. We'll let her know that I'm her father and that I had to go away for a very long time, and that Fernando agreed to take care of her in my absence." He stroked her hair gently. "When she's older and can understand more, she'll know the whole truth of the situation."

Closing her eyes, Pilar pressed her face into his shirt. His arms were shoring her up, nurturing her. "I'm so tired, *mi querido*. So tired...."

Culver kissed her hair. "I know you are, sweetheart. Come on, I want you to go back to bed and rest. I'll be here. I won't leave you...."

Chapter Fourteen

Pilar stood at the entrance to their hut and watched as Aurelia took Rane's small hand. Today she was going to take her great-granddaughter deep into the jungle to begin teaching her about the herbs that could save lives. All those who walked the medicine path were taught from an early age about such things, and Pilar was grateful Rane would have the chances that she had not.

Eight weeks had passed since her release from the hospital. Culver and she had been married by a priest in Tarapoto before leaving for the village. She gazed at the plain gold wedding band on her finger, still not daring to believe Culver was her husband. It was a dream she'd had for so long that she still didn't quite trust it to be real. Aurelia's wise care and the love of Culver and her daughter had worked miracles on Pilar's healing process. Moving her shoulder a bit, she could feel stiffness, but it was no longer painful.

The morning was cool without being cold, the fog suspended like white gauze between the second and third canopies of trees. The village was just awakening, the timid light of early dawn making the fog glow like a radiant ceiling above the huts. The calls of the birds announced the break of day, their music enlivening everything around them.

Pilar stood absorbing the beauty of her home. The younger men were already in the fields above the village, working with hoes or shovels, while the wives and widows hovered around cooking pots. The children were just coming awake, their sleepy faces evident as they stumbled from their huts, rubbing their eyes. Dogs barked and played among the pigs, chickens and noisy roosters.

Pilar recalled that sometime in the night, Culver had left her and gone outside. Then Rane had come in from her own room and had snuggled into her arms on the thick floor mat. Had Pilar dreamed that Culver had then come back, kissed her on the brow and whispered he'd be back later? With a sigh, she savored the quiet joy she'd experienced ever since Culver had returned fully to their lives.

Each day, he went with Grandfather Alvaro to the fields, to work with the men. He left very early in the morning, when it was still cool, and returned around noon to eat lunch. Then it was siesta time—they spent the hot, muggy afternoon snoozing outdoors in hammocks until early evening, when the heat dissipated. Culver then would sit with the men of the village, drinking a locally made beer, telling stories, laughing and talking about the events that made up the fabric of their lives.

Yes, it was a good life, Pilar thought. Culver would return to their hut for the evening meal, to eat with her and Rane. They always talked about the day's events in detail during dinner. Rane had accepted Culver as her father far more easily than Pilar had ever thought possible. Perhaps it was because Culver made sure his daughter was with him every day, in some way, and he listened carefully to her youthful, bubbly talk.

Fernando, Pilar realized now, had cheated Rane of much. Culver was not only interested in what Rane had to say, but he talked with her at length, respectfully, as if her ideas and thoughts truly counted. Fernando, bless him, had never held such conversations with Rane. Despite his love for her, she'd been a mere child to him, therefore incapable of serious discussions or worth the time it would take to answer the many questions she asked about things that caught her curiosity and attention. Culver, on the other hand, took great pains to explain carefully when she asked him a question. Pilar did not fault Fernando, for he'd been an old man, his heart giving him many problems. She'd understood when Fernando would wave his hand and ask Rane to leave him alone, for her daughter was an impetuous, terribly curious child.

But now Pilar's heart swelled with quiet happiness as she moved out to the cooking pot. Culver had already made a grain cereal and added water and honey to it. A blackened kettle was set high above the coals of the fire. The dish was fragrant, and Pilar stirred it gently with a wooden spoon. Her thoughts drifted back over the past eight weeks. Each night had been beautiful to look forward to. The people of the village had built them a three-room hut, so that Rane had her own room, she and Culver had a bedroom and they shared the main room, where they ate and welcomed their many visitors. When Culver had driven her back to the village, the entire population had stood waiting to greet them.

Pilar had cried as her grandparents embraced her. Rane had clung to her, her slender arms wrapped tightly around Pilar's skirt, her small head pressed against her mother. Culver had stood back, tears in his eyes. Pilar hadn't expected a new home, or the warm, heartfelt welcome she re-

ceived. The hut was completely furnished with the items
they needed to set up a household, and the generosity of the
people made her weep with gratitude. And each night, Culver would put Rane to bed, tell her a story, kiss her on the
brow, then come to their bedroom.

How Pilar looked forward to that. Because her wound
was still mending, he would not love her. She understood,
but she reveled in the feel of his powerful arms about her,
drawing her gently against him. And she waited in sweet
anticipation for his mouth to settle on hers. How badly she
wanted to love him fully!

Pilar was so caught up in her heated thoughts of Culver
holding her and kissing her that she did not hear his approach. However, her other sense—the jaguar medicine
within her—felt his presence. She was sitting on a log near
the cooking pot, the bowl of cereal in her hand, when she
felt him arrive. Her brain told her that was silly, since Culver would be out in the fields at this time of day.

But as she lifted her head, her eyes met his. He stood a
little off to one side, watching her, tenderness in his eyes.
The expression sent a thrill though her. Pilar felt heat suf-
fuse her heart, then streak downward like jagged lightning
hurled from the sky into Mother Earth. The look in his eyes
told her of his love, of his burning need of her—in all ways.
He was dressed in a loose, white cotton shirt, the sleeves
rolled up to his elbows. In his hand was a hoe. The jeans he
wore were threadbare, outlining his magnificent lower body.
Like all the men, he wore thick leather sandals to protect his
feet, and she could see he had been in the fields by the dark
soil clinging to his feet.

His gaze touched her, silent yet evocative. Slowly lowering the bowl to the log, Pilar watched his mouth curve
slightly in greeting. When Culver walked, he reminded her
of the silent jaguar, who owned the jungle on his own terms.
Culver possessed an incredible masculine grace, and the

eight weeks of hard field work had somehow brought a level of relaxation to his movements. Where before he'd been tight, almost rigid in his walk, now there was a fluidity about him that was beautiful to watch.

"I thought you were in the fields," she said a little breathlessly as he approached.

Culver placed the hoe against the side of the hut. "I was."

Pilar's mouth curved as he came and sat down next to her. "Are you not feeling well?" She searched his face, darkly tanned from the sun that shone brightly on the slopes above the village, where the terraced fields lay. So much of the tension that had been in Culver's expression had disappeared. Although his face remained as rugged as the granite Andes, at the same time it mirrored a relaxed quality.

"I feel great." Culver studied Pilar in the warm silence that hummed between them. She had braided her thick hair as she did every morning. Then at night, he would unbraid it and brush out the silky strands. It was a special time for them. "We're going somewhere," he said enigmatically. "Aurelia has packed us a lunch." He reached over and caressed Pilar's cheek. "All I need is you."

Surprised, she gazed up into his light blue eyes and saw amusement in them—and longing. Her skin tingled deliciously where he'd barely grazed her cheek. "Where are we going?"

Culver's mouth stretched. "Now, if I told you that, it wouldn't be a surprise, would it?"

Her lips parted. "What about Rane?"

"Aurelia is taking care of her all day. They know we won't be back until dusk."

Pilar studied him. "You have planned this carefully, haven't you, *mi querido?*" She saw Culver flush.

"Somewhat . . ." he managed to say, trying not to smile.

A deep, throbbing sensation began in her lower body. The look he was giving her was one a man gives his woman when he wants to love her—fully. Without reserve. Without regret. She felt a secret heat coiling tightly within her as she began to understand. "You are taking me somewhere that is private?"

"Very private."

"I see..."

"I think you're beginning to." He flashed her a slight smile. "Don Alvaro told me about this place."

"Oh?"

"It's a secret. Only the men know about it."

"Ahh," Pilar teased, standing up, "one of those." The Quechua had places for men and places for women. Each gender had unique, special places to go for healing, for ceremony or for time to think, uninterrupted. She knew that wherever Culver was taking her this morning, no one would interrupt them. Today he would love her. The thought made her go weak with desire. How many times had she ached to fulfill him with herself, her body like an anguished candle incomplete without him as her flame?

"I'll go over to their hut, pick up the knapsack and be back," Culver told her, rising. He saw her cheeks flush, making her look even more desirable. Pilar wore a simple white blouse and a pale blue skirt that brushed the tops of her slender ankles. She was barefoot and looked so much a part of this beautiful land—as if she belonged here for the rest of her life.

"How soon will we be there?" Pilar asked as she walked with Culver down a very old, rarely used path through the jungle. They had walked for more than two hours into a portion of the jungle she was unfamiliar with. She knew of all the women's places, the sacred places where they went for their monthly moon time, to spend five to seven days singing, dreaming, weaving and being close to the Mother, but she did not know this path.

Culver squeezed her hand. "Not much farther, according to Don Alvaro." It was nearly ten in the morning, and the fog was burning off, allowing dappled sunlight, like droplets of golden rain, to shimmer and dance through the thick canopy above them.

Pilar saw the jungle thinning in front of them, and she felt Culver's hand tighten momentarily around hers as they stepped out of the wall of foliage. Her breath caught. There in front of them was a waterfall nearly thirty feet high, the water gushing over the black-and-white-granite rocks into a huge oval pool below. The water was crystalline—a deep emerald green so clear that she could see fish swimming in its depths. Around the pool, water lilies extended their white petals skyward like slender arms embracing the sunlight.

"Oh!," Pilar whispered, her fingers going to her heart. "This is like a dream!"

Culver looked around, appreciating the beauty of the pool. "Don Alvaro told me about this place right after we brought you home," he said as he led her forward. Thick green grass covered the rounded banks. "He said this was the pool where a young man brings the woman he loves. A lovers' hideout, where they can have complete privacy."

Pilar halted at the pool's edge and gazed up at Culver. Her eyes filled with tears as she absorbed his tender look. "This is so much like the pool where we first met and loved...."

"Yes, it is." Culver released her hand and shed his pack, then took out a large sleeping mat and spread it beside the water. The rush of the waterfall mingled with the melodic songs of birds and the harsher calls of parrots that flitted like rainbows within the jungle wall. Culver saw the tracks of many animals, and knew the pool was a main water source for many jungle inhabitants.

Leaning down, he picked up a bright red Macaw feather. "Here, this is for you...." He knew how Pilar loved the brightly colored feathers. She was weaving a shield of ones she'd found on her daily forays into the jungle. Now he watched the delight in her eyes as he handed her the long crimson plume.

"Thank you!" Pilar stroked the feather lovingly and watched as Culver crossed to a very old rubber tree that leaned over the pool. Stretching upward, he picked a string of pink-and-white orchids that hung from the trees like a small cluster of stars. The look he gave her as he settled the necklace of orchids around her throat made her feel faint with need.

"These don't begin to do you justice," Culver murmured thickly as he began to slowly unbutton her blouse. He saw her lips part as his fingers lightly grazed her flesh. Pilar wore no bra under the faded white cotton, and her nipples began to harden beneath the fabric as he opened it. His voice grew hoarse with desire. "I wanted to bring you here, *mi querida,* to love you. I wanted to have you to myself for just a few hours, to make you mine again."

Heat swept through Pilar's breasts as he slowly opened the blouse to reveal them. She swayed unsteadily. Gripping his arms, she whispered, "Yes . . . please, love me, Culver. I—I've waited so long . . . dreamed so long of this moment. . . ."

His hands slid beneath the fabric, and she felt the calluses as his fingers cupped her straining breasts. His skin was toughened by long hours of work, powerful sunshine and unrelenting wind, while hers was soft, her flesh molding and fitting into his strong hands. Her fingertips dug into his upper arms, and her eyes closed as Culver moved his thumbs teasingly over her nipples. The sensation was electric. A gasp escaped her, and she felt his hands gently draw her forward until his mouth fitted hotly against hers, his tongue moving boldly into its depths. Breathless, Pilar raised her arms to his neck and sagged against his strong frame.

His mouth drew fire from her. Before this, at night in their bed, he had kissed her gently. Tenderly. But now, as he eased the blouse from her shoulders and worked the clasp on her skirt free, he was neither gentle nor tender. No, this kiss was hot and seeking. Pilar felt her skirt pool around her feet. When his fingers molded against her flared hips and traveled down her body, she felt her lingerie join the skirt. Then she stood naked, fitted tightly against his clothed form feeling his masterful hardness pushing strongly against her belly to let her know just how much he wanted her.

Without letting his lips leave her mouth, Culver picked her up and carried her to the mat, where he gently deposited her on her back. His mouth was rich, giving and taking. She felt the prickle of his recently shaved skin and dragged into her nostrils the scent of his body, slightly sweaty from the hard labor he'd performed in the fields earlier this morning. Her fingers frantically worked at the buttons of his shirt, and she ached to tear his clothes off so his naked body could mold and fuse with hers. Finally the shirt fell away, and with his help, his Levi's soon joined it. In one hot, burning movement, he settled at her side, one arm beneath her neck, his other hand ranging up and down her naked body.

The moment he pressed her fully to him and she felt his male hardness insistent against the apex of her thighs, Pilar moaned with pure pleasure. He tore his mouth from hers and lowered it to one hardened, uplifted nipple. Pilar tipped her head back, her throat exposed in exquisite surrender as he suckled her. Simultaneously, she felt his callused fingers moving downward, sliding between her thighs and easing her legs open just enough to give him entrance. Her body seemed suspended, waiting for his touch. As he slid down into that moist crevice, she shuddered, and an electrical sensation bolted up through her as he eased his fingers between the folds of her womanhood.

Instinctively, she curved tightly against him, her breasts pressed to his chest wall, her arms rigid with tension around his neck as he stroked her with velvet intensity. Her thighs opened wider, of their own accord. The fragrance of the pink-and-white orchids surrounded her and mingled with his very male scent. He suckled her other nipple, and she felt herself spiraling out of control, heat gathering rapidly wherever he stroked her. The hot liquid of her body spilled across his searching fingers like nectar produced by the fragrant orchids that lay around her neck. As his mouth fitted commandingly across hers once more, Pilar cried out, and a white-hot bolt seemed to shoot to her very core. But her cry was absorbed into his mouth as his tongue plunged again and again into her.

Culver smiled to himself as Pilar surrendered entirely to his ministrations. Her mouth was as wet and hot as the opening to her womanhood. He eased his fingers away from her, laid his hand on her small, curved thigh and opened her even more—to receive him. Laying her back on the mat, his mouth still clinging hotly to hers, he rose above her, covering her with his larger body and feeling her shift languidly beneath him in welcome. How long he'd waited for this moment! Culver had dreamed torridly of this coupling for eight endless years, and now, unbelievably, Pilar was here beneath him, her body writhing restlessly goading him to take her, to brand her as his.

The ache in his loins was nearly unbearable as he grazed the slickness of her moist inner thighs. His lips pulled away from his clenched teeth. He didn't want to hurt her, knowing she'd not lain with another man in eight years. She would be small and tight, just as she had been the first time he'd taken her virginity at the sunlit pool. Her mouth was pouty, soft and provocative against his. Did she realize that she was disintegrating his control with each movement of her hips? A hiss issued from between his teeth, and he froze above her, but she did not freeze in turn. With one twist of her hips, she slid upward, enfolding him, inviting him in.

It was too much. Culver hadn't expected her to be so bold, so assertive. Beads of perspiration popped out on his forehead as he tried to control himself. His rigidity made him tremble as she continued her gentle assault upon him, undulating her hips in an ancient rhythm that further crumbled his restraint. Heat was building inexorably within him, and he knew he would explode at any moment. Blindly, he plunged into her silken depths, the tightness overwhelming. His fingers curved and followed the shape of her head, and he felt her hands settle firmly upon his hips, pulling him closer, inviting him more deeply into her.

Dizziness exploded within him and he became mindless. He became the male jaguar taming his female. The fragrance of the wild orchids mixed with the raw, primal odor of their bodies, all conspiring against him. Groaning, Culver took her deeply, hard—plunging into her again and again, a little farther with each thrust. Suddenly white-hot heat surged through him, exploding like the power of the sun itself. Gripping her fiercely to him, he froze deep within her, and in that moment, she moved her hips, sucking the blazing energy out of him and into herself. With each graceful, undulating movement, he felt the power bleeding out of him like the waterfall that thundered into the womb-shaped pool below.

Within moments, he was spent, and Culver groaned and relaxed onto her smaller form. Kissing her soft, pouty lips, he drowned in the honey of life contained within her mouth. Moving his hips raggedly against her softer, more-provocative ones, he felt as if he were dying and going to a heaven he didn't deserve. The richness and depth of their recaptured love had made this time even better than eight years ago. They had been forged by the fires of life, shaped by intense and powerful emotions, and their lovemaking had gained an exquisite facet that had been missing before. The moments, golden and molten, spun together like a beautiful spiderweb that had captured the dew of the night and was now being shot through with sunlight. A deep glowing heat throbbed within him as she milked the last of his power into the depths of her moist, receptive body.

The love he felt for her in that moment was so rich, so intense, that Culver nearly drowned in the beauty as he moved off her and brought her alongside him, remaining deep within her, his hand flattened against the base of her spine to hold her hips captive. She held him in turn, a tender prisoner of love within her. Her hardened nipples grazed his chest wall, and he felt her ease away. Tunneling her fingers through his hair, she guided his head downward until once again his mouth fitted over one of those straining peaks, and he suckled her. A fine tremor moved through her as he held her in his arms in that moment, and he felt Pilar become boneless in his embrace, felt her release a sigh of utter womanly fulfillment, at one with the man she loved.

Culver could imagine nothing beyond this moment, and having this brave, warm and loving woman in his arms again at last. As they lay, locked together, he felt himself hardening again within her, filling her with his love. He felt the renewed honey of her liquid confines bathing him as his strength returned. Her belly was soft against him, and as he lay there, suckling her, holding her tightly, Culver wanted to give her another baby—a second child formed and fashioned out of this exquisite love that had never died.

As her fingers ranged through his hair, sifting the dampened strands, he lifted his mouth from her hardened nipple and gazed deeply into her lustrous, half-opened eyes, burning jaguar gold with love for him. He had no words. His throat constricted with tears as he absorbed her gaze, her touch. He loved her fiercely, as a jaguar possessed his mate—ferocious and territorial. For he was certain now: she was his mate for life, and he'd gladly fight to his death to see that she was protected and cared for, and never became separated from him again.

Pilar's lips parted, slick and glistening from his kisses, the corners lifting tenderly. She raised her hands and settled her small, slender fingers on the sides of his face. The love shining in her eyes shook him to the depths of his soul, and for the first time, Culver realized just how much Pilar loved him—had always loved him. Her love was fierce, he discovered, and no less loyal than his for her. His smile was very male, very tender, as he leaned down and barely touched his mouth to hers.

"I love you," he whispered thickly against her lips. "Forever..."

Epilogue

Culver tried to contain his surprise when they arrived back at the village that evening. Major Mike Houston was standing near their hut deep in conversation with several of the village elders. Culver's grip on Pilar's shoulders tightened momentarily, and she gave him a worried look. No one had expected to see Houston again. Why was he here, in their village?

Grimly, Culver quickened his pace. His hand dropped from Pilar's shoulder and he captured her hand, squeezing it gently to convey his support.

"There you are," Houston said, looking up.

Culver sized up the Special Forces officer, dressed in his fresh, tiger-striped utilities, a dark red beret on his head. Houston's pistol was at his side, and his black jump boots gleamed with a high polish. "What's going on?" Culver growled, halting and holding out his hand in greeting.

Houston smiled a little, nodded deferentially to Pilar, then devoted his attention to Culver. "I've been waiting a couple of hours for you, Lachlan." He gestured toward the clearing near the village where a U.S. Apache helicopter had landed, fully loaded with weapons. "I decided to drop in and let you know that the Peruvian government has taken out Ramirez."

Culver's brows dipped. "Taken him out?"

Houston's face grew hard. "Remember the fortress where he kept Morgan?"

"Of course."

"It's been leveled. The government decided to go after the son of a bitch—" He broke off abruptly, giving Pilar a distressed look. "Pardon me, ma'am, I didn't mean to be so graphic...."

Pilar nodded. "I understand, Major."

Relieved, his mouth twitching with the hint of a smile, he held Culver's assessing gaze. "Ever since you two rescued Morgan, the Peruvian government has been working overtime to locate Ramirez. Our spies told us he'd returned from Bogota. We found out he was planning to completely destroy this village as an act of revenge." With a shrug, he said, "When I found that out, I suggested to the general that we ought to do a little leveling of our own first. Of course, the Apaches were flown by Peruvian pilots. I just went along as an observer." His smile broadened. "Too bad you weren't there, Lachlan. You'd have been our cheering section. Those Apaches destroyed the army of choppers Ramirez used to ferry the cocaine in and out of the country. Not only that, but the chief was there and got caught in the cross fire."

Culver's eyes narrowed. "Ramirez is dead? How can you be sure?" The drug lord had the nine lives of a cat. Over the years, Culver knew, the Peruvian government had tried many times to capture him.

"I saw it with my own two eyes." Houston settled his large-knuckled hands over his narrow hips. "After the Peruvian pilots leveled the fortress, we landed and went in with a company of land-based troops to finish the job. Whoever had survived was taken prisoner at that point. We found Ramirez's body in some of the rubble near the hacienda. He was dead."

Culver saw the glitter in Houston's eyes and understood the officer's pleasure in finding the drug lord dead. He felt Pilar's reaction and looked down at her. She'd gone pale. Automatically, Culver placed his arm around her small shoulders and drew her gently against him.

Houston sobered. "One of the women from the village, who had watched the attack, came up to us. She asked for a pistol from one of the officers and he gave it to her. She and her daughter had been raped by Ramirez. She put the gun to the man's head and pulled the trigger. So I know he's dead."

"Justice," Culver muttered, "finally."

Houston nodded gravely. "I was telling the elders of the village that they're really safe now. And so are you. One of Ramirez's men spilled the beans. During interrogation, he told us there was a mole in Hector Ruiz's office—it was his secretarial assistant, Manuela. She's in jail awaiting trial."

Pilar's eyes widened enormously. "Manuela gave us away, then?"

Culver nodded. "We were attacked by Ramirez's men at Hotel of the Andes," he explained to Mike. "And I thought Ruiz had sold us out. I was wrong." He gave Pilar an apologetic look.

Houston's eyes narrowed speculatively on Culver. "I understand you're going to stay down here and make your home in the village?"

Culver nodded. "For now. We may decide to alternate years between the village and my family's home in Colorado. We can have the best of both worlds for our daughter that way. My parents want to see Rane grow up, too."

With a shrug, Mike grinned a little and looked around. "Not a bad way to live, really. You've got the sun for light, clean water from the Andes and good volcanic soil to raise food." He smiled down at Pilar. "And a good woman. Wish to hell I had one."

"Someday, if you get lucky like me, you might, Houston. Until then, you'll be another lone wolf."

With a sigh, Houston took off his beret to wipe the sweat from his forehead, then settled it back on his head. "Yeah, I was afraid of that. One more bit of information and then I'll leave you to your safe, idyllic life here, Lachlan. I called Perseus the other day to check on Morgan's condition."

"How is he?" Culver asked. The man had never been far from his thoughts in the past two months.

"The same, I'm afraid. He spent eight weeks recovering in the navy hospital at Bethesda. The doctors have written him off. Nothing they do seems to bring back his memory. He doesn't know his name. He doesn't remember Perseus. Worse—" Houston grimaced "—he doesn't recognize his wife, Laura, or their two children. Helluva sad situation, isn't it? It's going to be a pleasure to make a call to Jake Randolph. He's still running Perseus, and I can't wait to let him know we've taken Ramirez permanently out of the picture."

"How sad," Pilar whispered, tears in her voice, "for Morgan and his family. What will his wife do?"

"I guess she's planning on taking Morgan to a special place he loves—a cattle ranch in Arizona. Morgan made friends with the rancher's son in Vietnam, and the family has offered them a cabin on their property that's fairly isolated, so they can have time to get to know each other again. Jake said that Laura's extended family will take care of their children while they take some time off together. I think

Laura's hoping that relaxing surroundings and getting him out of that hospital setting will help jog his memory. Quality time alone, you might say."

Pilar shook her head and pressed her hand to her lips. "Oh, I feel so badly for Laura. How awful to be with her husband, who once loved her and now sees her as a stranger. How hard it must be for her...."

Culver squeezed her gently. "We know from experience that love is never easy."

Pilar wiped the tears from her eyes as she absorbed Culver's tender, loving look. "No, it's not. But love, if it's true, will never die."

Houston sighed. "At least there's one happy ending in this ongoing mess. I've got to get back to Lima before they start wondering where the hell that Apache helicopter is." He smiled a goodbye to Pilar, then held out his hand to Culver. "Stay well and happy, Lachlan. Since I'm permanently assigned to Lima as a military attaché, let me know if there's anything you need, okay?"

Culver gripped the officer's lean, spare hand. "You bet I will. Thanks, Mike—for everything." With Ramirez dead, Culver knew, people of the region could breathe a huge, collective sigh of relief.

"I hear from Pilar's grandparents that they're hoping you're going to be a papa—again—real soon," Houston teased.

Culver had the good grace to blush. He looked down to see Pilar blushing, too. Automatically, she placed her hand on her belly in response, and the elders surrounding them chuckled indulgently.

With a hearty laugh, Houston clapped Culver on the shoulder and left, striding toward the waiting helicopter. Culver turned with Pilar to watch him walk away.

"I cannot believe all this," Pilar whispered as they saw Houston disappear inside the helicopter, the door shutting behind him. The blades began to turn slowly.

"What? About Ramirez?" Culver asked, his gaze on the helicopter, but his heart centered on Pilar.

"Yes. It's like a prayer that's been answered. He was such a monster, Culver."

With a sigh, Culver turned and led her toward their hut. The elders nodded, the group breaking up and heading to their homes for the evening meal. As the helicopter took off, the noise echoed against the slopes above the village. At the door to their hut, Culver turned and watched the dark green aircraft lift into the sky, hazy now as the sun rode low on the horizon. Pilar's arm went around his waist, and she leaned on him.

"Major Houston is a good man. I don't understand why a woman hasn't fallen in love with him yet."

Culver chuckled. "Sweetheart, Houston is a professional soldier."

"You are a mercenary. What is the difference?"

"Was," he corrected as he led her into the hut. Someone had left a vase filled with colorful wild orchids in the main room. The soft dusk light filtered through the windows, and Culver seated himself on one of the wooden chairs. Pilar took a seat on the straw mat at his feet and began to prepare the evening meal.

An incredible peace blanketed Culver. He had everything, he realized humbly as Pilar leaned against his knee. Her legs were crossed beneath her skirt, her bare feet hidden by the material. As he looked around the simple hut, he realized he was the richest man on earth. He'd seen the envy in Houston's eyes—for the man didn't have a good woman to love and accept him. Culver had recognized that look of longing, and it made him feel damned lucky.

Reaching down, he caressed Pilar's hair. "Rane will be here soon. Grandmother Aurelia said she would bring her home at dusk, if you're worried."

Pilar looked up and smiled tenderly at him. She tied off one long, thick braid with a scrap of red yarn. "I am not worried, *mi querido*." She caught and captured his hand. Guiding it down to her belly, she placed her two hands over his one large one. "Do you wish for another child?" she whispered, holding his burning gaze.

Culver gently ran his hand across her belly. "Sweetheart, I want all the kids we can support. And I'll love every one as much as I love you." He sighed and sat up again, looking toward the opened door. In the distance he could see Grandmother Aurelia and Rane, hand in hand, coming across the clearing, each carrying a sack filled with what he was sure were many varieties of herbs. "I hope we have two more beautiful daughters exactly like Rane and a couple of strong, healthy sons to round out the family." He shifted his gaze back to Pilar, thinking how radiant and exotic she looked in that moment as she sat next to his legs, her hands still pressing against her belly. "What do you want?" he whispered thickly.

"Just you—and our love that never died," she said softly, tears in her eyes. "Our babies, no matter how many, will always be babies of love...."

Gently, Culver leaned down and touched her mouth with his. Her lips were swollen from the power of his earlier kisses, so he was tender with her. "I'll love you, Pilar, forever...."

* * * * *

Silhouette®

SPECIAL EDITION™

COMING NEXT MONTH

#1003 JUST MARRIED—Debbie Macomber
Celebration 1000!

Retired soldier of fortune Zane Ackerman's hard heart had been waiting for someone to melt it. Lesley Walker fit the bill so perfectly, he asked her to marry him. But when he needed to right one final wrong, would he have to choose between his past and a future of wedded bliss?

#1004 NEW YEAR'S DADDY—Lisa Jackson
Holiday Elopement/Celebration 1000!

Ronni Walsh had no plans to fall in love again, but that didn't mean her four-year-old daughter, Amy, couldn't ask Santa for a new daddy. And although the sexy single dad next door, Travis Keegan, had sworn off romantic entanglements, Amy was sure she'd found the perfect candidate....

#1005 MORGAN'S MARRIAGE—Lindsay McKenna
Morgan's Mercenaries: Love and Danger/Celebration 1000!

After a dramatic rescue, amnesia robbed Morgan Trayhern of any recollection of his loved ones. But Laura Trayhern was determined to help bring her husband's memory back—and hoped they could renew the vows of love they'd once made to each other.

#1006 CODY'S FIANCÉE—Gina Ferris Wilkins
The Family Way/Celebration 1000!

Needing to prove she'd been a good guardian to her little brother, Dana Preston had no choice but to turn to Cody Carson for help. But what started as a marriage of convenience turned into something neither one bargained for—especially when their pretend emotions of love began to feel all too real....

#1007 NATURAL BORN DADDY—Sherryl Woods
And Baby Makes Three/Celebration 1000!

Getting Kelly Flint to say yes to his proposal of marriage was the easy part for Jordan Adams. Winning the reluctant bride's heart would be a lot tougher. But Jordan was determined to show her he was perfect husband material—and a natural-born daddy!

#1008 THE BODYGUARD & MS. JONES—Susan Mallery
Celebration 1000!

Mike Blackburne's life as a bodyguard had put him in exciting, dangerous situations. Single mom Cindy Jones was raising two kids and had never left the suburbs. The only thing they agreed on was that they were totally wrong for each other—and were falling completely and totally in love....

MILLION DOLLAR SWEEPSTAKES (III)

Are your lips succulent, impetuous, delicious or racy?

Find out in a very special Valentine's Day promotion—THAT SPECIAL KISS!

Inside four special Harlequin and Silhouette February books are details for THAT SPECIAL KISS! explaining how you can have your lip prints read by a romance expert.

Look for details in the following series books, written by four of Harlequin and Silhouette readers' favorite authors:

Silhouette Intimate Moments #691
Mackenzie's Pleasure by *New York Times* bestselling author Linda Howard

Harlequin Romance #3395
Because of the Baby by Debbie Macomber

Silhouette Desire #979
Megan's Marriage by Annette Broadrick

Harlequin Presents #1793
The One and Only by Carole Mortimer

Fun, romance, four top-selling authors, plus a **FREE** gift! This is a very special Valentine's Day you won't want to miss! Only from Harlequin and Silhouette.

MORGAN'S MERCENARIES: LOVE AND DANGER

by Lindsay McKenna

Four missions—save Morgan Trayhern and each member of his family. Four men—each battling danger. Would rescuing their comrade help them discover the glory of love?

Watch for the next exciting title in this new series from Lindsay McKenna:

MORGAN'S MARRIAGE (SE #1005)

After a dramatic rescue, amnesia now robbed Morgan Trayhern of any recollection of his loved ones. But Laura Trayhern was determined to help bring her husband's memory back—and hoped they could renew the vows of love they'd once made to each other.

Don't miss the emotional conclusion to this series from Lindsay McKenna and Silhouette Special Edition!

Silhouette SPECIAL EDITION

THE FAMILY WAY™

Gina Ferris Wilkins

When their beloved Gram begins to play matchmaker,
four cousins find love in the new series by
Gina Ferris Wilkins! Meet Adam—and the rest of his
family—in Book Three,

A HOME FOR ADAM
(SE #980, September)

Dr. Adam Stone's rest and solitude were interrupted
when a very pregnant woman appeared on his
doorstep. He helped bring Jenny Newcomb's daughter into the world—and from the moment he looked at
mother and child, he wondered if they could provide
the love he needed....

Don't miss the warm and wonderful THE FAMILY WAY
series! Only from Gina Ferris Wilkins, and
Silhouette Special Edition!